The **Sweet,** Terrible,
Glorious Year
I Truly, **Completely**
Lost **It**

a novel by
lisa shanahan

the Sweet, Terrible, Glorious Year I Truly, Completely Lost It

delacorte press

Published by Delacorte Press
an imprint of Random House Children's Books
a division of Random House, Inc.
New York

First published in Australia in 2006 by Allen & Unwin
under the title *My Big Birkett*

Educators and librarians, for a variety of teaching tools, visit us at
www.randomhouse.com/teachers

Library of Congress Cataloging-in-Publication Data
Shanahan, Lisa.
[My big birkett]
The sweet, terrible, glorious year I truly, completely lost it / Lisa Shanahan.
p. cm.
Summary: Fourteen-year-old Gemma Stone struggles to understand her shifting emotions as her older sister plans her wedding, she overcomes her nerves and tries out for the school play, and she gets to know one of the most notorious boys in her class.
ISBN 978-0-385-73516-2 (trade)
ISBN 978-0-385-90505-3 (lib. bdg.)
[1. Theater—Fiction. 2. Schools—Fiction. 3. Shakespeare, William, 1564–1616. Tempest—Fiction. 4. Family life—Australia—Fiction. 5. Weddings—Fiction 6. Australia—Fiction.] I. Title.
PZ7.S52827Sw 2007
[Fic]—dc22
2006101158

The text of this book is set in 12-point Garamond BE Regular.

Book design by Angela Carlino

Printed in the United States of America

10 9 8 7 6 5 4 3 2

First American Edition

for
Keiran

one

When Debbie told Dad she was marrying Brian, her new boyfriend of one month, Dad went ballistic.

"Not Brian!" He leapt from his chair. "Anybody but Brian. I'd prefer that bloke who stole and hocked my tennis trophies . . . what was his name?"

"His name was Bruce, Dad," said Debbie, with a sniff. "And he didn't steal your tennis trophies. You gave them away to St. Vinnie's."

"I certainly did not!" Dad switched off the television. "One of those trophies was for the 1974 Buranderry Tennis Premiership and I certainly wouldn't have given it away. That was the year my backhand slice was so fierce and fast it took a piece out of your mother's backside. Hospitalized her, I did."

"Only because you couldn't get your backhand over the net that year," said Mum, peering up from her cross-stitch. "And all the other women on the team were too scared to be your partner."

My mum is always cross-stitching. The sunroom at the back of the house is full of cross-stitched fruit. Watermelon, grapes, a green apple, a Jonathan, a Red Delicious, a rockmelon, a mango, an orange and a lychee. Dad reckons it makes him feel like he lives in a fruit shop. Mum says it makes her feel peaceful. She can only cross-stitch fruit. She's tried veggies, but they never work out.

"Dad," called Debbie. "We're not talking about tennis now, we're talking about Brian."

"Oh blimey, him again! How did we get back to him?" Dad sank back into his recliner and closed his eyes.

"He's asked me to marry him," said Debbie, strands of blond hair floating with static. "And I've said yes."

Mum stood up. She put her arms around Debbie and gave her a big squeeze. "That's nice, Deb. He's a lovely boy, in his own way."

"Where were you?" I asked.

"In O'Riley's," Debbie said with a sigh. "He asked me at the spice rack."

O'Riley's is the only supermarket in Buranderry. It's small, dim, overpriced and understocked, but everybody shops there because there's nowhere else to go.

"He planned it carefully. He told me he wanted to buy

Chinese five spice for the spice rack that he gave his mum for Christmas, and even though they only had out-of-date nutmeg, it was there he got down on his knees and said, 'Deborah Stone, will you spice up my life and be my wife!' "

Dad slid the recliner back. "Why didn't you leave him there? You could have put a quick-sale clearance sign on him."

"Very funny, Dad," said Debbie.

"So you said . . . yes?" said Mum.

"Of course," said Debbie. "They even announced it on the PA."

For some reason, Stan O'Riley had installed a PA system even though the place is the size of a largish corner shop. The only time he ever uses it is when he's shouting out for his brother Ted to get off his bum, stop watching *Oprah* and serve customers.

"Stan even gave us a gift voucher," said Debbie, as if she couldn't believe it.

I've never liked Stan O'Riley. There is something grubby about the way he licks his pointy finger when he's trying to separate the plastic bags. Ted is my favorite checkout rooster. He likes ballroom dancing and when he's working, the place is full of music and the noise of his feet tapping on the linoleum.

"When are you planning to get married?" asked Mum.

"Sometime in spring," said Debbie.

"How come Brian didn't ask me for your hand in marriage?" asked Dad.

Debbie twirled her gold chain around her finger. "Oh Dad, nobody asks for permission anymore! That was only done in the Dark Ages when women were viewed as possessions."

"I asked Bob for your mother's hand in marriage."

"See what I mean!" Debbie shrugged. "I am so happy! Brian said it was the most original thought he's ever had—his idea of how to propose. He's adorable!"

And she snatched the phone off the coffee table and ran upstairs to call all her friends.

We sat in silence.

"That's his most original thought!" whispered Dad. He lay still in the leather chair, looking at the large patch of damp on the ceiling.

Mum licked her cotton and tried to rethread her needle.

"What sort of bloke is he? He didn't even turn up with her to give us the news," said Dad.

"Well, love . . . ," said Mum. "Debbie did tell me that Brian is frightened of you."

"Frightened of me!" cried Dad. "What's there to be frightened of?"

"Whenever you see him, you grunt, Dad," I said.

"As far as I can tell that's the only language he speaks. He's hardly said a word with a syllable since I've met him."

"He's shy," said Mum.

"Bloody odd, more like it," said Dad.

Mum stroked Dad's arm. "Oh well, love, at least she isn't marrying Birkett."

Birkett was Debbie's last disastrous boyfriend. She met him the previous Christmas at the Buranderry Markets after he set up his bookstall near the rubble of the Buranderry fountain, right next to Mum's craft stand.

He recited his own love poetry without stopping for the whole morning. When he finally paused for a drink, Debbie tossed him a five-dollar note, mainly to keep him quiet—but it only encouraged him to pack up his books and spend the rest of the afternoon describing her silvery gilt hair and her pond-green eyes and her smooth, creamy skin.

Their relationship was doomed. Debbie was a girl who liked to be in bed at eight sharp and Birk was a bloke who didn't wake up until dusk. After two weeks of traipsing into the city and visiting late-night, smoky dingy poetry haunts, listening to Birk's rants against meat, sport, rhyming poetry, dairy products, America, white bread and the scent of fresh grass, Debbie was exhausted. She wrote Birkett a note saying she didn't want to see him anymore.

That night, at midnight, he appeared on the footpath outside our house, wearing a leather loincloth with a black snake draped around his neck. He stood on Dad's lawn and recited twenty different acrostic poetry renditions on the word "Debbie."

"Debbie—Delicate, Energetic, Beautiful, Broody, Inamorata, Emerald. Come back to this fool, my precious jewel." He flung the words out so vigorously the cords of his neck stuck out and torpedoes of spit sprayed the front garden. All the lights went on in the street, one after the other like a Mexican Wave. Heads popped out of bedroom windows and people snuck out onto their lawns in their pajamas.

Birkett barely paused to draw breath. He was the type to ride the wave of his emotions right through to the very end, until he had seaweed up his nose and sand all through his swimmers.

If it hadn't been for his pet snake coiling around his neck three times and squeezing so hard that the only sound that came out of his mouth was a wheeze, he would still be on our front lawn.

These days, in our family, when anyone starts riding the big wave of their emotions, we say they're chucking a birkett. The actual quality of the emotion is not so important—whether it's anger or love or sorrow or fear—but what does matter is whether the emotion has the necessary monstrous power to drive out all of your common sense. When that takes place, when the emotion is larger than you are, you can be certain you're in the middle of a big birkett.

The other telltale signs are: redness around the cheeks, shortness of breath, slightly bulging glassy eyes, increasingly agitated speech, and a prolonged outburst marked by silliness and illogicality.

Some people are more prone to birketts than others. Those sorts of people are also usually easily provoked. It's like they have a San Andreas Fault running through their personalities and even the smallest thing can set them off. How else can you explain those drivers that flip their fingers and toot their horns the moment someone in front of them hasn't turned left when the traffic arrow has flashed from red to green?

In my family, you're more likely to see Dad and Debbie chuck a birkett than you are Mum or me. Sometimes when I watch them in full flight, I can't help wondering if maybe they're a little addicted. Why bother getting towed onto waves as big as skyscrapers in Hawaii when you can have all that fun in the safety of your own home?

• • •

Later that night, Brian came over. Dad cracked him a beer and they sat on the front fence for about an hour, staring at Dad's prizewinning roses, grunting about the heat, the chance of rain, army worm and Dad's latest attempt to thwart the local dogs from pooing on his lawn.

Dad works at a nursery and he is passionate about lawn. He was about to launch in and explain the benefits of kikuyu versus common couch grass, when Mum called them in for dinner.

When Brian sat down at the table, his face had that faint queasiness of someone who had just had their appendix removed without an anesthetic.

"Let's propose a toast," said Mum.

"Right," said Dad. "To Debbie and Brian."

Mum lifted her glass. "To Debbie and Brian! And to lots of spice and all things nice!"

"Mum!" I said.

"It's an important part of marriage," said Mum, clinking her glass against Brian's. "Sometimes a spicy love life can be the only thing that keeps a marriage going. . . ."

"Shhh! Mum! You're grossing me out."

The idea of Mum and Dad having a spicy love life made my stomach turn. I always imagined they slept with an invisible Great Wall of China running down the middle of the bed. The idea of Mum and Dad . . . no. It didn't bear thinking about.

I often daydream at the dinner table. It helps block out the eating noises.

"Anyway," said Debbie. "We'd really like it if Gemma could be a flower girl. Brian's sister is going to be one too."

"Isn't she a little old for a flower girl?" asked Mum. "She'd be better as a bridesmaid."

"It's the only role left," said Debbie. "She can't be a bridesmaid, I've already asked Rochelle, Renee and Rachael, and Brian's only got three mates. What do you think, Gem?"

Spurts of air rolled out of my mouth. The very idea of people staring at me made my skin prickle. I took a deep breath. "I'm not sure. What would I have to do?"

"Nothing! You don't have to do anything. You only have to look cute and pretty."

"Just make sure you don't stand with your arms crossed the whole time," said Mum. "You've got a nice set of strawberry creams and you should be proud of them."

"Mum!" I tried to imagine myself as a sausage, parentless, sizzling alone on a plate.

"Er," said Brian. "What are strawberry creams?"

"He speaks a sentence!" grunted Dad.

"Breasts," said Debbie.

"Oh!" I groaned.

Brian choked. Debbie slammed him on the back so hard his head wobbled and a snippet of carrot shot out of his nose and into the water jug. It floated like a small boat among chunky icebergs.

"It's true, love," said Mum. "When you were at the swimming carnival, you had your arms crossed over your strawberry creams constantly. You looked ridiculous in the backstroke."

"Please Mum," I begged. "Be quiet."

Brian was the color of grated beetroot.

"And you won't be wearing something sloppy to cover them up either," said Mum. "You'll be wearing something that shows off your figure. Something with lace and ribbon."

"Oh," said Debbie. "It's going to be fantastic!"

"Fantastic!" said Brian, in a faint, sick echo.

"We'll see . . . ," said Dad. And he poured a glass of water and drank it all down, carrot and all.

two

The next morning, I went down to the river at Sandy Beach, the only decent swimming hole in all of Buranderry. At one end is the Buranderry Swim Club, a decrepit wooden building, where a group of old people called the Buranderry Ice Chips meet each day to swim laps, their skin hanging loose around their hips like handbags. At the other end, on the bend of the river, is the place where I always go with Jody, my best friend.

We lay half in the shade, watching the cockatoos perch in the gum trees like giant white bows.

I rolled over. "Debbie's getting married."

"What?" exclaimed Jody. "Debbie?"

"Debbie," I repeated.

"Whoa!" said Jody, flicking off a fly. "But they've only been going out a month! I haven't even met him."

"I know."

"I would never marry someone that quick!"

"Debbie reckons that when love hits, you know." I sifted the soft, quartzy sand with my fingers. "And once you know, you know!"

"Where did he propose?" asked Jody.

"At O'Riley's," I answered. "Near the spice rack."

"What! And she accepted him!" said Jody. "If I had a boyfriend and he proposed to me there, I'd smack him out."

"Debbie didn't mind."

"I want it to be somewhere exotic," said Jody. "Like on top of a cliff above a wild sea or in a balloon at sunrise."

"Some people might think O'Riley's is exotic," I said.

"Only if you don't have a life!" Jody smeared coconut oil all over her arms.

She wiped her hands on her towel and slipped on her sunglasses.

"Is he hot? He must be hot! You'd only say yes to a proposal like that if he was absolutely hot-hot!"

"I wouldn't say he was hot," I said. "He looks sort of . . . haggard."

Even though Debbie reckoned that Brian was athletic, there was something about him that reminded me of a brown, parched rubber band.

"Haggard!" said Jody. "What's Debbie thinking?"

"I guess she's not worried about his looks."

"She has to wake up to his looks every morning!" said Jody. "The first thing she's going to think when she rolls over and sees him is, 'I feel tired.' "

Most of the time having an opinionated best friend is a good thing. It saves you from having to have opinions yourself, but sometimes when Jody gets on a roll, she's hard to stop.

"Debbie's asked me to be a flower girl," I said. "They're getting married in spring."

The cicadas screamed in the gum trees and the magpies chortled in the distance. I watched a fish jump and plop back into the river. Jody was deathly silent.

"Brian's sister is going to be one too," I added.

Jody stared at me over her sunglasses. "You!"

"Yes."

"But you can't stand people staring at you," said Jody. "You vomited over the guest speaker in assembly in Year Seven when Mrs. McMahon made you say thank you."

It was true. I did have a tendency to vomit at inappropriate moments, particularly if I was experiencing extreme stress.

"How come Debbie wants you to be a flower girl? You're too old. You're fourteen. You should be a bridesmaid."

"She's asked the Three Rs to be bridesmaids," I said. "And Brian's only got three mates."

"Oh you poor thing!" said Jody.

Debbie is ten years older than me, and Rochelle, Renee and Rachael (or the Three Rs as Dad always calls them), have been Debbie's friends since preschool. They all call me the "Love Child" when Mum and Dad are around, and the "Big Mistake" when they're not.

"It's not so hard," said Jody. "All you have to do is wear some fizzy dress, walk down the aisle and throw rose petals."

"Oh no," I said.

"And you get good presents," she finished.

"Really?"

"Really!" said Jody. "See this emerald ring, that was from Janie, my aunt." She patted my shoulder. "You'll be fine."

A group of kids poured down the bush track onto the beach. I spotted Lauren, Jody's sister, in the center of the crowd. Lauren is the most beautiful girl in our school. Everything about her is petite and golden and perfect. Even though Jody is pretty, it's a pale lunar prettiness that goes fuzzy around the edges whenever her sister is nearby.

Lauren unhooked the rope and swung out over the river, her long, blond hair streaming out behind her.

"Oh great," grumbled Jody, sliding her sarong over her legs.

"There's Craig!" I said.

Craig Bennett is the footy star of Buranderry High. His shaved head is as shiny as a glazed apricot and he wears his aftershave like an imperialistic force. You can always smell him before you see him.

"Look at his calf muscles," hissed Jody.

"Don't be pathetic!"

"No wonder he can run! Oh, his chest!"

"Spare me!"

"It's glistening . . ."

"Please!"

"With little pearls of sweat!"

"You're a sad sack."

"He has evolved," said Jody. "Not like your ape."

Nick Lloyd, the best actor in our school, has a face that could be minted onto an old Greek coin, but according to Jody, any bloke with even three strands of hair on their chest qualifies for the title of "Caveman."

"I don't know why you're so into him," said Jody. "It's hopeless. He's in Year Eleven and you're in Year Nine, which is virtually saying he lives on the North Pole and you live on the South. You should go out with someone closer to your . . ."

"Closer to my what?"

"Capacity," said Jody. "Raven De Head likes you, big time."

"I'm not going out with anyone just for the sake of it."

"I don't know why you don't," said Jody. "You need kissing practice."

"I'm not going out with anyone to get kissing practice."

Jody adjusted the straps on her bikini. "It's a kiss! An exchange of saliva! My first kiss was so not romantic. I pulled away and there was a long string of drool swinging between us like a bridge. I didn't know what to do with it. Should I have chopped it with my finger? Or licked it back up?"

"You are so gross!"

"Anyone would think that your first kiss is going to be

the most meaningful moment of your life," said Jody, shaking sand off the edges of her towel.

"I'm allowed to think what I want," I said. "As long as I'm not trying to make you think the same. There's nothing wrong with waiting for the right guy for my first kiss!"

"As long as it happens before you're seventy," she shrugged. "Because if you leave it that long, you'll be removing your dentures."

We watched Lauren race Craig out to the pontoon. Jody squinted.

"I'm telling you, if my sister gets it on with Craig, I'm going to kill her."

•   •   •

In late summer, the Buranderry bus always stinks of sweat, suncream, dead fish and rotten eggs. Everyone is dependent on it though, despite the fact that Terry Dole, the driver, has no idea about customer service and the seats are old and hard; the tough vinyl sutured and puckered with scars.

"There's your man," said Jody, as we swayed down the aisle.

Raven De Head and his little brothers were spread out along the backseat. Everybody in Buranderry knows the De Head family. Back in the seventies, when Mr. De Head was refused service at Pete's pub, he packed the town fountain with a lead pipe bomb and blasted the head off the statue of our town founder. But because Mr. De Head was boozy and forgetful, he also blew off three of his own fingers.

If that wasn't enough to make the De Head family

notorious though, Mr. De Head also called his five sons after birds. Raven's two oldest brothers Crow and Magpie have been in and out of detention centers for stealing and the youngest boys Sparrow and Robin are always running the streets.

Raven is basically the delinquent of our year, too. He's been suspended at least three times, but it never makes much difference. He's always the same after suspension— probably worse, because he spends more time with his older brothers.

"Don't you think he's cute?" asked Jody as we slid into a middle seat. "Just the tiniest bit!"

I turned and looked. Raven was sitting on the backseat like he owned it, his black hair straggly at the ends. Even in the heat, he was wearing jeans. He nodded at me. Two dimples punched his cheeks like deep wells.

All the De Head boys have dimples.

Debbie reckons it's unfair that a family so ugly could get something so adorable. Mrs. Wilton, the owner of Wilton's Quilt On, where my Mum works, calls their dimples "the sign of the devil." But then Mrs. Wilton wears a white, foamy cravat and is always seeing visions in the quilts she sews.

Raven quirked an eyebrow.

"Not even the tiniest bit," I said.

three

At lunch the next day at school, while Jody was at swim squad trying to get near Craig Bennett, I wandered around the playground trying to look meditative rather than friendless. This is harder than it seems. Firstly it requires concentration, because in the playground it's easy to feel like a reject when everyone else is sitting with friends. Being meditative also requires physical coordination, because you are more likely to trip over bin lids and stray apple cores.

So it wasn't surprising I bumped into the trestle table that Nick Lloyd was sitting at in the vestibule area.

"Hi there," he said. He was smiling at me, and his skin

had that glow, that special olive confidence that he didn't even have to work at.

"Sorry." I hid my sunburned arms behind my back.

"Would you like to sign a petition?"

I looked over my shoulder. "Me?" My legs felt numb, as if I'd had surgery to remove all my nerves.

He grinned. "Why not?"

"What for?" I asked.

"For the restoration of the Buranderry fountain to its former glory. Here are some pictures of the new design."

He handed me a folder. I opened it and studied the sketches of a stone man sitting on a stone horse. Despite the artist's best intentions, the horse was plainly miserable. "Have you got many signatures?"

"Not yet."

I handed the folder back. "How many?"

He ran his hand through the cowlick in his fringe. "None."

"That's too bad."

"People aren't as excited about this as they are about whales and starving children."

I nodded. I tried to think of something clever and interesting. Nick picked up a pen and drew a squiggle on top of the petition page.

"You don't have to sign if you don't want to."

"Old Hairy Buranderry wasn't a nice man," I blurted. "He was horrible to his five children."

"He's still the town founder."

"So!" I shrugged.

"You don't think he should be remembered?"

"Why don't we have people who live quietly, but majestically, made into statues and fountains?"

"Because . . ."

I struck a pose. "Here stands Joe Dalloway, who faithfully fed the ducks at Sandy Beach each day of his life and gave all his money to the poor and never had a bad word to say about anyone for as long as he lived."

"Yes . . . but . . ."

I posed as a woman holding a child on her left hip. "Here is a memorial for Maria Carvelli, who stayed at home and brought up her children without complaint, who minded her children's children and her children's children's children, who never had a day off in her life and who died in their service."

Nick put down his pen.

"Sometimes," I said, "the people who get all the acclaim after they've died are the ones who got enough of it while they were alive."

I was teetering on the edge. A prolonged outburst of silliness and illogicality was not too far away. I placed my hands against my cheeks and slowed down my breathing. It's always unseemly to chuck a birkett in my opinion. But it's actually insane to chuck one in front of a complete stranger. Especially if that stranger also happens to have the most cutely crooked nose in the universe.

Nick stood up slowly. "You're making me wish *I'd* blown up the statue."

"I'm not encouraging vandalism."

We stared at each other. Nick wore his school uniform with the easy grace of a fashion statement. All the creases and folds lined up right. His brown hair was curling over his collar and a little upside-down triangle of hair was peeking out of his shirt.

"So I guess you won't be signing," he said. "Even though I've spent most of my lunch hanging out in this heat."

A thread from my hem tickled the back of my left leg. He was so sweetly hangdog that for a moment I couldn't help thinking I'd sign my own death sentence.

"Maybe not this time."

"You know," he said, leaning towards me, "you should do debating or drama."

"I don't talk in public."

He raised his hands. "What are we doing now?"

"In front of large groups," I said. "It makes me vomit uncontrollably."

"But you're good!" he said.

The school bell buzzed. Hordes of kids poured across the grounds, heading for the main entrance. Screeches and shouts echoed around the vestibule as hundreds of feet shuffled back to class.

"Listen," said Nick, "on Thursday there's a meeting for the school play. It's called *The Tempest*. It's great. It's the last play Shakespeare wrote. It's full of magic, revenge, hope, hate, forgiveness and love at first sight."

"Wow."

"I'll see you there."

"I don't know."

"Come on! Be adventurous," he said. "I'll hold your hand."

And the thought of Nick Lloyd holding my hand made my head go dizzy. My stomach fizzed as if a large aspirin had been dropped in it.

"I'll see."

"After school," he said. "The hall."

I allowed myself to be swept up in the stream surging through the front door. People elbowed, pushed and shoved, but I couldn't care less.

• • •

That afternoon, I caught the Buranderry bus home from school. It takes the same route every day, up through Buranderry East, down through Buranderry Flats, over into Buranderry West and up the curvy roads to Buranderry Heights where all the fancy houses perch on the cliffs like thickly iced wedding cakes.

I'd borrowed a copy of *The Tempest* but it was too hard to read. The language was thick and creamy. And it was so hot. Even in the late afternoon, the road was full of shimmer. The petunias in Buranderry Memorial Park were flopping over in their beds as though they'd been up partying all night.

"Saw you talking to Nick Lloyd today."

I turned around. Raven De Head lounged behind me.

"Are you spying on me?"

"Don't flatter yourself," he said, grinning. "I was on detention. I could see you out the window."

"Right."

"That whacker's trying to get the town fountain restored."

"What's so bad about that?"

"Better off without it," Raven said. "My dad did the town a favor. Hairy Buranderry was an arsehole and the fountain was dead ugly. Ask anyone."

"Nobody's perfect," I shrugged.

"So did you sign?"

"What?"

He lifted his eyebrows. "Lloyd's petition."

"Oh that."

"Well?"

"None of your business."

"I knew you had good taste."

"You've got no idea," I said. "The fountain should be restored. But not with Hairy Buranderry."

Raven tapped out a drumbeat against the rail. His fingernails were bitten short. "So what are you reading?"

"I'm sorry?"

He leant over the seat and nodded. "What's the book?"

"It's a play."

"What play?"

"*The Tempest.*"

"Oh yeah."

"Shakespeare."

"Right." Raven shook his head and laughed. Even though he had a smile on his face, his eyes had that ripped-off look he and his brothers carried around like birthmarks.

"I'm thinking of trying out for the school play," I said.

"You!" he said.

"Why not?"

"Didn't you vomit over Mr. Suzuki's legs in Year Seven in assembly . . . ?"

"Mr. Daihatsu!" I said, with emphasis.

"Whatever."

"That was a long time ago," I said.

The pong of the town tip flooded through the bus.

Everything that's ugly in our town is located in Buranderry Flats. The worst part by far is the town tip. It's been closed for a couple of years since the Buranderry Village Progress Association lobbied the government to open a new tip at Sesquith. Meanwhile the old one festered while the council argued about what to do with it, and it smelled, always, like wet, dead dog.

I reached out and jammed my window shut. The sound of windows slamming ricocheted up and down the bus.

"Why would *you* want to audition?" asked Raven, pushing his window wide open.

"It's a great play."

"What's so great about it?" asked Raven, jutting his right elbow out.

"You know . . . it's . . . I haven't finished reading it yet. But . . . you know . . . the idea of those characters . . . they fall in love at first sight and there's magic and revenge and hope and everything."

"Get your elbow in, De Head," shouted Terry Dole, the bus driver.

"It's bloody amazing how he can drive without looking at the road."

I couldn't help laughing. It was true. Terry Dole always

knew what was going on at the back of the bus because his eyes never moved off the rear vision mirror.

Raven watched a blowfly buzz against the window. "What's so great about love at first sight?"

"If you have to ask, I can hardly hope you'd understand," I said.

"Hear my soul speak," said Raven.
*"The very instant that I saw you, did
my heart fly to your service; there resides,
to make me slave to it; and for your sake
am I this patient log-man."*

I stared at him. "What's that?"

"Shakespeare," said Raven, cupping his hand around the fly and flicking it out. *"The Tempest."*

"Oh."

He closed his window. "What made you think I wouldn't know Shakespeare?"

I could feel myself go red. I wasn't up to confessing my theory that the only reason people like him got into trouble at school was because they were too stupid to do anything else.

He leant forward, waiting. His face was so close I could see the different segments of blue in his eyes and the small crescent of black pores at the sides of his nose. I looked away.

He laughed and pressed the buzzer. "See ya, Queen of Naples."

four

"You need to put on some makeup, Mum," said Debbie.

Debbie handed over her makeup bag. Mum fumbled around and pulled out a battered case and dabbed some rouge on her cheeks.

"You need lipstick too," said Debbie.

"But blush is all I ever wear!"

"Come on, Mum," said Debbie, with a sigh. "Tonight is very important."

"What's wrong with the way I look now?"

"You're meeting my in-laws, Mum," said Debbie. "I want them to think they're marrying someone from a respectable family."

"But how does wearing lipstick make me respectable?"

"Think of it like this," said Debbie. "At the moment, you're a black-and-white television. With a dash of lipstick, you're a color one."

"I don't know, Debbie," said Mum, patting her cheeks. "Sometimes it's best to stick with what you know."

"All I'm asking for is a little effort." Debbie's voice cracked. "But don't worry, Mum . . . if it's too much trouble . . ."

"It's not too much trouble," said Mum. "But why do I have to pretend?"

"I'm not asking you to *pretend*!" said Debbie loudly.

"I don't see—"

"I'm just asking you to put on some lipstick!"

"There's no need to shout, Deb," said Mum.

"Wearing lipstick is a sign," cried Debbie, "that coordinating a wedding will be no problem for you because you know how to organize your own two lips in a satisfactory manner."

Debbie had all the telltale symptoms. She was red around the cheeks. Her eyes were bulging. Her speech was increasingly agitated. She was teetering on the edge of a birkett. If someone didn't intervene, the night was going to be ruined.

"Mum," I said. "Maybe you should let Debbie do your makeup. Think of it as a practice run for the wedding."

"That's a good idea," said Mum. "A practice run."

They were in the bathroom for twenty minutes. When they came out, Mum's face looked like a paint display for Dulux.

I hesitated. "I thought wearing blue eye shadow was out now?"

"What would you know?" said Debbie.

Dad walked into the kitchen, his hair slicked down with baby oil. "Bloody hell!" he said. "Did you fall on your face?"

Mum's bottom lip flickered. "Debbie gave me a makeover."

"With a plank?"

"No," said Debbie.

"She can't go to Brian's like that," said Dad. He wiped the oil off his hands onto a tea towel. "They'll think I bash her."

"All right, Dad!" cried Debbie. "It was an experiment."

"She looks like a rainbow trout."

"All right Dad! You don't have to go on!"

Mum raced off to the bathroom. I went to the door. I could hear the sound of rushing water and some sniffling. "Mum?" I called. "It's not too bad." I tried to think of something good to say. "You look . . . tanned."

Mum opened the door. Black mascara ran down her cheeks in rivers. "You tell Debbie, that if I'm not good enough to go as I usually am, then I'm not good enough to go."

Debbie's voice floated down the hall. "Come on!" she cried. "We have to go! They'll be waiting for us. Brian's dad gets upset when people are late!"

I turned to Mum and patted her shoulder. "Of course you're good enough to go."

Debbie stormed up the hallway, her turquoise pantsuit flapping and her fringe slicking up. "Are we ready to go or what?"

It's a sad truth that people who chuck birketts rarely stop at one. Usually they are never as exhausted by the emotional fallout as the people who have to watch.

Mum smiled and took a deep breath. She pulled up her pantyhose and smoothed down her skirt. "All ready then."

Debbie came closer and stared. "You've still got mascara—"

"Shut up," I said. "She can fix it in the car."

five

Meeting the Websters started badly, mainly because Dad got lost trying to find the quickest way there.

The Websters live in Buranderry East. That's where the government built identical fibro houses to hide returned ex-servicemen and their widows. It's close to Buranderry National Park, which is full of scrub, blackberry, lantana and wild deer.

To make matters worse, Debbie forgot to warn us that the Lieutenant Colonel had a missing right leg. So Dad spent the first ten minutes making one faux pas after the other; talking about how he doesn't drink full strength beer anymore because it's easy to get legless and how he's the best wicket-keeper for the Buranderry over thirty-fives because he's so brilliant at stumpings.

Fortunately, the Lieutenant Colonel and Mrs. Webster were so busy fussing with the drinks and peanuts and a platter of dried apricots with cream cheese that Dad's conversation eddied around them. But Debbie was mad. You could tell she wanted to lean over and scratch Dad's eyes out.

The Websters' dining table was decorated with little Australian flags and candles. In pride of place, behind the head of the table, above a maple dresser, hung a picture of the Queen, lit by a small wall lamp.

A large tapestry hung on the side wall. There were soldiers on horses, stabbing the enemy straight through the heart. There were dead bodies and decapitated heads rolling around the hillside, all done in neat little stitches.

"It's wonderful, isn't it?" said Mrs. Webster, as we sat down for dinner.

The horses reared with foam-flecked lips and wild eyes. Pools of blood drenched the dirt. The dark shadowy faces of the enemy sneered at the noble glowing soldiers.

"We're into war," she confided. "It's in our blood."

Mrs. Webster was so sweetly pretty, with her silvery cinnamon perm and her soft, pink cheeks and her faded blue gingham apron, that when I heard those steely words I felt like I was watching a badly dubbed film.

"Brian!" said the Lieutenant Colonel. "Get your sister. She knows what time it is. This'll be ten demerits for her!" He gazed around at us and smiled smugly, satisfied that he had everything in his life conquered.

Brian opened a door at the end of the lounge room. "Jackie!" he called. "Dinner's on."

"Jackie's been studying very hard," said Mrs. Webster, taking off her apron. "She wants to go into the army as soon as she can. She even took a summer school subject on military warfare. Topped her class."

"She was the youngest in her year," said the Lieutenant Colonel. "She outperformed everyone in the practical unit. She's a fighting machine. She can strip and load a gun faster than the flick of a lizard's tongue. Not bad for a girl."

Jackie charged through the door. She was small and lean, with a long, dark plait hanging limply over her shoulder. She was dressed in army fatigues with a black beret perched on her head.

"This is Jackie," said Mrs. Webster proudly.

"You're late, girl!" said the Lieutenant Colonel.

"Sorry, Sir," she said.

"This is Debbie's family," said Mrs. Webster. "This is Debbie's mum, June, and Debbie's dad, Barry, and Debbie's sister, Jim."

"Gem!" I said.

She pulled out her chair. "I know you," she said. "You go to my school."

"Sorry?" I said, my mind cataloging.

She sat down and flipped out her serviette. "Yeah," she said. "You hang out with Lauren Tebbutt's younger sister, Jody."

"That's right."

"I'm in the year below you," she said.

"Right," I nodded, trying to place her.

"Apparently you guys call us 'the Barmy Army,' " she grunted.

"Oh," I said, at last.

Buranderry High is built on reclaimed swampland and a whole group of war fanatic kids built trenches down near the mangroves at the bottom of the school oval. The fact that there were mosquitoes as big as birds didn't stop them from mucking around down there.

"That's okay," she nodded. "Sometimes we call you girls 'the Pound.' " She screwed up her nose and for a moment I saw her standing above me with a bayonet, ready to disembowel me.

"She's going to be the army's secret weapon," said the Lieutenant Colonel.

"That's right," she said, and she gave me a glare so lethal I could feel my heart frizzle and shrink.

"Well, isn't that lovely," said Mrs. Webster, "to think you two already know each other."

"Well, Barry!" said the Lieutenant Colonel to my dad. "I'll let you give the toast.

Dad stumbled upwards, sloshing champagne onto Mrs. Webster's crisp, white tablecloth. "Right then!" he said.

Everyone stood up.

"Um . . . Yes! Let me see! It gives me great pleasure to toast . . . the future Mr. and Mrs. Webs—"

Debbie flinched. "Dad!" she whispered. Her head jerked towards the top of the table.

"What?" Dad asked.

She rolled her eyes sidewards. Dad's forehead was a fan of wrinkles. "Are you all right, Deb?" he said.

"The Queen!" she whispered.

Dad swung around. The Websters were facing the Queen, their glasses slightly raised. Their faces were somber and reverent, as if the Queen were sitting at the head of the table. They obviously had a complicated pre-dinner ritual that was ceremonially important.

Dad's Adam's apple bobbed up and down. Mum gave his arm an encouraging pat. "It gives . . . me . . . great . . . pleasure," he dithered. "To propose . . . a toast to . . . the Queen. . . ." He looked around at Debbie. She nodded. "Who as we all know . . . surely understands more about . . . marriage than most of us . . . after spending many long decades . . . with that old grump of hers. . . . To the Queen, God save her!"

Dad took a long drink and sat down with a thud. The room was quiet. The Lieutenant Colonel dug his tongue around the bottom of his lip as if he had an irritating ulcer.

"G-God save the Queen," stuttered Brian.

Debbie, Mum and Mrs. Webster chinked their glasses. "To the Queen!" they said.

Jackie glowered and said nothing. I gulped my thimble of champagne.

"Aubrey," said Mrs. Webster. "Would you mind if we left the anthem for later?"

The Lieutenant Colonel rubbed his chest and then nodded. "All right," he said. "But before coffee!"

Mrs. Webster walked soberly over to the maple dresser. "I've got your knife ready for carving."

The Lieutenant Colonel caressed a long, gleaming sharp sword. He puffed warm air along the blade and then he wiped it carefully with his serviette. He took a deep breath, then carved the lamb as swiftly as if it were a sponge cake. "It's in the technique," he said, glancing at us. "And the practice! Perfect practice equals perfect pleasure."

"Having a good leg doesn't go astray either," said Dad.

Debbie's fork fell off the table.

"Of lamb," he added hastily.

Mum squeezed Dad's shoulder until he moaned and then she launched into a long monologue on the therapeutic benefits of cross-stitch for the elderly.

• • •

Dinner was going reasonably well until the good food and wine went to Dad's head and he got to that stage of the night when he was in the mood for some pontification.

"She's had a terrible couple of decades," he said, gesturing to the Queen. "What with that whinger of a husband and those sniveling sons and that horsy daughter and that great castle burning down and having to pay back those taxes and those divorces in the family, then Diana dying like that and her sister and the Queen Mother popping off and those blasted corgis pooing in the palace and that ex-daughter-in-law of hers lazing around the Bahamas—it's amazing she's lasted as long as she has."

The Lieutenant Colonel winced and sat up straighter at each item in Dad's long litany of catastrophe. It was clear he viewed even a minor difference of opinion as a threat to his authority.

"After spending an evening under the watchful eye of

our monarch," said Dad, with a nod, raising his glass of port to the Queen, "I realize that even if you're rich, famous and powerful, it can't save you from your family!"

Anger blanched the Lieutenant Colonel's cheeks.

Dad opened an after-dinner mint. "If I was the Queen, I'd scowl too!" he added. He leant back in his chair and popped the chocolate into his mouth. "We've got a lot to be thankful for," he said magnanimously, his teeth turning brown. "We've got nice normal families in comparison to hers!"

Mrs. Webster scraped the dessert dishes frantically and piled them on top of each other. "Why don't we adjourn to the lounge room," she said. "We can talk about the wedding in comfort there."

Brian began clearing the dishes away. "Leave that, love," said Mrs. Webster. "Jackie, why don't you show Gemma the backyard while we talk. She must be bored stiff."

The Lieutenant Colonel stood up. Brian handed him his crutches. "Take her out the back, girl," he said to Jackie, his cheeks now mottled red. "And show her some action."

I did not want to be left alone with Jackie.

"Go on, love," Mum said. "Out you go!"

"It'll do you good to get some fresh air," said Dad. "Your face is as red as Aunty Beryl's after a night on the booze."

Jackie stared at me like I was an annoying insect she was longing to crush.

"Make sure you time her," the Lieutenant Colonel called, as I followed her out.

six

The sky was a deep purple, freckled with stars. A bat flew overhead, its wings whooping. The night air was dank and rotten, quiet but for the popping of frogs.

Jackie leant on the balcony railing, her face closed up like a paper puzzle.

"About the Barmy Army thing," I said.

"Do you know that the word 'engagement' has a number of different meanings?"

"No," I said.

"It can mean betroth, or to pledge oneself to another, to interlock, or bind by contract or promise." A thin silver bullet and some dog tags swayed on a chain around her neck. "But to those of us with war in our blood, it means to enter into conflict, to fight."

What can you say to a fanatic?

"Tell your sister," she said, "I'm not wearing a dress."

"I can see that."

"At the wedding."

"Oh right," I said. "Okay."

"I don't wear dresses," she said. "Ever!"

"Look," I began, "sometimes you don't get . . ."

"My dad reckons your family's soft," she said, flicking her long, skinny plait over her shoulder. "He's worried your bloodlines are going to muddy ours. We've been warriors since time began."

"Oh."

"Dad was hoping Brian would make an alliance with someone from a naval background."

"Debbie likes the water," I said. "She's taken the tinny out on the river a few times."

"It's unfortunate," said Jackie. "But Brian won't listen to reason."

Her supercilious, condescending air made me want to punch her lights out. How dare she talk about Debbie as if she were an animal and not a person with real feelings?

"Debbie has a lot to offer, you know."

It felt weird to be speaking so positively about Debbie, after all the years I had spent bagging her. "She's vivacious and fun," I said. "She's caring and sensitive."

"That's not going to help us win a war," said Jackie.

"Well, I don't think Brian's going to be much use either. He can barely stay awake most of the time."

"I know," said Jackie. "It's a disappointment. Dad was hoping a good alliance might rectify it. Cadets didn't. But the right girl might have. My mum says Brian takes after Dad's great grandmother. She was a civilian. Soft as they come. Muddied bloodlines. . . ."

A spotlight blazed on and the backyard was stripped of shadow.

Directly below the balcony was a large ditch. It was as wide as the backyard and filled with dirty water. There were no stairs leading down to it. There were no stairs anywhere off the balcony. Just three ropes swinging across the black water, attached to a thick steel pole on the other side.

"What's that?" I asked.

"A rope bridge."

"What's it for?"

"This is an advanced military training ground. My dad believes constant training is needed if we are going to stand against the enemy. Perfect practice equals perfect performance."

"What enemy?" I asked, gazing at a long patch of barbed wire behind the ditch, thick as a blackberry bush.

In the middle of the yard a weird net, covered in leaves, soared high between two wooden trunks. A row of tires led up to a brick wall, almost as tall as the house. The only trees, two big red angophoras near the side fence, had a single rope tied between them.

"We have enemies everywhere," she whispered.

She was freaking me out. "Where's your Hills Hoist?"

Jackie bounced the rope with her foot. "We have an underground drying room."

On the back wall, I could see the outline of round targets.

"I bet you can't!" she said.

"Can't what?"

"Walk across the rope."

"Across the rope!" My voice rose ridiculously higher in pitch.

"Are you scared?"

"No!" I said. "I'm not. How deep is the water?"

"Over my head," she said.

"You're kidding."

Jackie stretched her arms and cracked her knuckles. She stared at me with her dark, sharp eyes. "We don't kid in our family."

"We don't stop kidding in ours."

"You're family is a product of popular culture," she said. "You need to be constantly entertained."

"I won't go across it."

"So you *are* scared."

"No, I'm not."

"Well, then!" She jumped the balcony railing and climbed out. She stood springing on the rope. She was like a tightly coiled hose, craving water, aching to flick and slide and fly and whack, her aggression leaking out in a hundred long fizzing spits. She licked her lips and stared at me triumphantly, her arms flared out in sharp triangles.

"I'm not into war," I said.

"Not into war." She shook her head as if she'd been made to swallow medicine. "So you're a coward?"

"You might like to think so," I said. "But I reckon peaceful action works better than fists and guns. Have you ever read about Gandhi?"

The Lieutenant Colonel popped his head out the back door. "How's she going?" he called.

"She's too scared to do it," said Jackie.

"Too scared?" bellowed the Lieutenant Colonel. "Where's your gumption, girl?"

Mum and Dad came out onto the balcony. Their eyes slid left and right, as they tried to check for an outdoor setting without looking too competitive.

"What a huge yard!" said Mum.

"A bit of grass wouldn't go astray," said Dad, nodding. "You might like to think about Winter Green Couch."

"I didn't realize you had a swimming pool," said Mum.

"This is not a pool, Madam!" hollered the Lieutenant Colonel.

Mum put on her glasses. "Oh," she said.

"This is an advanced military training ground!"

"I see," said Mum.

"The only way we're going to survive an invasion is if every house in Australia has one. They should be as common as barbecues. We must be prepared for the rigors of war!"

"Surely a game of squash would suffice," joked Dad.

"I beg your pardon," said the Lieutenant Colonel, whirling around.

"I . . . well . . . I can't help thinking that a squash ball would be almost as unpredictable as a bullet," said Dad, slipping his hands in and out of his pockets. "Least it is when I play."

"Your daughter is unable to complete the easiest obstacle in the whole course," cried the Lieutenant Colonel. "If she had any grit about her, any pluck, spirit, daring and fortitude, not to mention intelligence, she'd manage that obstacle in a second. I hope whatever her problem is, it's not genetic!"

"Of course it's not genetic," said Dad.

"There's nothing wrong with our genes!" said Mum.

"That remains to be seen, Madam," said the Lieutenant Colonel.

"My husband has been the Buranderry Senior Sportsman of the Year three times running. He's got three trophies to prove it. He's a very fit man. He won his squash competition for the Waratahs this year and the Buranderry Public School Primary Fun Run for the over-forties. He could cross that rope in a minute. It'd be as easy for him as sliding down a slippery dip!" cried Mum.

"Would it?" said the Lieutenant Colonel.

"Now, love!" said Dad, clearing his throat.

"He's a fantastic sportsman! And both my daughters have inherited his genes."

"Perhaps he'd like to have a go then?" said the Lieutenant Colonel.

"He certainly would," said Mum.

"No!" said Dad.

"Now, Barry," said Mum. "Don't be modest."

Dad's bottom lip puffed out ineffectually like a blowfish caught on a hook. "Now, love . . . I really don't think . . ."

He wilted under Mum's icy gaze. "You must defend the girls," she said. "And their honor!"

Dad nodded. He undid his shoes with fumbling fingers and handed them to Mum.

"And your trousers. They're tan," she said. "They'll stain if they get dirty, and they're your only good pair!"

Dad unzipped his trousers and slid them off. He stood under the blaze of light in his white shirt and love heart boxers. His brown legs poked out jauntily, as skinny as the legs of a flamingo. He climbed the railing and stood at the beginning of the rope bridge. His shorts fluttered in the breeze.

The Lieutenant Colonel took out his stopwatch. "On your mark," he said. "Get set. Go!"

Dad stepped out confidently onto the rope.

"Don't look down," said Brian. "Aim for the other side."

"Be quiet," cried the Lieutenant Colonel.

Dad sidled out like a crab. The rope danced and his legs began to tremble. When he reached the middle, he stared down and came to an abrupt halt. His left leg shook uncontrollably, as if it was experiencing an earthquake.

"Go, you great stallion of a man," called Mum.

Dad's leg was shaking so hard it looked like it was completely separate from the rest of his body.

"Keep going," bawled the Lieutenant Colonel. He gave the bottom rope a flick.

A wave jolted Dad as he took a step. His right foot slipped. He lunged forward, his arms outstretched. The rope hit his face and he bounced and slid round, his right leg hooked over the line. He hung like a wounded fruit bat.

Brian scurried out along the rope. Dad's body joggled in time. Brian grabbed the side rope. "Give me your hand, Mr. Stone," he cried.

"I . . . can't," grunted Dad.

Brian reached over. "Bugger!" he said.

"Give him your hand, you silly-billy," called Mum.

"Look," said Brian, urgently. "I'm going to get you into a sitting position, then you can turn round and grab hold of the side ropes for balance, and when you're ready, you can stand up and we'll go back to the balcony."

"There," said Mum. "That sounds easy."

Dad stretched out his hand. Brian grabbed it and pulled Dad up so fast and hard that his backside slid off the rope with a twang. Now Dad was dangling in midair, his boxers spangling in the light like a disco glitter ball.

"Bloody hell," muttered Brian. "Your hand is sweaty."

Dad's hand slid. Palm passing palm. Brian's fingers scrabbled. And then Dad was falling. He hit the water with a gigantic crack.

"Barry!" cried Mum.

White froth swirled on the surface like the bubbles on a chocolate milkshake.

"This is the genetic inheritance you're going to subject your children to," yelled the Lieutenant Colonel, as Brian scrambled back across the rope. "Can you live with that?"

"I can live with it fine," said Brian, as he stripped off his shirt. He dropped a rope ladder down into the ditch.

"You might be able to," called the Lieutenant Colonel, "but can your children?"

"They'll just have to be grateful for what they get," said Brian and he jumped into the ditch and fished out Dad.

Dad was black with mud, the whites of his eyes fluorescent. He crawled under the railing and straggled across the balcony like a wet newborn kitten. Brian slammed him on the back and water burst out of Dad's mouth and nose like a volcanic eruption.

Mum slipped her arms under Dad's shoulders and lifted him up.

"They're gormless, Val," said the Lieutenant Colonel. "I told you they would be. Why couldn't he marry Lance Corporal Emmeline Friday?"

"That's enough, you little rodent!" hissed Mum.

"Rodent!" said Mrs. Webster. "Who are you calling a rodent?"

"Your husband!" said Mum. "He's a walking, talking, useless showbag!" And she dragged Dad through the back-door, into the kitchen.

"My husband is not a rodent," said Mrs. Webster, following hot on Mum's heels. "He is the reason that you and your family are standing in this free land!"

"Come on, Gemma! Come on, Debbie!" Mum called. Dad was slumped against her like a war-wounded soldier. "We're going."

Debbie trailed behind Mrs. Webster, sobbing openly.

"But we haven't sung the national anthem," cried Mrs. Webster.

Mum twirled around and faced Mrs. Webster. Her cheeks were bright red. Her eyes bulged and she could barely breathe. "You can shove it," she wheezed. "Along with your decorative swords, your horrid little obstacle course, your lousy Queen and your foul tapestries!"

It was the first time in my life I had ever seen Mum chuck a birkett.

It was also the first time I had ever considered that at the right time and for the right reason, a birkett could be a beautiful thing.

seven

In our school, the same people do the school play every year. They are always confident, outrageous and sure of each other. Even the backstage people tend to have a gothic splendor that makes them untouchable.

On Thursday afternoon, when I pushed the door open to the school hall, I felt like I was going to my execution. There is something very scary about fronting up to a meeting and speaking in front of a group of people who are so glamorous and capable. I feel strangely drawn to them, like an insect bedazzled by light and yet still always aware of a certain danger, of the ability that glamorous people have to snap you into insignificance if you make even one mistake.

Everyone was sitting in a circle. They turned and stared. I was about to slide back out, when Nick stood up. "Hey, you came," he said.

"Hi."

"Mrs. Langton, Ms. Highgate, and everyone, this is . . ." He bit his lip. "I don't know your name," he said.

"Gemma," I said, quickly. "Gemma Stone."

Sometimes I can't help thinking the world is divided into two sorts of people: those who expect to be known and remembered and those who expect to be unknown and forgotten.

"Hi," I croaked.

Most of the students hanging around were in the years above me. There was a scattering of younger kids from the years below, those aspiring actors who auditioned for everything chronically and were totally thrilled when they got into the chorus.

"Welcome, Gemma," said Mrs. Langton. "It's wonderful to have a fresh face in our group."

Mrs. Langton was the senior drama teacher at Buranderry High and she inspired the type of loyalty that the Lieutenant Colonel could only dream about.

"Hi there," said Ms. Highgate, the junior drama teacher, tossing an orange corkscrew curl over her shoulder.

The stage jutted out like a large tongue, waiting to gulp me down. Bile rushed into my throat. I swallowed hard. I did not want to be sick in front of these glittering, competent people.

"Um, actually, I was hoping, I could, maybe, do some backstage work or something," I said, my stomach churning.

"Don't be shy!" said Ms. Highgate, arching her eyebrows. "We like everyone to try out, even if it's only a few lines. We're very egalitarian." Her voice was loud and had the twang of a basketball when it's slammed on the court.

I tasted sour milk in my mouth. "I'd like to give it a go . . . but . . . I   think . . . performing . . . might   make me . . . vomit," I said.

"Really?" Mrs. Langton tilted her head and looked at me. I'd never seen her rush. She walked rather than charged around the school and she did everything with an intense gravity, as though she wanted to draw the most out of each minute of her life.

"Do you feel like vomiting when you're speaking as someone else?" she asked.

"I don't know," I said. "I've never spoken as someone else."

"I've heard her give a speech," said Nick. "She's good."

"Well, often being in character can make a difference," said Mrs. Langton. She slid her glasses on top of her head. "I've known people who've stuttered terribly offstage, but when they're onstage in character, they can speak without a problem. So have a go. And if it's too much, we'll find you a backstage role."

Nick put his hand on my elbow and guided me to a gap in the circle. I sat down, clutching my legs. He gave my hand a squeeze. "Don't worry," he said.

Ms. Highgate took a deep breath and closed her eyes. When I did drama in Year Seven, she was into crystals, astrology, dolphins and getting in touch with her inner child.

On the outward breath, her eyes popped open. "It's time to warm up," she said.

The door banged and Raven slouched in. There was no need for introductions.

"Do you have a message?" asked Ms. Highgate.

"Nope."

"Detention's been moved to the science lab," she said.

"I know," he said. "I've just come from there. That's why I'm late."

Ms. Highgate's eyebrows squiggled up and down. "Well, how can we help you?"

"I'm here for the play."

"For the play?" Ms. Highgate cleared her throat. Her eyes flicked to Mrs. Langton for support. She toyed with the amethyst around her neck.

"Why wouldn't I be?" asked Raven.

Ms. Highgate took another deep breath. It was clear that her notions of egalitarianism were now in fierce conflict. "This meeting is only for students who are serious about performing," she said at last. "So perhaps . . ."

"How do you know I'm not serious?"

"Because . . ."

"Julie." Mrs. Langton's voice was barely audible.

"I've read Shakespeare," said Raven. "Even *The Tempest.* Are you going to critique colonialism in your interpretation?"

Mrs. Langton laughed. "Why don't you sit down and find out," she said, indicating with her head that he should join the circle.

Raven shuffled around and squeezed into a spot by my side.

Ms. Highgate glared at Mrs. Langton and then at Raven. She tugged the crystal around her neck so hard I wouldn't have been surprised if a unicorn had suddenly appeared, reared its great hooves and knocked Raven senseless.

"Where was I?" she asked, her right cheek stained red.

"Warm-up," said Nick.

"Ah, right," said Ms. Highgate. "Thank you. Let's begin."

And we played games. Tag games like we did in primary school. "Stuck in the Mud," "Cat'n'Mouse," "Granny's Footsteps" and "Fruit Salad." Everyone was screaming and charging across the hall.

This was more fun than drama in Year Seven and Eight where we used to spend most of the lessons on the history of theater or watching videos on the building of the Globe or making fiddly masks with gold sequins and pink feathers.

After we finished the tag games, we played trust games.

The scariest one was the trust circle. In this game, we stood in a circle and the person in the middle had to close their eyes, keep their body in line and fall forwards and backwards into our arms. As the person's confidence increased, so did the speed, until they were whizzed around the circle like a special delivery parcel.

Raven was hopeless. He found it hard to keep his eyes closed and whenever he fell backwards, he'd take a step. No matter how hard he tried. In the end he couldn't stop sniggering but it wasn't a brash who-cares snigger. It was the kind of snigger that someone might slip out before putting his neck on the chopping block.

After that, Mrs. Langton led a vocal warm-up. We got in touch with our breath, our diaphragms and intercostals. We pummeled our chests and massaged our nasal resonators. We lifted our soft palates at the back of our mouths and sirened up and down scales like demented opera singers. Mrs. Langton wanted us to think of our soft palates as domes in a cathedral. My soft palate felt like a saggy bed.

When we finished warming up, we sat in a circle again. I made sure I was on the opposite side from Raven, as far away from him as possible. Mrs. Langton and Ms. Highgate sat with us on the floor and we talked about the play.

"The plot is fairly straightforward," said Mrs. Langton. "But it's good to understand some history in order to make sense of it."

"Prospero was the rightful Duke of Milan," said Ms. Highgate, taking over, her eyes alight as if she had juicy gossip. "He was too caught up in his studies, in his own head really, to pay attention to his kingdom. So he left the practical running of his state to his brother Antonio." She leant forward, as if she was getting to the good bit. "But Antonio was rotten to the core, a right royal backstabber. He was so riddled with ambition that he plotted to usurp Prospero, and he did so by doing a secret deal with Prospero's enemy, Alonso, the King of Naples."

I tried to keep the connections from getting muddled. But Shakespeare could have been a little more helpful by not giving all Prospero's enemies names that started with "A."

Nick clicked his fingers. "So Antonio organized for the King of Naples to raise an army and those guys kidnapped Prospero, the rightful Duke and his baby daughter Miranda."

"That's right," said Mrs. Langton. "Rather than risking

bloodshed and rebellion, they hurried Prospero and his baby daughter aboard a sturdy boat and carried them out to sea, where they deposited them in a leaky boat on a roaring ocean with no rigging or tackle."

The image of a father and a tiny baby in a small boat, abandoned, whipped by wind and washed over by waves, was haunting.

"How did they survive?" I asked.

"Because of 'Providence divine,' " said Raven, pressing the flapping sole of his left shoe together. "That's what Prospero says."

"There was that nobleman from Naples," said Nick, reprovingly, as if he was irritated that Raven had dared to speak. "Gonzalo was in charge of sending them off. He secretly gave them food, fresh water and volumes of books on magic from Prospero's library. They wouldn't have survived without his help!"

Raven smiled and shrugged, as if he wasn't going to take Nick on, but his eyes had an "I'll make up my own mind" defiance.

"They arrived safely on a deserted island," said Ms. Highgate.

"It wasn't completely deserted," said Raven. "Caliban lived there, and some spirits—one was called Ariel."

"That's true," said Ms. Highgate, grudgingly. "But it might as well have been."

"The play begins with a tempest—a violent storm conjured up by Prospero," said Mrs. Langton.

"Prospero summons the storm because, by a strange

accident, Lady Fortune has brought his enemies nearby," said Ms. Highgate. "Prospero knows it in his bones. He feels it in his psyche. Or maybe he's seen it in the stars."

"So his brother Antonio and Alonso are just offshore," added Nick, with relish.

"With Alonso's son on board," said Raven.

"Prince Ferdinand," said Mrs. Langton. "Good pickup, Raven. It's a nice twist. It means Prospero's enemy, Alonso, and his son are as vulnerable as Prospero and Miranda all those years ago in that leaky boat."

"What happens next?" asked Tea, a girl from the year above. "Does he kill them?"

"With the help of the spirit Ariel, the ship is wrecked," said Mrs. Langton. "And as the groups of survivors wander the island, Prospero orchestrates his strange revenge. And it's not what we expect. Alonso's son falls in love with Miranda, others plot murder but nearly all undergo a sea change."

"Wow," I said.

"What if you've never auditioned before?" interrupted a younger girl who had rainbow-colored braces.

"Well, we want to be fair, so we're going to give everyone a chance to get acquainted with the play and the audition process," said Mrs. Langton. "All roles in this play are up for grabs. Nothing's been pre-cast. If someone convinces me they're ideal for a role, even a role I would not naturally cast them in—the role is theirs. But first, let's get used to the language. Pair up."

Pair up. Those words were like a lighted match to dry

grass. Everyone snatched at each other like greedy shoppers in a New Year sale. Nick was mobbed. Girls dived at him from all over the room. It was as if he was a dangling leg in a piranha-infested river.

By the time the echo of those two small words had faded, everyone was in a pair, except Raven and me.

"Well," said Raven. "I guess you've got to be quick to get the good ones."

"Quick sticks! Pair up!" ordered Ms. Highgate, flicking her fringe.

Raven loped over. "Hey there, Queen of Naples."

How could it be possible to join the drama group to get close to Nick, only to be lumbered with Raven? Life was not fair.

Mrs. Langton handed out scenes. Raven and I were given Scene One, from Act Three.

"Well," said Raven. "We've got your favorite 'love at first sight' couple."

"Yeah," I said, with a sigh.

"You're going to have to be a little more convincing than that." He grinned, his dimples shallow half-moons.

I couldn't say anything. I felt smashed, as if I'd run a marathon, only to be sideswiped by a spectator as I was about to cross the finish line.

eight

That night, Debbie cooked dinner for Mum, Dad and me. She only cooks one dish and Mum only lets her cook it once a month. Not many people can stomach charred steak, mash, beans and salty carrots more often than that.

While we were crunching our way through the carbon, Debbie announced, "Brian and I have found a reception venue."

"I thought everything was off?" I said.

"Why?" asked Debbie.

"Because of the other night!"

"Everything's patched up," said Debbie. "Dad and Mum went back to the Websters' place and sorted it out."

"Mum?" I said. "When did this happen?"

"Today. I couldn't stand it a moment longer," said Mum. "Debbie was so miserable and I've never called anyone a rodent before."

"Don't forget the walking, talking, useless showbag!" said Debbie.

"There's no need to keep bringing it up, Debbie." Mum stabbed a carrot. "Even though the Websters were wrong, in fact even though I think they were *appalling*, suggesting *we* would sully *their* genes, there was no excuse for me behaving so outrageously."

Mum was clearly not a true birkett chucker.

A true birkett chucker never thinks twice about whether their birkett is justified or not. They don't worry about whether their behavior is appalling or uncalled for because they're too busy focusing on the behavior of the people they think provoked them in the first place.

"What do you think, Dad?" I asked.

Dad was like an old man in a nursing home, his big, veiny hands clutching the table for balance, his eyes fixed in a glaze, as if the days ahead could only promise disaster and death.

"Oh," I said.

I couldn't help feeling disappointed. Of course I was glad for Debbie. It would have been horrible to have a broken engagement before there had even been time for an engagement to take place. But I hadn't realized that when a person got married, they actually had to say "I do" to the whole family.

"The Lieutenant Colonel is giving Dad a wonderful peace offering," said Debbie, patting her mashed potato flat.

"Oh yes!" said Mum.

"An antique miniature silver cannon," said Debbie.

"It belonged to his great-grandfather," said Mum.

"Where are you going to put it?" I asked.

"In the front garden, of course," said Debbie.

"We'll be able to hold our own Anzac ceremony at dawn," whispered Dad.

"The Lieutenant Colonel says Dad will never have problems with dogs again," said Debbie. "It's just: Ready! Aim! Fire! from here on in. He reckons it works a treat on possums too."

Dad put down his knife and fork and rested his forehead on his hand.

"And Mum gave them a cross-stitch of a mango," said Debbie, beaming.

"They loved it," said Mum. "The Lieutenant Colonel said it reminded him of the time he served in Darwin."

"So we're going to have the reception at the Buranderry RSL," said Debbie.

"No way!" I said, choking on a soggy bean.

"Yes!" Debbie said, her fingernails clicking against her knife and fork. "Of course!"

"But it overlooks the tip," I said, stunned.

"So!" Debbie said, chewing hard on her steak. "It's where Brian and I went on our first date. That's why we want to hold the reception there. In the Jungle Room."

Dad fiddled with his carrots. "Why the Jungle Room?"

"Because of the serviettes!" said Debbie.

"Serviettes!" said Dad.

"The serviettes," repeated Debbie, speaking in the slow voice she always reserved for Dad. "They do wonderful origami with them. Each serviette is crafted into a wild animal. A different one for each guest. Storks, bears, dogs, flamingos!"

"How much extra does that cost?" interrupted Dad, picking up his glass of water.

"Nothing," said Debbie, irritated. "Anyway, the night Brian first took me there, I had a zebra. They used two serviettes for that. It was so special I didn't use it the whole night!"

"You didn't use it the whole night?" I asked.

"No," whispered Debbie. "It looked beautiful in the candlelight." She slid her knife and fork together. "We've approached the management and asked them if they could do serviette origami of animals that mate for life, you know, as a theme for the wedding."

Dad coughed and water ran down his chin. "Animals that mate for life?" he cried. "As the theme for your wedding?"

"Everyone has a theme, Dad," said Debbie. "You can have a medieval theme. You can have a fairy-tale theme. You can have a cave-people theme. You can even have a Star Trek wedding."

"Really," said Mum. "Fancy that!"

"I know of a couple who were into vampires," said Debbie. "They had black invitations with embossed red rosebuds and silver ankh seals, gothic organ music and custom-made fangs for the formal pictures of the wedding party."

"How much extra do custom-made fangs cost?" asked Dad.

Debbie rolled her eyes. "I don't know."

"I'll tell you what," said Dad. "It must have made kissing the bride bloody messy."

"That's not the point, Dad," said Debbie. "The point is the wedding reflected who they were as a couple."

Dad dug his finger into his ear and swirled it around. This was always a sign that he was thinking hard. "What animals mate for life?" he asked, leaning back in his chair.

"I've done some research," said Debbie. "Swans, gray geese, peacocks, pelicans, kookaburras, storks, doves and albatrosses . . ."

"They're all birds," interrupted Dad.

"Well, there's the American beaver," Debbie rattled on. "And the silvery gibbon and an African antelope known as the dik-dik. They live in stable, monogamous pairs. And apparently foxes and wolves won't service other females either."

Mum placed her knife and fork together with a ting. "How fascinating," she said. "That there is an African antelope known as the dik-dik!"

"I have to do more research," said Debbie thoughtfully. "Did you know that monogamous birds outnumber mammals nearly ten to one?"

Dad rubbed his teeth with his serviette. He was always

uncomfortable with the idea he might be called upon to give us a little talk on sex.

"If I can't find enough mammals, I could look at insects too," added Debbie.

"It sounds clever," Mum said, stacking up the dishes. "You could give the serviettes some real texture with some cross-stitching."

"Don't worry about the serviettes, Mum," said Debbie. "You're going to have enough cross-stitching to do on the veil and train."

I pushed my plate away. "Wouldn't you prefer the Buranderry Fishermen's Club as your reception center? That's where Jody's aunt had her reception. Most girls from Buranderry have their receptions there!"

Debbie stared at me as if she had been slapped. She stood up. "I don't want to be like everyone else," she said. "This is *my* wedding and I have a vision for it. Now, you're either with the vision, or you're not!"

She stared at me. Dad screwed up his nose and lifted his eyebrows. Debbie leant over the dining table like an executive in a boardroom waiting for an explanation.

"I'm with the vision," I said, nodding my head.

"Good," said Debbie. "Because this is *my* wedding."

"That's what everyone says, dear," said Mum.

The phone rang. "I'll get it," said Debbie. "I'm expecting a call from a photographer."

Ever since Debbie had announced her engagement, she had monopolized the phone. Whenever it rang, she presumed it would be for her. It didn't enter her head that it might be for one of us. For a while, I kept racing her to the phone, so she would know we still existed, but after speaking to a hundred different people, all with a quote on some aspect of the wedding, I had given up.

"The thing is," said Dad, "when you have kids, you have a 'vision' of how they're going to turn out, too. . . ."

Debbie appeared at the door, her hand clasped over the mouthpiece. Her thick mascara was crumbling, each eyelash studded with small blue balls. "It's for you," she said, horrified.

"Who is it?"

"Raven De Head." She scrunched her head forward, as if some charity had asked her to remember them in her will.

"Oh."

"What's he want?" asked Debbie.

"How would I know," I said. "I haven't spoken to him yet."

She held out the phone as if it were a disease. "He's a thug," she hissed.

The green-tinged copper picture of an angel on the dining room wall stared down at me. Her head was in profile and too large for her body. The wings were like small buds.

"And his brothers are crims!" Debbie said loudly, her hand slipping off the mouthpiece.

I snatched the phone. "Hello?" I said.

"Gemma?"

Debbie stood with her hands on her hips. "Well?" she mouthed.

"Yes," I answered.

"Hi!" said Raven.

"Don't you care who she's hanging out with anymore?" whined Debbie loudly. "If it was me, I'd be grounded. You let her get away with so much!"

I hurried into the lounge room and closed the door. I felt wriggly and agitated. I wanted to hurry Raven off the phone before he had a chance to speak a sentence. I wanted to cut him off, as if he were a person ringing up from a call center to conduct a survey on toothpaste.

"I'm sorry," I said. "I didn't quite hear you."

"All I said was hi."

"Oh. Well. Hi."

"Have you had dinner?"

"Yeah."

We listened to each other breathe. His nose whistle had a fierce and melancholic sound, although vaguely soothing at the same time.

"What did you have?" he asked.

"Sorry?"

"What did you have for dinner?"

"Oh," I said. "Steak."

"Steak! Mmm. Delicious."

"It was burnt."

"Well done!"

"Very funny," I said.

We were silent again. He nose whistled some more.

"Is there something wrong?" I asked.

He sighed and I could hear his breath shake. "Well. I

was wondering if you'd like to come over tomorrow night to rehearse?"

"What?" I said, my tongue catching on a piece of meat in my teeth.

"You can come for dinner, if you like."

"Oh." I flicked Dad's recliner back. "Oh," I said. The patch of damp on the roof was the exact shape of an upside-down molar with long roots. "I'm pretty busy."

"It'd be good to go over our lines."

"Maybe another time. My sister's getting married. I've got to help her with stuff."

"Is she getting married tomorrow night?"

"No," I said. "But you'd think she was, the panic she's in."

Raven was quiet. "Right," he said. "Okay then . . ."

I heard a thwack. The phone sounded like it had crashed to the ground. I could hear groaning and the buzz of a TV in the background, and the sound of a voice shouting, far away.

"G'day, this is Magpie. Raven's brother."

"Oh."

"Raven says to tell you he'll buy *premium* mince in special recognition of you coming for dinner!"

Magpie hooted in my ear, a raucous, wild, abandoned sound.

"Put Raven back on."

"Please! I'm begging you," said Magpie. "We love premium mince in our house! And do you know how often we get it? Once a year. Save us from best mince please!"

There was muffled laughter in the background and another thud and a groan, as if someone had been punched hard in the stomach.

"Hello. It's me. Sorry about that."

"That's okay."

"Are you sure you can't come?"

I stared so hard at the damp patch that for a second, it took shape as a coat of arms. I didn't know what to say. I couldn't make it any clearer. I'd already said no.

"I'm starting with a disadvantage. You know, not having done a play before," he said. "I don't want people to think I'm a complete no-hoper."

"It's never bothered you before," I said.

The moment the words were out, I regretted them. Insulting him came so easily. Whenever I was near him, the first thing that came into my mind slipped out of my mouth.

"How would you know?"

He said it so quietly it sliced into me.

How did I know? I didn't. I just presumed.

And at that moment, I heard myself say, "You know, maybe it would be good if we did rehearse."

"Really?" said Raven. "Great. You can come home with me straight after school." And he hung up before I could change my mind.

I lay on the recliner for an hour, every now and again wincing and moaning out loud. I felt uneasy and disgusted. The only reason I was going to Raven's house was because I felt guilty and sorry for him.

nine

Raven's house was the way I imagined it, except that there were only two burnt-out car shells in the front yard.

It was white fibro with speckles of mold rising up the panels like an invading army. The tin roof was saggy and rusted. Someone had tried to brighten the walls by putting up four red window shutters but the paint had blistered and peeled and two of the shutters were hanging off their hinges, flapping in the hot westerly wind. Amputated car doors were strewn against the front fence and the grass was knee-high. Steel drums were dotted around the front yard, filled with metal and junk.

"Well," said Raven. "Welcome to De Head Manor."

He strode up the path, stepping over two sleeping ginger cats. One opened an eye and the other twitched a tail, but they didn't get up. I followed him tentatively, frightened that the cats might lurch up and attack my legs.

"Don't worry about them," he said. "They don't move. Not even when there's a dog chewing on their tail. The only time they wake is when they hear the rattle of food in their cat bowl."

Three blue butterfly lights hung in duck formation on the wall next to the front door. They were gaudy and tropical, flying in retreat from the march of the mold.

I didn't know where to look. My head felt full of mean thoughts; they clustered over me, the way flies huddle over roadkill. Everything I saw kept confirming my worst opinions.

Raven pushed open the front door. "I'm home," he yelled.

Nobody answered. The walls hummed with the sound of a TV game show and the throb-throb of a stereo. "Are you coming in?" he asked.

The house was dark. It smelt of dust, cigarettes and cat wee. The floor was carpeted in bedraggled, thick, blue shag pile. Two gray cats wound down the hall towards Raven. They took turns wrapping their thin bodies around his legs, whining constantly.

"Hey there," murmured Raven, stroking them around their ears.

"Raven!" cried a voice. "You're late. Did ya get the meat?"

"We've got a guest, planet dung," said Raven.

A tall, skinny bare-chested man sauntered into the hallway. He had long, greasy hair, a big jaunty Adam's apple and a silver nipple ring. "Hello," he said. "Didn't think you'd come."

"This is Maggie," said Raven, nodding. "And this is Gemma."

"Hi," I said.

Maggie grinned. "Would you like a smoke?"

"No, she wouldn't," interrupted Raven. "Or would you?"

"No thanks," I said.

"You wanker."

"Just being friendly," said Maggie, punching Raven on the shoulder.

"Just being an arsehole more like it," said Raven, hitting him back.

"Do you want to take me on?" asked Maggie. "I'll do ya!"

"Bugger off," said Raven. He pushed past Maggie, with the cats trotting behind him.

"Did you get the mince?" Maggie asked again. There was a huge tattoo of a Magpie on his right shoulder blade and a fire-breathing dragon on his left. Underneath the dragon was the word "Mum."

"Yep," said Raven.

"Ah! Premium!" called Maggie. "Nice work."

I followed behind them. Raven fished the bag of mince out of his backpack.

The kitchen was a psychedelic swirl of silver and tangerine. The benches were brown, teeming with dirty plates and cups.

"How much?" asked Maggie. "Was it on special?"

"Thirteen bucks a kilo," said Raven.

"That bloody robber," said Maggie. "How much did you get?"

"Three quarters of a kilo," said Raven, shoving the dirty plates into the sink. "Egg Tuffy said to say you owe him money."

Egg Tuffy is the only butcher in town. He's big and bald with a bottom lip that sticks out like the rind of a fatty pork chop. If there's a choice between serving a grandpa and a pretty girl in his shop, he'll serve the pretty girl every time.

Maggie lit up a cigarette. "Bull," he said. "I don't owe him a thing."

"Where's Dad?" asked Raven.

"Sleeping," said Maggie, puffing smoke at the ceiling.

Raven stared at his brother. "Did you put bets on for him?"

"Yep," said Maggie. He sat down at a white, plastic table. He put his feet up on another chair and took a long drag.

"You're a whacker," said Raven. "You know Mum doesn't want you to do it."

"Well," said Maggie. He rolled his cigarette along a round, yellow glass ashtray. "He was a miserable wretch and my heart ached for him."

"How much did he pay you?" asked Raven. He opened a tin and shoved some cat food in a bowl underneath the sink.

"Enough for a beer or two," said Maggie, grinning. "And a hamburger and some chips."

The back door slid open and Raven's two little brothers

and a large, scruffy dog came charging in. The dog pushed past the boys and went straight for the cat bowl and ate the meat in two gulps. He looked up, licked his chops and dived straight at me. He was like a sniffer dog on a drug bust.

"Get him out of here!" shouted Raven.

"This is Sparrow and this is Robin," said Maggie.

"Where's Mum?" asked Robin.

"She's working an extra shift," said Maggie.

"Aw, no," said Sparrow. "Who's making dinner then?"

"Ravin' Raven," said Maggie.

"Aw, yuck," said Sparrow. "I hate Raven's cooking. He always sneaks in veggies."

"Would you help me get Dozer out of here, you fat wood duck," yelled Raven at Maggie.

"Dozer! He doesn't seem sleepy," I said.

"It's short for Bulldozer!" said Maggie.

"Bulldozer! Bulldozer!" shouted Robin, his freckly face grinning.

"Come on. Come here, boy!" screeched Sparrow, his rat's tail all frayed and uneven.

"Sorry, Gemma," said Raven. He grabbed the dog by the scruff and tried to yank him off.

Mr. De Head stumbled into the kitchen, through the lounge. His face was sleepy and flushed. He was wearing blue shorts and a grubby white singlet.

"What the blazes is going on here?" he yelled. "What's the bloody noise about?"

"Dog's gone berko," said Maggie.

Mr. De Head stared at me and then at the dog. His thinning gray hair was standing up on his head as if he had been given an electric shock. One side of his face was crumpled. An imprint of a single button was pressed into his cheek. He shuffled over and gave the dog a swift kick in the ribs. "Get out of here, you mongrel," he shouted. "Before I put you down!"

The dog yelped and ran out the back door, his tail between his legs. The two younger boys chased after him, shoving and pushing each other.

"Sorry about that, love," said Mr. De Head. "That mongrel's two bricks short of a load. Who are you?"

"Gemma," I said.

"Ah, yeah," said Mr. De Head. "Raven said you'd be coming over. How do you do?"

"Good, thanks," I said.

"I'd shake your hand," said Mr. De Head. "But it's a bit hard getting a grip." He lifted up his right hand and waved. He was missing every finger except the middle one. He grinned at me—there was a big gap between his front teeth which were yellow and stained. "I've still got the finger that counts," he said.

"Cut it out, Dad," said Raven.

"Raven said you're doing some play together?" Mr. De Head said, and winked. He rested his left hand on his gut and belched. "He says you've got a lot of talent."

Maggie jabbed Raven in the ribs. "A play?" he said. "Are you a poof now?"

"Shut your clap trap," said Mr. De Head, opening up

the fridge and pulling out a beer. "Raven knows what he's up to. A play's the place to pick up the real good sorts. If you'd known that when you were at school, you might not be where you are today, you great bozo."

"I'm doing all right with the girls," said Maggie.

"You're a droob," said Mr. De Head. He popped the can open. "The only girl who'd look at you would be a dead scrubber."

"What would you know!" said Maggie.

"I know," said Mr. De Head, taking a swig. "I lost my fingers, not my brain."

They stared each other out. Maggie's eyes were like slits. Mr. De Head's eyes twinkled like a jolly Santa on a Christmas card.

"I'm going out," said Maggie.

"Where to?" asked Mr. De Head.

Maggie snatched his wallet from the top of the fridge. "Wherever I want."

"Get me a pack of ciggers," said Mr. De Head. He handed Maggie a ten-dollar note. "Keep the change."

Maggie glared at Mr. De Head. Mr. De Head grinned back. "Give your Dad a hug, you lug," he said.

"I'm no poof!" said Maggie.

Mr. De Head followed Maggie out into the hall. "Be back for dinner," he said. "And tell those nippers too."

Raven started sorting and stacking the chaos.

"Can I give you a hand?"

"Nah. Won't take a sec. Have a seat in the dining room."

There were two resin doors separating the dining from the lounge room. They were plastered with goldfish. A whole variety—black and orange, pure orange, even white fish—surrounded by little seashells.

"Those doors were Crow's final project for woodwork when he was in Year Ten," said Raven, emptying ashtrays into a bin.

"The fish look real," I said.

"They are," said Raven. "He got most of them from the ponds in the Buranderry Memorial Park. That was the year the council thought they had a bad problem with cranes. They put up steel netting after the first fifty went missing. Mum had to buy out the pet shop so Crow could finish the doors."

"How did he make them?" I asked. The doors were smooth like ice.

"He poured a layer of resin then flopped them in," said Raven. "Then he poured another layer on top and when it was dry slotted the panels into the door frames. Mum's always wanted doors between the dining and lounge rooms. She reckons it makes the rooms classy. When the lights are off and the telly is on, the fish glow."

"They were dead, weren't they?" I asked. "The fish?"

"Most of them," said Raven.

"Oh gross!"

"That's Crow for you," said Raven. "He's into stuff like that. He was always the type of kid to pull the wings off flies and other insects. That's what Mum says."

"How did he go?" I asked.

Raven stacked more dishes in the sink. "What do you mean?"

"What mark did he get?"

"Oh, not too good. He had Mr. Crabtree," said Raven, flicking on the taps. "He's a closet environmentalist, even though he's a woodwork teacher who loves using materials from old-growth forests."

There were photos hanging up on the wall behind me. "Where's Crow now?" I asked. There was a picture of two boys wearing striped overalls, sucking two big lollipops. They both had front teeth missing. Their faces were scrubbed and their dark hair was cropped short.

"He's in the clink," said Raven. "He got caught in a stolen car. He's twenty-three, so he was charged as an adult."

"Oh," I said. "That must be hard for your mum."

"She's used to it," said Raven.

There didn't seem to be as many photos of Raven and Robin and Sparrow—just a few small ones of them playing in the mud and running nude around a sprinkler. "You can go and watch telly if you want," said Raven, as he wiped down the benches.

I peeked into the lounge room. The TV was new. Gray chrome, flat screen and huge. It was switched on and a game show was kerchinking, but no one was watching. The couches were threadbare, faded purple velvet. Two gray cats were entwined on one armchair. The carpet was the same blue shag as the hall, but not as worn. There were two windows on the side wall but the curtains and venetian blinds were drawn. The room was hot and smoky.

I felt sick—almost as if the stink of those cats, the filthy ashtrays, the festering dishes and the smell of stale unwashed clothes had somehow covered me in a thin layer of dirt.

"No, it's okay," I said. "There's nothing on at this time of day."

I stared at the photo of Mr. De Head and Mrs. De Head on their wedding day. Mrs. De Head had a crooked silver coronet perched on her head with a fluff of veil. She was dancing with Mr. De Head, clutching at his shoulder, looking up at him as if she thought he was the most handsome thing on two legs. Mr. De Head's arm was tight around Mrs. De Head's white silk dress and he was laughing a big belly laugh, as if he'd been told the best joke in the world.

The one thing that stood out about the photos was how old they were. There were no new ones on the wall. It was as though the best memories had happened when the family was young and there was nothing worth preserving of the present.

"I'll set the table if you want."

"Okay." He handed me a plastic tablecloth.

"How many places?" I asked, removing the ashtray.

"Six," he said.

I stretched the red checked tablecloth over the table. Raven slid six chipped glasses and tarnished knives and forks across the bench.

"Do you make dinner every day?" I asked.

"Not if Mum's around," said Raven. "Only if she's working. Dad's no good in the kitchen. He can't even boil an egg."

He turned to the fridge and pulled out a bag of carrots and some zucchinis. He took out six carrots and began peeling them.

"I can do that," I said, quickly.

73

"Okay. Thanks," he said. "Robin and Sparrow hate veggies but if you cut them up small, they don't notice them much. And it makes the mince go further."

Raven oiled a pan on the stove and started chopping garlic. He slid the garlic on a knife and brushed it off into the pan. The oil hissed and fizzed. I diced the carrots, as he poured out clumps of mince from the plastic bag, straight into the pan. He hovered, turning and flipping the mince, as if he was tending the world's most fragile baby.

"I never imagined you as a chef," I said.

"I'm thinking of getting a show together," said Raven. He opened a tin of tomatoes. "I'll ride around town on my push-bike, the camera will follow me dashing into Tuffy's meats, and O'Riley's as I pick up my produce. Then they'll follow me home and I'll cook up every international variation on mince known to humankind. I'm thinking of calling the show *The Prince of Mince*."

There was something rueful about the way he said this, as if he was apologizing for his home being such a shambles, without putting it into so many words.

"How many mince dishes are there?" I asked.

"More than you think!" he said, laughing.

• • •

Having dinner with Raven's family was like sitting at a table with a bunch of headless hens. They talked loudly with their mouths full, competing against each other.

As soon as I picked up a fork, one of them would ask me to pass the salt or the pink lemonade. The cats kept jumping up onto the table and getting knocked down like bowling pins.

"I can't believe you wasted premium mince on spag bol! What were you thinking?" said Maggie.

"How come we didn't have hamburgers?" asked Sparrow. "I like hamburgers much better."

"Why not chilli con carne?" asked Maggie. "Now there's a dish deserving the honor of premium mince."

"How come ya didn't make lasagne?" said Robin. "Lasagne's gas."

"Too much gas for you," snickered Sparrow.

"Shut up, ya spaz!" cried Robin, knocking over his glass as he punched Sparrow in the arm.

"You're a dolt," shouted Maggie. "Watch what you're doing!"

"Shut your gobs, the lot of you," said Mr. De Head, smacking Robin over the head. He smiled at me, his eyes twinkling.

"You could've made tacos," said Maggie.

"You should be bloody grateful to get anything," said Mr. De Head.

"I got better food in jail," said Maggie with a snort.

"And no doubt you'll get it again," said Mr. De Head.

"The carrots are crunchy," said Robin. "I nearly broke a tooth."

"Sorry about that," I said. "My fault. I diced them too thick."

"Ya better fix your chopping," said Robin. "Or no one will marry ya!"

"Who says she wants to get married," said Mr. De Head. "She might be a career girl."

"Ya got to be smart for that," chirped up Sparrow.

"Raven'll marry ya!" said Robin. "He's not fussy."

"Shut up," hissed Raven. "Or I'll knock your block off."

• • •

After dinner, Raven tied Bulldozer to the tap and we sat on the back deck.

The yard was as full of junk as the front. There were old bike carcasses and another car without a roof, rusting under a tree. A corrugated garden shed, grown over with weeds, was sloped like an old man.

"Have you learnt your lines?"

"Not yet," I said. "What about you?"

"Some."

I slapped at a mosquito on my leg and accidentally kicked a pot plant off the deck.

"I'm sorry," I said, standing up and peering over the edge.

"Don't worry about it. Those violets were dead anyway."

Bulldozer whimpered and started biting the base of his tail. Then he licked his chops and rested his head on his paws and gazed up at us, his face meek and pleading.

"I'll have to go soon," I said.

"We might as well read," said Raven.

The readings were ugly and stilted. Nothing flowed. It was impossible for me to be tender with Raven, even if he was in character. I didn't want to hear his voice cry out how he loved me.

I was horrible. There was obviously something wrong with me. Maybe I had a disease. How else could I explain how automatic it was for me to despise Raven because his life was shabby?

Raven picked paint flakes off the deck railing. "When you're saying your lines, you sound like we've been married for twenty-five years," he said.

"I do not."

"It doesn't sound like I'm the 'third man you've ever seen in your whole life and the first you've ever sighed for.'" He grinned.

He was funny and clever, and yet for some reason he made me feel angry, so annoyed I felt like donking him on the head so I could make a quick getaway.

"When Miranda sees Ferdinand for the first time she says that nothing ill can dwell in such a temple," he said. "That's high praise."

"I know," said. I wanted to burst into tears.

"Maybe we need to set the scene more. You know, Prospero's given Ferdinand the job of piling up wood, to test his love and endurance and Miranda wants to help because she can't stand to see him work so hard. We could go down near the shed to make it more real," said Raven. "There's a woodpile there. If you think that would help."

"Okay."

"Just don't touch the wood because if you do, the shed'll fall down."

We walked past the dog, through the rubbish, to the shed. A ragged pile of wood was stacked up against the back wall. There were lorikeets swooping and the last cicadas of the summer blurting in the distance.

We began the scene again.

Maybe it was because we were behind the shed, with

the whole, huge sky stretching above us, or maybe it was because dusk was falling fast and everything was veiled in blue, but this time the scene *was* different, and it was easier to pretend that we were the only two people on the island.

Raven was so close; I could hear him swallow. I could smell garlic on his skin and the tang of pine from the woodpile.

"O heaven, O earth," he whispered, *"bear witness to this sound,*
And crown what I profess with kind event,
If I speak true! If hollowly, invert
What best is boded me to mischief! I,
Beyond all limit of what else i'th' world,
Do love, prize, honor you."

He spoke so softly the words floated like incense. He was oddly awkward and gentle, and I felt dizzy. For one moment, I placed my hand against his chest and felt the warmth of his skin through his shirt.

"Hey, you two," shouted Robin, his freckled face peeking around the woodpile. "What are you doing behind the shed?"

"They're being lesbians, you moron!" shouted Sparrow.

"Lesbians," I said, snatching my hand away. "What does he mean by that?"

"He means thespians," muttered Raven.

A cat meowed from the back fence. The wind blew and the pong of the tip hung in the air like sweet vomit. The sound of a train clacking across the tracks echoed around the yard.

"I'd better go," I said. "I feel a bit off."

"I hope it wasn't the spag bol."

"The spag bol was fine," I said.

"Maybe we can fit another rehearsal in before next Thursday," said Raven.

"I'll have to see," I said. "My sister's got me on a tight schedule."

ten

On Saturday morning, Debbie dragged the whole of her bridal party to the annual Buranderry Bridal Fair.

We were greeted at the entrance by a harpist angel. "Welcome," she intoned. "Enjoy!" Two silver cherubs stood by her side, playing panpipes. For a few moments, I wondered if we had died and gone to heaven.

We bought our tickets and walked through a gigantic heart archway of pearly white and silver balloons, past two monstrous balloon swans with golden bows.

The air was woolly with a thick, floral scent.

"Don't you think it's funny how brides and grooms are called hens and bucks," I said to Jackie, desperate to make conversation. "Why aren't they called petunias or gerberas? Or forks and knives? Why a hen and a buck? Why not a hen and a rooster?"

"This is sick," grunted Jackie, stalking off to stare disdainfully at an exhibit of tiaras, pearl chokers, gold-plated pendants and diamanté earrings.

"What's wrong with her?" hissed Rochelle. "And why is she wearing that outfit?"

Jackie was distinctly out of place in her fatigues, black boots and red beret.

"Where's her bazooka?" said Rachael.

"Did you tell her we're not going to boot camp?" asked Renee.

"Shhh!" said Debbie. "Be nice."

"When are we going to check out the fashions for flower girls?" I asked.

"Enjoy yourself. Soak it in." Debbie's nails bit into my arm. "We've got the whole day."

• • •

We toured five exhibits spouting bridal dresses, and a stand for magic bubbles. We paused at a hissing steam iron stall and then watched a presentation on kitchen hygiene by the Country Women's Association. We wandered through two photographic displays and past an aviary of white doves.

We were about to scoot around an exhibit called the King of the Cadillacs when a gentleman in a fire-engine red suit came rushing up to us.

"Good morning ladies," he crooned, his coal black hair swept up in a wave. "A more beautiful bevy of brides I have never seen."

Debbie and the Three Rs giggled. He stared at Debbie pointedly.

"Stunning!" he winked. He flicked his glance again at the Three Rs. "A wedding is a special day," he murmured. "A once-in-a-lifetime event for some."

He pounced on Rochelle and scooped up her hand. "My dear," he whispered. "I'm sure you want to look your best for that special day! Like a princess out of a fairy tale, am I right?"

Rochelle nodded her head. "Definitely!" she said, her eyes shining.

"Some brides call me their fairy godmother," he murmured. "Because I get them looking their best. Now the last thing a fairy-tale princess wants is to look like the pumpkin, isn't that right?"

Rochelle flushed bright red.

"It's a big day," he said. "And I'd hate for it to be a 'big' day for you, too! Perhaps you might consider losing a kilo or three to bring out your curves!"

Rochelle's eyes flooded with tears and her bottom lip curled down as she read his badge. LOSE WEIGHT QUICK OR MY NAME'S NOT RICK!

"Rack off, sleaze bag," declared Debbie, pushing past.

Rochelle let loose a sob. Rachael and Renee surrounded her like bodyguards. The man slid out a card and handed it to Debbie. "If she's not interested now, she might be later!" he said. Debbie pushed him in the chest and I heard the pop of his breath.

Rochelle's face crumpled. All the good things she

believed about herself zoomed around the entertainment center like little swallows, just out of reach.

"I'm fat!" she whimpered, her nose running. "I told you so. I'm never going to get married. No one will ever want me. I'm a great big balloon!"

People were staring at us.

"I'm a monster," she cried. "I've got more fat rings than Saturn! I'm a slug." She staggered forward. "I'm a dugong!" Her face was a patchwork of red and yellow. She sunk down to her knees. Her back shuddered.

"Shhh . . . shhh," said Rachael. "You're beautiful!"

"Divine!" said Renee.

"You're not going to trust a freak dressed up as Elvis, are you?" murmured Debbie.

"No one will ever love me," heaved Rochelle. "No one."

"Are you ladies all right?" A woman bustled forward, dressed in a red mink coat with a fluffy purple cocktail hat.

"My friend's had a fright," Debbie said.

"She's met Rick then, has she?" murmured the woman. She shook her head. "Would your friend like a drink?"

"Thanks," said Debbie.

"Come with me to my stall, love," she said. "Your friend can sit on my chair and get her breath back."

Debbie helped Rochelle to her feet and we scurried after the woman, through the crowd, to a large exhibit filled with ice sculptures: blue ice swans, cupids, pink doves and hearts, yellow dolphins, gray horse heads, translucent bride and groom statues, huge purple seahorses and a white dragon.

Debbie settled Rochelle on a chair underneath a giant ice castle.

The woman poured a drink from a little tap sticking out of the bellybutton of an ice sculpture of a female torso. "We call her Susie. The boys like to drink straight out of her belly button. She's very popular for buck's nights," she said. "But drinking out of a belly button is not sanitary for a bridal fair, so we have a tap."

Rochelle took a sip. Her sobs softened.

"This is a wonderful display," said Debbie.

"Thank you, dear," said the woman, with pleasure. "My husband is a master carver!"

"I'd like to get your card," said Debbie enthusiastically. "My fiancé and I are having a theme for our wedding night. We want animals and birds that mate for life. We could have an ice sculpture of a mating couple on each table."

"You couldn't have them mating on the table, Debbie!" I said, aghast. "Uncle Bert would have a heart attack!"

"No, not mating, you great drongo," sighed Debbie impatiently. "The two mates on the table. You are so dense sometimes!"

"Well, love," said the woman. " 'Say It Nice With Ice' can create almost anything. We've done spread-winged eagles, even a kangaroo and a joey. So give us a call and we'll fix it for you!"

Rochelle finished her drink. She looked better, even though her eyes were swollen like puffy apple turnovers.

Debbie took the woman's card and we all wandered on to the next display.

"If one tenth of this money was spent on the poor, we could erase world hunger!" said Jackie suddenly.

It was the first time I had heard Jackie say something I agreed with.

• • •

"When are we going to look at flower girl dresses?" I asked early that afternoon as we weaved our way through the crowds of women. I was completely exhausted. The bright lights and the high-pitched voices made my head pound. "You said we would check out our options!"

"Soon," said Debbie. "Soon!"

We sat in the coffee shop and had lunch.

The Three Rs and Debbie ordered salads and skinny lattes. I ordered a hamburger with chips and mud cake for dessert. If I had to hang out in a place I hated, Debbie might as well pay for it. Besides, I couldn't stand the way they self-righteously crunched on their celery and carrots, as if what they ate would change the fabric of society.

Jackie pulled out a package of food and a water bottle from her backpack. She snapped open a tin of Spam and started eating it with a fork. The Three Rs stared in horror, as if Jackie had just bitten the head off a rat.

From where we sat, we had a bird's-eye view of the Grand Bridal Parade. Models as skinny as poplar trees sauntered down the catwalk. They wore skimpy bridal dresses made of curtains of lace. Foamy veils sprouted like waterfalls from their heads. They weren't like normal models though. They were smiling for a start. But it was clearly fake, pasted on. They were like brides at the end of their big day; their stale faces about to crack off from having too many photos taken.

After the bridal parade finished and I had licked up every skerrick of chocolate icing, we roamed down to the beautician aisles.

The Three Rs and Debbie volunteered for makeovers. It took ages because the beauticians wanted to work out their colors, whether they were spring, autumn, winter or summer. A whole pack of whispering brides gathered round to watch. Debbie and the Three Rs relished being the center of attention.

"When are we going to look at dresses?" I grumbled.

"Don't be impatient," snapped Debbie, as the beautician squeezed her blackheads.

"It was a big mistake to bring the Big Mistake!" said Renee, with a sniff.

When they had finished their makeovers, we moved on to fake nails, push-up bras, lingerie, stationery, bridal registry lists, reception center displays, honeymoon packages and breast implants. "This looks fantastic," said Renee, waving a breast implant around so it wobbled indecently.

"Is she all there?" muttered Jackie.

"It's never been confirmed," I said.

Debbie made us try five different types of fruitcake with marzipan icing and then tons of after-dinner mint chocolates. We sat in five limousines and two white Mercedes. Then we rode in a horse-drawn buggy around the entertainment center. The Three Rs waved at the throngs as if they were royalty.

"Can we look at dresses now?" I asked, staring at a large nappy wrapped around the horse's bum.

"You and Jackie go," said Debbie. "We'll catch up with you after we've been to the clairvoyants' tent."

Jackie and I zigzagged back through the entertainment center towards the designer aisles. Flocks of brides, with their mothers at their shoulders, pushed past us, their faces intent and hard.

"I'm never getting married," said Jackie.

"It doesn't have to be like this," I said. "I'm pretty sure you can get married without ever attending a bridal fair."

"Yeah! You don't see blokes charging off to groom fairs," said Jackie. "Or worrying about implants and whether autumn or spring colors bring out their eyes."

"True."

"I'm not filling my mind with this junk," said Jackie. "Not when there are border disputes to be resolved, territorial waters to be protected and strategic alliances to be forged."

Just when I was thinking she might be okay, she came across like undiluted green cordial.

"Did you know that in days gone by the bride stood on the groom's left because the groom's right hand was his sword hand!" she said.

"No," I said.

"I bet you didn't know the groom used to steal into an enemy camp and kidnap a bride of his choice while the groomsmen fought off the other contenders."

"No," I said. "I didn't know that either."

Jackie picked up a feathered cocktail hat. "That's the way it still should be."

"What's wrong with love?" I asked.

"Love makes you idiotic," she said. She tossed the hat back on the table.

"Let's check out the dresses," I said. "That way we might get to choose a style we're both happy to wear."

Most of the flower girl outfits were bristly toilet brushes spangled with sequins, butterflies and flowers. The only trouser options were pantaloons, and there was no way I was going to wear a clown outfit.

By the time Debbie and the Three Rs emerged from the silk circus tent, they were cranky and uptight.

"Every single clairvoyant," said Renee. "Every single one. We must have seen at least ten. And all of them predicted romantic doom!"

"I could've told you that for free," I said.

"Why did you make her a flower girl?" asked Renee. "You've made a Big Mistake, Debbie."

"Did you know that the tradition of having bridesmaids dates back to the Druids," said Jackie suddenly.

"No," said Rachael. "Really?"

"Yes," continued Jackie. "Back then bridesmaids were included in the wedding ceremony, so they could act as decoys for evil spirits. One minute there were four girls walking down the aisle and then BANG. The evil spirits attack! The odds were on that one of the bridesmaids would get it instead of the bride."

The Three Rs were deathly silent.

"In contrast the tradition of flower girls began in ancient Greece," said Jackie, adjusting the beret on her head.

"After the wedding feast, everyone walked the bridal couple to their new home as flower girls littered the path with
rose petals to ensure the future happiness and fertility of
the bridal couple."

"Where did you find that out?" snapped Renee.

"In some bridal book," said Jackie.

Silence. Beautiful silence.

Rochelle shuddered, as if someone had walked over her
grave. "What's the age limit on being a flower girl?"

eleven

Everyone at drama was pleasant to Raven. But it was the condescending politeness some people show the disabled. When Raven walked by, they leapt out of his way as if they had to make way for his wheelchair. If he cracked a joke, everyone laughed like hyenas, even if the joke was only mildly funny.

On Thursday, when Raven and I rehearsed our audition scene, I caught their expressions when they thought we weren't looking—their raised eyebrows and their tight, sneaky smiles. They made me mad. They didn't know him. Their sophistication was artificial, as brittle as a shell.

And yet I knew I was like them.

As Raven and I rehearsed, I found myself wanting to

stand far away from him. I wanted to keep a distance between us. I wanted it to protect me. Because even as I despised the way most people treated Raven, I still wanted to be saved from their snide condescension.

I was so like them. I was worse. I felt a surge of loathing. It rolled and churned. It lathered and thickened, the dirty gray foaminess of it swelling, rising, filling me up.

"Are you ready to start?" asked Raven. "Let's go from the middle of Miranda's speech to Ferdinand: 'I would not wish any companion in the world but you.'"

"In a minute," I said.

I couldn't concentrate. Nick was rehearsing the identical scene with Tea on the other side of the room. He was so regal. He was princely from the tilt of his shoulders to the tip of his big toe. He was full of confidence and authority and Tea was saying those words to him, the very words I wanted to whisper in his ear.

"Let's go," said Raven.

"I would not wish any companion in the world but you." The words shot out like bullets.

He held up his hand. "Stop! You're not making me think love. Right now I'm thinking armed hold-up."

Nick was clasping Tea's hand. He was noble, his body a holy temple.

But Tea was hopeless! She was playing Miranda like an American cheerleader. She twirled her dank, split, overdyed blond hair round her finger and gazed at Nick like a moonstruck cow. She was so carried away she forgot her cue. Then she had to shove her piece of chewy out of the way so quickly, she choked on her own saliva.

"Do you lo-ove me?" she asked, recovering. Her voice was simpering, her line a cute advertising ditty.

Why couldn't a plank fall down from the ceiling and crush her flat?

"Our scene's not working," said Raven, sitting down. "You're playing Miranda like she's a grump!"

"I am not."

"She's meant to be full of wonder. Not a pessimistic cynic."

"You don't know what you're talking about."

"Why are you so angry?"

"I'm not!"

"Well, you're playing her like she's got PMS."

"What would you know about PMS?" I said.

"One minute you're up," said Raven, "the next you're down!"

"Bull!"

"Do you want some chocolate?" He grinned. "Fruit and Nut? Or just plain Dairy Milk?"

"Get stuffed!"

Tea clutched Nick's arm as if she was lost in a jungle, threatened by tigers. Raven glanced across the room. He laughed.

"I'll tell you something for free," he said. "That guy is the type to save the whole world, but love no one."

"What would you know?"

"Nothing," said Raven. "I'm just a delinquent."

Mrs. Langton roamed the room, her silver skirt swishing around her ankles. "How are you two going?"

"Fine," said Raven.

"Okay," I said.

"You need to get the scene up to scratch," said Mrs. Langton. "After the holidays, you'll be presenting it as your official audition piece."

"Yeah," said Raven. "We know."

"If you need any help, it's a good idea to ask for it now." She waited, glancing at both of us.

"I don't think I'm any good," I said. "Maybe I should stick to backstage stuff."

"Maybe," said Mrs. Langton, rubbing her neck. "Or maybe you're suffering a failure of imagination." She gave a half-laugh and patted my shoulder before weaving her way over to Nick and Tea.

"Was that meant to help?" I said.

Raven shrugged.

"What do you think she meant?" I asked.

"It's simple," said Raven. He leant his chair back against the wall.

"Oh yeah."

" 'I might call him a thing divine; for nothing natural I ever saw so noble,' " he said, grinning.

"Don't quote Miranda's lines at me."

"If you could at least imagine you believed it, then we'd have a decent scene."

"You are so up yourself!" I gave him a shove and his chair tipped on its side and he crashed to the floor.

"Oh, woman," he groaned. " 'Get thee to a nunnery.' "

twelve

"**W**here've you been?" asked Debbie. "I told you to be home tonight to help make the Chinese lanterns for the engagement party."

"I had a drama rehearsal," I said.

"This is the year of getting married," she said. "And I don't want some piddling school play interrupting my plans."

"You're the one getting married," I said. "Not me."

"You're my flower girl!" Debbie slapped down her bridal folder. "And it's your job to help out with whatever needs to be done."

"What about the Three Rs?" I asked. "Where are they? Shouldn't they be helping too?"

"They're coming to my dress fitting!" said Debbie. "I've set up the stuff for the lanterns. You and Mum should be able to knock out fifty between you."

"I'm beginning to understand what it's like to be Caliban," I muttered.

Mum took my warmed-up dinner from the microwave and put it on the table.

"Who's Caliban?" asked Dad. "Is he a mate of yours?"

"He's in the play!"

"What part?" asked Dad.

"He's the bad guy, Dad," I said. "He tried to rape Miranda. So her father, Prospero, enslaved him with magic, and from then on Caliban was made to do every *ugly*, *dirty* and *despicable* job."

Debbie humphed, and collected her bag, keys and folder and stomped out of the room. She slammed the front door so hard the copper angel swung on the picture rail.

"She's in a good mood tonight," said Dad.

• • •

After dinner, Mum and I cut and pasted Chinese lanterns, using red cardboard, red cellophane, glue, and lots of stapling to make the bottoms sturdy so tea light candles could be inserted into them.

Mum kept stapling and gluing bits in the wrong places, including her fingers. "Oh this madness," she said finally, after botching her tenth attempt. "Would you like a cup of hot chocolate?"

"Okay," I said, peeling dried glue from my fingers in big sheets.

Mum bustled into the kitchen and filled the kettle. "I'm worried about you, love." She put chocolate powder in two mugs. "You seem peaky, and a little more snappy than usual!"

"I'm fine," I said.

"I haven't seen Jody in ages. You haven't had a fight with her, have you?" asked Mum. "You should ask her over. We could have a big pizza night, just like we used to."

"No," I said. "We haven't had a fight. She's busy. She's in the swim squad and I'm caught up with the play and stuff."

"Mmm," said Mum. She tightened her old pink dressing gown. "That's a shame." She carried my mug over and slid it towards me. "Is everything at school all right?"

"I guess so."

"Is it the wedding?"

"No."

I traced my hand over the scratches on the dining table. I hesitated. "Does . . . does life get easier as you get older?"

Mum hugged her mug and leant back in her chair. Her slippers whispered over the lino. "Oh," she said. "Well, you know, as you get older, life becomes like . . . like marbled chocolate. When you're younger, it's like Top Deck. The white chocolate sits flush on the dark chocolate, but separate from it. The joyful things in life are clear and distinct from the sad. But as you get older, it gets muddled. The good comes with the sad. The sad with the good. And it's not so clear. Life's not harder or easier. It's just both, all whirled into one."

I sighed and rubbed my forehead. "Don't you wish life could stay Top Deck?"

Mum fished around in her pocket. "Not really." She piled up little scraps of old tissue that had been living in the depths of her dressing gown pocket. "Marbled chocolate is richer, creamier, sometimes harder to take in one go, but in the end much more satisfying. And that's what life is like when you get older too."

I ran my finger around the rim of my cup. My throat felt scratchy. "When you were my age . . . did you ever . . . was there anyone . . . did you ever really like a boy who didn't know you existed?"

Mum sighed. "I liked a different one every week."

"I mean a serious one."

"Oh, a serious one," she said. She blew her nose on a tattered tissue remnant. "I did like one boy when I was your age. His name was Lambeth Box."

"Lambeth Box," I said. "The funeral director?"

"Yes," said Mum.

Whenever Mr. Box shops at O'Riley's he wheels his trolley around the aisles like it's a coffin. He even signs his credit card slip with a grand flourish, as if he's authorizing a death certificate. I shuddered at the idea of him being my father.

"He was gorgeous!" said Mum. "He had black hair back then, with little white splotches. It was very unusual. There must have been something wrong with his genes. At the time it made him dashing and mysterious. Your Uncle Bert reckoned he looked like a Dalmatian—but your Uncle

Bert's not one to recognize romance, which is probably why he's still living with his sister. . . ." She took another sip. The clock ticked. The house creaked. I could hear Dad blow out a small fart in bed.

Mum often has dreamy pauses mid-conversation. Sometimes they last as long as ten minutes. Dad reckons that once when he and Mum went away for a weekend, she had a pause that lasted an hour and a half. He timed her. Just after they drove through Jindleburra, she started talking again, as if she had never stopped.

"His family was rich," she said.

"Whose family?"

The problem with Mum's pauses is that although she remembers what she is talking about, everyone else moves on.

"The Boxes," Mum murmured. "They never ran short of customers." She tapped her spoon against her cup as if she was striking a tiny church bell. Then she drank the dregs of her hot chocolate and sighed. A line of chocolate fuzz shadowed her top lip.

"How do you know when you're in love?" I asked.

Mum stood up and popped her cup in the sink. "Oh that's easy. I know a good test. You'll know you're in love when you meet someone and—despite his faults and flaws—you'll happily clean his shoe for him after he's trodden in dog poo."

"That's the test?" I asked. "Dog poo? That's the test you used on Dad?"

"Your father had a lot of flaws," said Mum. "He hocked

up his phlegm in a way that made my skin crawl. He wasn't a good listener. He was tight with his money. His hair was oily and he always seemed to have a speck of red capsicum caught in his front teeth—but one day we went for a walk and he trod in a mountain of poo, and I couldn't clean it quickly enough. It was a delight. A pleasure. After that, I knew he was 'the one.' And twenty-six years later, he's still 'the one,' even though his flaws are the same if not worse." She dipped her hands into her pockets and beamed at me. "The moment that something like the dog poo happens to you and you don't care, you'll know you've found 'the one'!"

"But what about the fireworks, the heart thudding and the legs trembling like jelly?" I asked.

"They're important," said Mum. "But they're not always the most reliable hallmarks of enduring, true love." She patted my head. "No, Gem. You can't go past the dog poo test."

thirteen

On Saturday, I met Jody at Thea's Milk Bar.

Although the veneer of the shop is chintzy and cute, everything on the inside is worn. The curvy formica tables are dotted with singed spots from the days when smoking was allowed and all the ice-cream posters are faded from decades of afternoon sun. Even the newest posters look like they're advertising ice cream from the 1980s. But it is the best kind of worn, like comfy old jeans.

"There you go, girls," said Thea, plonking two frothy chocolate milk shakes on the table. Her gold chain with the blue eye swung like a pendulum.

"How's the play?" asked Jody, swizzling her straw.

"We haven't auditioned yet," I said, running my finger through the trailing beads of water on the formica.

"How's Raven?" asked Jody.

"He's okay."

"Is he any good?"

"How do you mean?"

"As an actor!" said Jody.

"I don't know," I said.

"Maybe you should give him a go," said Jody, slurping.

"No way."

"He hasn't had a detention in ages."

"Look," I said. "He's all right . . . but . . ."

"But what?" asked Jody. She squirreled the last bubble of froth from the bottom of her glass.

"He's hardly the man of my dreams."

"That doesn't matter," said Jody.

"It does to me," I said.

At the next table, two older ladies were tucking into fish. Behind them, a bloke was feeding his girlfriend chips in between pashes, and right down the back, a truckie was eating an egg roll and reading the paper.

"What's so good about the man of your dreams?" asked Jody.

"I'll answer that when you can tell me what the difference is between liking and loving," I said.

Thea was dripping with sweat. Her blue uniform was stained dark purple under her arms and her face was bright red. She was shouting at her husband, Carl, to hurry up with the hamburgers.

At that moment Magpie swaggered into the shop. He was wearing a pair of old ripped jeans, no shirt and no shoes. He stood at the back of the queue and scanned the menu. When the queue cleared he shuffled forward and slapped down his keys and cigarettes and tapped a five-dollar note against the counter. Thea salted chips, wrapped them and gave them to a waiting customer. Then she wiped the counter before serving a woman who had come in after Maggie.

"Four hamburgers with the lot, thanks," said the woman, flipping her sunglasses onto her head.

Maggie leant his arms on the counter. The soles of his feet were black with dust. He stubbed his toe against the bench.

Thea lifted a great big basket of chips out of the oil and set it to drain. She tipped a serve of chips from a smaller basket onto butcher's paper and powdered them with chicken salt. The muscles under her arms shook and her bracelets jingled. "Three dollars worth of chips," she called.

Only after there was no one else to serve, and Thea had turned the chickens and wiped the counter one more time, did she take Maggie's order. Even then she barely looked at him.

"What do you want?" she asked, tidying up the muesli bars.

"A battered sav, thanks," said Maggie. "And three potato scallops."

She held out her hand. Maggie handed over his five-dollar note. She ruffled around for change in her old green ice-cream bucket.

"Busy today?" asked Maggie.

"What's it to you?" she grunted.

She slid the coins across the counter. Maggie scrabbled

the money up, dropping a twenty-cent coin onto the ground. "You'll be able to go back to Italy," he said, "and visit your daughter."

"Greece," said Thea.

"Oh, sorry," said Maggie. "Right."

As he picked up the twenty-cent coin, he spotted me. I shrunk in my seat.

"Hi Gem." He walked over to our table. He smelt of sweat and beer. "What's up?"

A fleck of spit hit my cheek.

"Nothing," I said.

Thea watched him, her eyes hard. She whispered something under her breath, before tossing three potato scallops and a frozen battered sav into a basket and dropping them into the oil.

Maggie arched right over the table. His pale chest had a few straggly tufts of hair.

"I keep telling Raven he needs to work a snog into your scene. I mean, I've read it and it sucks. Nothing happens."

"Right."

"You're competing against the telly," said Maggie. "You need to cut to the chase." He sucked some loose saliva back in. He had no idea about personal space. He glanced at Jody. "Who's this then?"

I didn't want to have a conversation with Maggie in front of Jody. I felt like I'd be airing Raven's dirty linen.

"She's just a friend."

"Oh just," he said, in mock surprise. "Bet she feels good about that." He laughed and then coughed, wracked with spasms, his whole body emaciated from too many cigarettes.

Why couldn't he take a hint? "Her name is Jody."

"I'm Maggie."

"I know," said Jody.

"You're pretty," said Maggie. He was smiling, but he had a gleam in his eye that made the compliment seem more like an insult.

Jody turned her head and stared into the mirror. She twirled her ponytail. It was the cool, efficient dismissal of someone confident of her own beauty, something she had learnt from Lauren.

"Well . . . it was nice to meet you, too," said Maggie. "I'll catch ya, Gem."

Thea slid his package onto the counter without a word. Maggie picked it up and sauntered out, turning right.

"What a dropkick!" said Jody.

"Yep—Raven's brother."

"True. But you've got to give Raven the benefit of the doubt," said Jody. "After all, Raven's cute. If you squint at him, he could almost be a movie star."

I squinted at the truckie who was licking barbecue sauce from the corners of his lips. "Most people look like movies stars when you squint," I said.

"Shut up," said Jody.

Moments later, I saw Maggie cross over the road and head into the Buranderry Memorial Park. He sat alone, eating his battered sav, leaning against the rubble of the fountain, taking swigs from a brown paper bag.

fourteen

"**W**hat's wrong with this dress, for heaven's sake?" Debbie held up a lemon frothy, frilly meringue. "This one's lovely. See the fur sash and matching muff."

"I don't wear dresses," said Jackie, her chin tilted and pointy.

Iris, the dressmaker, tutted. She slipped a tape measure over her head like a stethoscope and tidied up the flower girl dresses, twigging them into line.

"Bloody hell," hissed Rochelle, poking her head out from behind the dressing room curtain. "Tell her she has to wear it or she's not in the bloody wedding party."

"Shut up, Rochelle," said Debbie. "You're not helping."

"What does she think a flower girl wears?" asked Renee, whipping her head around the curtain.

Debbie smiled patiently at Jackie, but her top incisor hung over her bottom lip like a fang. "Look," she said. "It's only one night. One measly night out of many."

"I don't care," said Jackie. "I've never worn a dress and I never will."

"But I have a vision for my wedding. I want it to be different, one-of-a-kind, so it reflects the unique love that Brian and I are so lucky to share," said Debbie, barely concealing her anger. "And it involves the wedding party. I want you all to be uniquely special."

"I have a vision of myself," said Jackie. "And it doesn't involve wearing a dress that makes me look like a custard tart."

"You can't wear fatigues," said Rachael. "It's a wedding, not a military ceremony."

"My dad's wearing his full military uniform," said Jackie. "With his medals and his great-grandfather's sword. So is my uncle, and all of my cousins."

"Now that's going to be different," I said.

"Oh, blimey," said Rochelle.

"Dad wants Brian to wear his Army Reserve uniform, too."

"He is not wearing an Army Reserve uniform," said Debbie. "Brian is wearing a purple velvet suit."

"Purple velvet!" I gasped. "Isn't that a bit seventies?"

"Shut up," said Debbie. "Nobody asked you."

"You'll have to speak to Dad then," said Jackie.

"Don't worry," said Debbie. "I will."

They glared at each other. Jackie's face was pinched

with great red flares running up her cheeks and temples. Her green T-shirt was dirty and her army trousers were floppy at the pockets, as if she was carrying something heavy around, like grenades.

"She shouldn't have to wear a dress if she doesn't want to," I said.

"It was a big mistake inviting the Big Mistake," said Renee.

"Stop calling me that," I said. "I was born out of a moment of wild passion. I am not a mistake. I am a celebration."

Renee collapsed into her change cubicle, weak with laughter. She sat on the stool, her breasts heaving in their corset. "Wild passion," she screeched. "I like that. Your mum and dad. Hilarious!"

"What's so hilarious about that?"

"They're hardly the type," she said.

Iris coughed and reorganized the flower girl dresses once more.

Although I don't like to think about Mum and Dad and their moments of passion, this was ridiculous.

"They can't get enough of each other," I said. "Every night, their bedroom door closes promptly at nine-thirty."

"Gemma, they close their door because Dad can't fix the toilet and Mum can't sleep with it running all night," said Debbie.

"That's what they tell us," I said. "But I know better."

"Too much information!" shouted Rochelle.

"Get serious," said Renee, slipping on her bridesmaid's dress. "They don't even kiss each other goodbye."

"I hate to tell you this, Gem, but if you check the dates, you'll find you were conceived on their anniversary," said Debbie.

"Which is probably the only time they, you know . . . ," said Renee.

"That and birthdays," said Rachael.

"It's a miracle you were even born!" said Rochelle.

Iris rushed forward with a clutch of dresses in her arms. "How about these ones?" she said. "This Little Red Riding Hood dress is very popular for flower girls. It's taffeta with a delicious gold brocade on the trim."

"I don't think so," said Debbie.

"Or this one?" said Iris. She held up a dress with a skirt like a bell. "It's called the Little Bo Peep ensemble. It's shantung with an organdy overlay and it comes complete with a shepherd's crook."

"I like it!" said Debbie.

"I don't!" I said.

"It's got a gorgeous bonnet," said Iris. "It's very cute."

"No way!" I said.

"The shepherd's crook is great for keeping the younger members of the bridal party in line," said Iris. "My friend had her flower girl dress up as Bo Peep and when the pageboy disappeared under the bridal table during the speeches, she hooked him around the neck and pulled him back into place in a matter of mere seconds."

"We're not having a pageboy," I said.

"That's a pity," said Iris. She fiddled with the tape measure. "Let's see . . . We have lovely ballerina dresses with lots of tulle. Or perhaps you could go for a Roman toga look."

"Anything else?" asked Debbie.

"Do you have a theme?" asked Iris.

"Yes," said Debbie. "Animals that mate for life. Swans, pelicans, the dik-dik, creatures like that. The RSL are doing the serviettes and we're getting life-sized animal and bird ice sculptures for each table."

"Why didn't you say so!" gasped Iris. "A couple of years ago, my husband and I were invited to my Great Aunty Edna's eightieth 'old duck' birthday party. Everyone dressed up. I made two beautiful white duck costumes."

"I don't know about ducks," said Debbie. "I'm not sure they mate for life."

"With some work, I could make them into swans, no worries."

"They sound wonderful," said Debbie.

"I'll dig them out," said Iris. "They're embroidered with sequins and feathers. I didn't scrimp."

"Debbie!" I whined.

"You'll be like the totems of our wedding!" cried Debbie.

"The mascots for mating for life," said Renee.

"Say something!" I begged, appealing to Jackie.

"I'd rather go to the wedding as a duck than wear a stupid dress," said Jackie, shrugging.

"Why don't we forget about the whole flower girl thing?" I said. "I'll ride on the bonnet of the wedding car instead of the bridal doll. Then you can just wrap me in tulle!"

"That would be hilarious!" said Debbie, her eyes widening. "Could we do that?"

Rochelle shook her head. "No," she said. "She'd dent the bonnet!"

"Oh," Debbie said. "Bugger!"

"Here they are!" said Iris, carrying two black garbage bags. "They'll need a bit of taking in, but you might as well try them on."

She dumped the costumes on the floor. Feathers flew up and spun down like snowflakes. White sequins glittered and winked. "I'll have to rework the necks and the bills," said Iris. "But that won't be hard."

Debbie bundled one of the costumes up and tossed it at me. "Try it on," she said.

"No."

"It's that or the Bo Peep."

"Give it to me." I stomped over to the dressing room and ripped open the curtain.

It took me ages to work out how to get it on and when I did, the duck's head sat on top of my head, its bill drooping over my forehead like a fringe. "I can't wear this," I muttered.

"Have you got it on yet?" asked Debbie.

"I'm not coming out."

"Give me the crook," said Debbie.

I clomped out, the feathers flurrying around me like a blizzard. "I look revolting."

"If Debbie wants you to wear a giant carrot suit with a shaggy green head, you'll wear it!" said Renee.

"You look cute," said Debbie.

Jackie waddled out. The eyes on her costume were crooked, as though her duck had been shot, mid-flight.

"What do you think?" asked Debbie.

"It's okay," said Jackie. "Better than a dress."

"You've got to be joking," I said. "We look ridiculous."

"You're charming. Quite fetching," said Iris. "Everything a flower girl should be."

"I'm not wearing the webbed feet," I said.

"You'll wear what I say," said Debbie, with a certain glower in her eyes. "Or I'll make your life so miserable you'll wish you were a duck."

I held my tongue. Debbie was on the edge of a big, big birkett and she had a myriad of ways of making my life miserable.

"At least you'll be warm," said Rachael.

"October can be cold," said Rochelle.

I sighed. "I feel so much better."

fifteen

In the school holidays, it rained nearly every day.

In between doing jobs for Debbie, I rehearsed with Raven under the she-oaks on Sandy Beach, their spindly leaves lit by hundreds of raindrops, while his brothers Sparrow and Robin dug trenches in the sand.

The clouds were swollen and dark. The clubhouse was shut. The Buranderry Ice Chips were probably warming up at Pete's pub with schooners of foamy beer, cracking their false teeth on salted cashews.

"Do you want to rehearse from the moment Miranda tries to stop Ferdinand lugging the wood?" asked Raven, as he watched his brothers run around the beach.

"Sure," I said.

Raven picked up a big eucalyptus limb and started dragging it behind him. I took a breath and ran after him, trying to grab it out of his arms.

"Alas now, pray you," I called.
"Work not so hard: I would the lightning had
Burnt up those logs that you are enjoined to pile!
Pray, set it down, and rest you: when this burns,
'Twill weep for having wearied you. My father
Is hard at study; pray, now rest yourself:
He's safe for these three hours."

Raven glanced over his shoulder as if, for a moment, he was considering whether it would be right to have a rest. Then he gave me a gentle push and held onto the log even harder.

"O most dear mistress," he said.
"The sun will set before I shall discharge
What I must strive to do."

He stalked off, dragging the log behind him, the leaves rustling in the dirt.

"If you'll sit down," I said, running to catch up.
"I'll bear your logs the while: pray give me that;
I'll carry it to the pile."

I sat on the log. Raven let go and crouched down by my side. His blue T-shirt had faded to green on the shoulders.

"No, precious creature;" he said.
"I had rather crack my sinews, break my back,
Than you should such dishonour undergo
While I sit lazy by."

Raven helped me to my feet. His right cheek was smudged with dirt and there was a clump of spiderweb in his hair. He held my hand and stared at my fingernails.

"It would become me," I said.
"As well as it does you: and I should do it
With much more ease; for my good will is to it,
And yours it is against."

Raven laughed and shook his head. He dropped my hands and picked up the log again.

"You look wearily," I said.

He lifted the log above his head like a weightlifter and grinned.

"No, noble mistress: 'tis fresh morning with me," he said.
"When you are by at night. I do beseech you—
Chiefly that I might set it in my prayers—
What is your name?"

Raven bit his lip, his dimples flashing, his arms shaking under the weight of the log. Both our characters knew the reason he wanted to know my name had nothing to do with his prayers.

And so I told him. I said my name out loud. Even though my father had forbidden me.

"Miranda."

It was delicious, like the murmur of the sea in a shell. In some way I *was* Miranda. The river was rushing and the smell of the mangroves was in the air. There was no Nick to compare Raven to, and no Tea. The nagging voices in my head were gone and Miranda's lines and my thoughts were no longer two different things.

And then Raven began that speech, the one where Ferdinand declared himself Miranda's slave; the one Raven had recited months ago on the bus on the way home from school. He said his lines plainly, examining his feet, as if he was too scared to say them to my face. But even so, my stomach clammed up. He glanced at me quickly, waiting, his face and shirt damp with sweat. His left eyebrow had a small patch of hair missing in the middle and his right eyebrow did a dogleg at the end.

"It's your line," he said.

"Oh, right," I said. "Okay."

"The line is, 'Do you love me?' " he said. He shifted the log in his arms.

"I know," I said.

"Can you hurry," he said. "I can't hold this log much longer."

But something about the line made me uneasy and I hesitated. I couldn't understand how Miranda could ask her question so freely. She was offering all of herself to Ferdinand. I admired her and one part of me wanted to be like her too—but to think someone could love you so quickly, after only a day—it didn't make sense to me. It was as silly as Jody wanting me to go pash boys I don't even like, just for the experience.

I was beginning to think I had an icy chunk inside that made me wary, that made me weigh everything up and hold myself back, and it was weird to know it was there even when I was pretending to be someone else.

"Bloody hell, Gemma," said Raven. "This is getting heavy."

I took a breath. "I . . . okay . . . do . . . you . . ."

"Watch out!"

He dropped the log onto my left foot.

I fell to the ground. "Oh!" I rolled around. "Oh!"

"Are you all right?" asked Raven.

"Oh!" I groaned.

"Are you okay?"

"I think you've broken my big toe."

"Oh, gees," he said. "I'm sorry." He crouched down. "Here let me take your shoe off." He undid my sneaker and slowly eased it off. He gently peeled off the sock. "Phhhooff," he said.

"Sorry." My voice was so tight and small.

"Don't be stupid!" he said. "Sheez, it's red!"

I started to cry. I couldn't help it. One part of me was

crying because my toe was throbbing and the other part was crying because I was a mean, horrible cagey person who was going to go through life never loving anyone with any passion. I could see myself as an old lady, bent over with rheumatoid arthritis, perched on a vinyl recliner, alone, in a sterile lounge room, waiting for the clock to chime every quarter of the hour, the TV a blur in the background, knowing that love had spilled through my blue-veined hands like raindrops no matter how hard I tried to catch it.

The image made me sob even harder.

"Do you want me to get an ambulance?" asked Raven.

"Don't be ridiculous," I howled.

"Can you wiggle it?" he asked.

I tried. It moved backwards and forwards.

"It can't be broken!" he said. "I'm pretty sure you wouldn't be able to wiggle it!"

Sparrow and Robin came running across the beach, so crumbed with sand they were like little veal schnitzels.

"What's she bloody bellowing about?" asked Sparrow.

"She's hurt her toe," said Raven.

"Aw," said Robin. "Did you kiss it better?"

"Don't be stupid," said Sparrow. "She might have ringworm."

"You'd better pray to Jesus, Raven," said Robin.

"What for?" I said, sniffing.

"That's what Mum does," said Sparrow.

"Mum's seen Jesus," said Robin. "Sitting on the roof of the dunnies at Lake Gunawarra." He peeled a gumleaf in two. "She said he was beautiful."

"But frightening, too," said Sparrow. He wiped his nose on his sleeve.

"He told her we were fishing in the wrong spot," said Robin.

"And he knew her name without her telling him," said Sparrow.

"That was on our first-ever holiday," said Robin.

"Dad doesn't like being told how to fish," said Sparrow, picking a bindy from his foot. "So when Mum told Dad what Jesus said, Dad cursed his head off, packed up the tent and drove home."

"So it was our last holiday, too," said Robin.

"And we didn't catch a single fish or prawn," said Sparrow.

"Jesus really fixed that," I said.

"Yeah, but he's the God of thieves and dumbheads," said Sparrow, "so he gives her hope."

"What hope?" I asked.

"You know, that everything's gonna work out good in the end," said Robin. "Like the tip."

Raven helped me stand up. I leant against his shoulder and limped over to the picnic shed. A spiderweb hung between two palings. With each small gust of wind it drifted towards us like a silver lace parachute.

Robin reached into Raven's black backpack and pulled out a paper bag. He fished out a sandwich. "Oh no," he groaned, "leftover rissole sandwiches."

"Did you hear how they're going to build a huge shopping center there?" asked Sparrow. "On the tip?"

"That's right," said Robin, shoving the sandwich back in his bag. "It's good, hey!"

I rubbed my toe. "What's so good about it?"

"You can tell you don't live with the stench," said Raven.

"Do you reckon the shopping center will have a Maccas?" asked Robin.

"Probably," said Raven.

"A huge shopping center," said Robin, doing a star jump. "With a flashing neon sign shooting up into the sky like a spaceship."

Raven flicked his finger against the spiderweb, so it dropped down suddenly, like a stage curtain.

"You find good stuff at the tip, but," said Sparrow, engraving his initials on the picnic table. "Me and Robin got our bikes from there."

"And Dad got the couches," said Robin.

"Aw come on!" said Raven.

"You're not supposed to tell people, ya dill!" said Sparrow, shaking his head.

"Don't worry," said Robin. "Mum steam-cleaned them."

"And she puts a cushion over the bloodstain that won't come out," said Sparrow.

Raven shot Sparrow a dirty look. "Mum's hoping she might be able to get a job at the shopping center when it's finished. Be closer than Jindleburra."

"And we'll be able to skateboard in the car park," said Sparrow.

I reached into my backpack for an apple. "But what will happen to the Buranderry Village shops if they build a huge shopping center on the tip?"

"They'll probably go bankrupt," said Raven. "Some of those shopkeepers are bastards. Like Egg Tuffy. He's always trying to palm off his old mince onto us."

"My mum works in those shops," I said.

"Oh," said Raven. He rolled his plastic wrap into a ball. "Oh, yeah. I forgot about that."

"I guess it might not turn out so good for everyone then," said Sparrow.

sixteen

In the first week back at school, Nick was on the move, rallying kids to sign petitions.

"I don't know why he's so upset," said Jody. "I think it's great we're going to get a new shopping center. We'll be able to get hundreds of flavors of lip gloss. Melon. Pawpaw. Kiwifruit. Strawberry. Passionfruit Fizz. That's better than a plain old Chapstick from Shane O'Connell's pharmacy." She licked her dry lips. "We might be able to get jobs as well," she added. "In the food court or something."

"I'll probably have to," I said. "Mum will most likely lose her job and I bet they won't employ her at the shopping center. Just teenagers they can pay crap wages to."

The poplars down by the oval had lost half their leaves and were like a line of witches' brooms. A liquidambar tree stood out like a bonfire.

"I probably won't even be paid enough to buy a tube of lip gloss," I said. "Let alone pay the mortgage on our house."

"I didn't think of that," said Jody.

"That's what happens when huge shopping centers move in," I said. "Little shopping villages become deserted ghost towns."

Jody peeled a banana. "Things have to move with the times!"

"Sometimes, Jody . . ." I said, picking up my school bag. "Sometimes, you're just plain heartless."

• • •

I limped over to the vestibule where the action was happening. Nick had organized a cake stall to help raise funds to fight the development. Two tables, covered in white paper, were spread across the vestibule. There were chocolate sponges, banana cakes, plates of bottle-green toffees, a tray of powdery pink Turkish delight, blueberry muffins, chocolate crackles, honey joys, pecan pies, baklava dripping with honey, a platter of oozing caramel slices, giant white chocolate-chip biscuits and a wobbly vanilla custard tart. It was a feast. A banquet.

Students milled around the tables, elbowing and jostling, as they bought as many slices of cake and biscuits as they could carry.

Most kids were keen to sign the petition, too, except for the ones who lived in the Flats and had to smell the tip day after day.

"Buranderry is being threatened by Rosefields," Nick shouted over the noise. "This corporation builds massive shopping centers around the country. They charge crippling rents. They control the council. Wherever they go they obliterate what is unique about a town and make it generic and bland. Home brand. No frills. No-name towns. Why should our town be another one to be ruled by the dollar?"

Some of the kids clapped and more of them lined up to sign the petition.

"What makes you think the dollar doesn't rule now?"

Raven stood at the edge of the crowd with some of the other kids from the Flats. He was eating a packet of chips and he had that bitter expression on his face, defeated and defiant at the same time.

"Buranderry Village is small," said Nick. "It's a community that values the individual."

"That's your experience of Buranderry," Raven scoffed. "But maybe for others, a shopping complex might get rid of the small-town mentality of this place."

"What do you mean 'small-town mentality'?" called Tea. She had chocolate cake crumbs hanging in her hair like a cluster of baby cockroaches.

"Buranderry has taken out Friendliest River Town three years in a row!" chirped Eloise.

"The bar staff at Pete's Pub won't serve my older brothers even when they've got the dough," called Raven.

"See!" jabbered Tea. "They're not worried about the dollar there!"

"They're just worried the cars might go missing from the car park," yelled Jago.

Kids clapped and wolf whistled.

"Egg Tuffy makes black kids wait in line until everyone else has been served!" said Raven.

"So," said Nick. "It still doesn't make the shopping center a good idea!"

"Why not?" asked Raven. "If they put in a shopping center, prices would get more competitive and some of us could upgrade from best mince to premium."

"And some of us would go out of business," screamed Tea.

A flash of anger ripped around the vestibule area.

"If they put a shopping center in," said Raven, "it might mean my mum could get a job in Buranderry, instead of her having to drive to the pet food cannery in Jindleburra."

"What makes *your* mum so special, dickhead!" shouted a boy with his hair gelled up into little horns.

"Why can't your mum get a job in Buranderry?" called Nick. "There's plenty of jobs around for people who are willing to work."

Lots of kids clapped. Lots of kids talking, talking; cake crumbs shooting out of their mouths.

"There's plenty of work for some people," said Raven.

"Well, sometimes the benefit to the majority outweighs the detriment to the minority," said Nick.

"I think I've heard that policy before," snorted Raven.

"It's called democracy," sneered Jago.

"This is the first time any of you have ever fought to stop something happening in the Flats," said Raven. He crumpled up his packet of chips. "We're normally the first place you people dump the things you don't want. Like the mobile phone tower, the cemetery and the tip."

"Right," called Tea, her face twisting as if she had had a stroke. "Thank you for your contribution. Why don't you go back to whatever hole you emerged from."

"The only reason you're up in arms is because a shopping center threatens your parents' jobs."

"Thank you," said Tea, clearing her throat. "Cake anyone?"

Raven's face was ugly, as if he'd found his best friend fleecing his wallet. "You dickheads think you're saving the world," he said. "But you're just saving yourselves."

"THANK YOU! THAT'S ENOUGH!" shouted Tea, her head reverberating like a struck bell. "CAKES ARE NOW HALF PRICE. GRAB YOUR SPECIALS!"

"But I guess the quality of your super-duper lifestyles is all you're mainly interested in," he sneered.

Some of the kids from the Flats clapped.

"LET'S EAT CAKE!" yelled Tea. "EAT CAKE." Her face paled, then went yellow with rage. I imagined her standing on the back step of a brick veneer mansion in fifteen years time, screeching for her children to come, a wooden spoon gripped so tightly in her hand that splinters dug into her palm.

And suddenly in the lull, Nick spoke. "Raven De Head!" he called. "You've got a chip on your shoulder larger than Lake Eyre."

Raven smiled, even though I could tell he was stung. As he turned to walk away, Nick said, "There must be an ocean in your house."

And Raven turned back and lunged through the crowd, pushing kids out of his way. He grabbed Nick by the shirt and smacked him hard in the face.

It was like a red nuclear war button had been pressed. Arms swept through the air like missiles. And at first there was smacking, kicking, whacking, skin-splitting, screaming, cursing and thuds.

And then there were cakes.

Sponge cakes splodged in faces. Carrot cakes spattered into a million different pieces with chunky walnuts out of control. I ducked a pecan pie whipping through the air like a brown discus. Toffees bounced and ricocheted off our heads and crunched underneath our feet like glass. Turkish delight flew through the air like pink comets followed by a soft powdery tail.

A girl from Year Eight, someone who I had helped once in the library, grabbed me by the arm, swung me round and mashed a vanilla slice in my face, wiping it all the way down my forehead to the bottom of my chin. Tiny passionfruit seeds lodged in my gums and the icing stuck to my skin like a mudpack.

"Yeeee-haaaaaaaaaaa!" she yelled, before she whizzed around and grabbed a Year Twelve prefect and slammed a Lamington into his chest.

"You've wrecked my badge, you little turd," he grunted, pinching her ear.

At the sidelines female teachers were screaming like coffee-fueled mums at a soccer match. Male teachers were throwing themselves into the melee like sacrifices and kids were splattering them with whatever cakes they had at hand.

The ground was spattered with swirls of icing and specks of toffee—an abstract painting in progress.

As I was wiping the icing out of my eyes, I heard the jingling scatter of coins.

And then silence.

That strange, deadly silence in the eye of a storm.

Everyone stopped and waited.

And there was Mrs. Langton standing in the middle of the mess, her arms outstretched, towering over everything. And she was like Prospero, the master puppeteer. All she was missing was a magical cloak. Her rage made the air quiver around her. Everyone shuddered, waiting for the wave.

"Get to class," she hissed, her eyes like coals.

The juniors scurried away like frightened mice. The prefects hurried forward: fixing the tables, picking up coins that had spilled from the overturned ice-cream buckets.

Other kids sidled away, all iced and sticky.

Mrs. Langton's body shook with a light tremor. She stared at the remaining students, one by one, taking our faces in. When she saw us, the kids from her drama group, the anger slid from her face like a death mask.

I felt so little, so wrong. I felt like a betrayer. Her eyes were giant pools of disappointment and I wanted to throw myself in them and drown.

"You two come with me," she said to Nick and Raven. Nick's left eye was rising up like a purple sunrise and Raven had blood streaming from his nose, down his shirt.

"The rest of you, clean up this mess!" Her voice was quiet with resignation, as if this was all she could expect from us. She turned and walked away.

My chest hurt. I felt like I had swallowed one of those jagged bottle-green toffees and it had lodged in the wrong place and was cutting me on the inside.

Jackie ran up and dumped her bag at my feet. "I can't believe it," she said. "Why does it happen like this? Why are the people who are into war playing stupid pretend games while the real thing is going on around them?"

It took everything I had not to thump her.

seventeen

I was scared to go to drama.

I didn't want to see Mrs. Langton's disappointed face. But when we turned up on Thursday, shuffling and shame-faced, Mrs. Langton sat waiting on the stage, her legs crossed, smiling at us.

I felt a gigantic, searing gladness.

After we warmed up, Mrs. Langton taught us a new game called "Hot Seat." In this game, we had to sit in a chair at the front and pretend to be our characters. Then people asked us questions like: What's your favorite place in the world? What's your favorite food? What's your first memory? What scares you? If you could be anything in the world what would you be? What do you do when you first get up? What's your last thought at night? What would your true love look like? What makes you angry? What makes you sad? What would make a perfect day?

It was hard work. Some of the kids giggled and flushed, rolling their eyes and frowning at the roof, hoping for an answer. Some stuttered and said they didn't know. Even Nick was subdued, stopping once and shrugging his shoulders at an impossible question.

But for some reason I played the game well. I was good at making things up on the spot.

I found it easy to imagine Miranda's world and spin it out and make it hover in the air like a silvery miniature globe.

Any sign of sickness, any hint of heaviness in my stomach, evaporated as I closed my eyes and saw the island. I could feel the warmth of the water, the way salt stung my eyes and nose as I surfed a wave. I could feel the pure delight in watching schools of jellyfish twirl past Rocky Point, their tentacles swirling out like silk tutus. I could hear the squeaking of hot sand. I could feel the fur of a mussel shell and the cool of green afternoons spent running though the coconut groves. I could taste the ripe berries fizzing on my tongue. And everywhere the sound of the sea, rushing, rushing, rushing, as regular as the swish, swish of the blood through my own heart.

I loved watching the faces watching me as I was knitting this world together. I loved the way Jago's mouth fell slightly open because he was so caught up that he forgot to breathe through his nose. I loved seeing those girls who had treated me like some dull gatecrasher, sitting with their heads bowed. But what I loved most was the way Nick stared at me, dumbstruck, as if he was seeing me for the first time.

It was so sweet, so terrible, and so glorious. I felt dizzy with possibility, just like I did when Dad let me drive around the national park without a license.

As I made Miranda's world shimmer, I couldn't help feeling that performing had the power to smash me free from my big, fat iceberg self or to swallow me up and spit me out.

When I finished, I felt sugary and high, as though I'd eaten half a pack of chocolate Montes in one go. Mrs. Langton nodded and I sat down, blushing, knowing I had surprised her too.

Ms. Highgate announced that auditions would take place the following Monday.

The whole hall started humming and buzzing.

We paired off to give each other a massage. Nick clapped his hands on my shoulders. "You were amazing," he said. "You made me feel like I was on the island."

Small shivers eddied and rippled down my spine.

"Really?"

"Really."

"It just clicked," I said.

"I know what you mean," said Nick. "One minute you feel confused and then it's like a mist lifts and everything's clear." He massaged my neck more deeply. "I was wondering . . . ," he said, bending his head close to mine, his mouth near my ear. "Would you like to come over to my place tomorrow night?"

I jolted forward as if a hundred bolts had been blasted through my body.

"Sorry! Did I hit a nerve?" he asked, taking his hands off my neck.

"No. I'm okay," I said. "It's fine."

"How about it?" he said. "Come for dinner."

Dinner. Candles. Me playing Miranda to his Ferdinand. My first kiss. Soft as sea foam.

"Gemma?"

"What? Oh? Great!" I said, my legs weightless and light as clouds. "Yes!"

eighteen

When I met Jody after swimming and told her Nick had invited me to his house for dinner, she ran up and down the street, squawking and flapping her arms.

"AAAAAAAAAAAAAAAH," she screeched. "AAAAA-AAAAAAAAAAH!" She stopped. "How did he say it?"

"Casually," I said.

"How did he look?"

"I couldn't see," I said. "He was massaging my neck."

"He was massaging your neck!" cried Jody.

"Everyone was doing it," I said.

"EVERYONE WAS MASSAGING YOUR NECK!" yelled Jody.

"No. We each had a partner."

"How come we don't do massage at swimming training?" said Jody. She tapped her nail against her teeth. "You're going to need help," she said. "Nails, hair, face, outfit, the whole package. I'll come to your place tomorrow and get you ready. Straight after school."

"I have a rehearsal with Raven after school tomorrow," I said.

"You can't do both," said Jody. "You need to focus. This is the most important day of your life. I can't believe it—no insult—this is almost as good as if Craigie had asked me out. How did you do it? What was your trick?"

"I don't know."

"Were you just yourself?"

A wave of guilt surged through me. Right then, for some reason, I'd never felt less like myself.

"Maybe you could help me get dressed after rehearsal," I said.

"No," said Jody. "You need to make an effort. Didn't you join this drama group so you could be near Nick?"

"Yes . . . but . . ."

"And now he wants to have dinner with you, you're hesitating about making sure you look great for what is going to be a momentous occasion in your life . . ."

"I know . . ."

"Have you lost your mind!" gasped Jody.

"It's just I want the part of Miranda . . ."

"More than you want Nick?" asked Jody. "Look, there's Raven. Go and tell him you can't meet him tomorrow."

Raven loped up to the bus stop from the bottom gate.

He was reading a book, his backpack hanging off one shoulder. His hair had been cut, the straggly bits shorn off. It made him look young and eager, as if he was getting ready to apply for a job in a fast food outlet and hoped to hoodwink the manager into believing he was trustworthy and reliable, despite his slightly swollen, bruised nose.

I walked up to him. I felt sick in the stomach. "Hey there."

"Hey!"

I turned back and glanced at Jody. She grimaced. I turned back to Raven.

"What are you reading?"

"*Romeo and Juliet.*" He flipped the book over and held it against his chest.

"How come?"

"For detention with Mrs. Langton," said Raven. "Nick and I have to learn a new soliloquy each Friday lunch for the next six weeks. That's how I first discovered Shakespeare. In detention. Maybe I'll get through the histories next. All those plays about Henry."

"About tomorrow arvo . . ."

"Oh yeah," said Raven. "Mum said to ask you to stay for dinner after we finish rehearsing. She wants to meet you. We're having roast lamb."

"Lamb?" I picked a piece of skin near my thumb.

"Have you gone vegetarian?" asked Raven.

"No," I said. "But what happened to mince?"

"Would you prefer mince?" asked Raven, anxiously.

"No. No. Lamb is fine."

"Lamb with rosemary and garlic."

"I'd like to come," I said. A whirlwind of autumn leaves cartwheeled around our feet. "But . . . I've remembered I've got something else on."

"The audition's on Monday," said Raven.

"I know."

"Is this because of the fight with Nick?" asked Raven.

"No. I really do have something else on."

"Are you sure you're not mad at me?"

"I think you're an idiot," I said. "But that's your choice."

"Thanks."

"Maybe we could do an extra-long rehearsal on Sunday arvo, on Sandy Beach," I said.

"I might have to bring Sparrow and Robin."

"That's okay."

"Where are you going?" asked Raven, chucking his book into his bag.

"Now?" I said.

"No, tomorrow night."

Lauren pulled up in a red Cortina. She bipped her horn. I hesitated. "It's a family thing."

"Oh right."

"My sister's engagement party."

I felt bad lying about Debbie's engagement. It was on Saturday night though and that was pretty close to Friday. I felt a yucky, prickly feeling under my skin.

"No worries then," said Raven, shifting his bag onto his other shoulder.

Lauren bipped her horn again.

"Come on, Gemma!" squawked Jody from the car. "I've got a clarinet lesson."

"See you," said Raven. "Have fun."

"Yeah. Bye."

I hopped into the car. Jody was arguing loudly with Lauren over what radio station she wanted on.

"Did you fix it up?" she asked, turning to me.

"Yeah," I said. "I did."

But no matter how hard I tried, I couldn't shrug off how one tidy lie could make me feel as hollow as an ice-cream cone with the bottom bitten off, the goodness slowly dripping out onto the cement.

nineteen

"It's simple," said Jody, the following afternoon. "I'm going to wax your legs first, then squeeze your blackheads and then pluck your eyebrows."

"Is that all?"

"No. That's not all. You don't have anything to wear." She flicked through my clothes. "Everything is too daggy or too dressy. Luckily, I've got a Plan B. I raided Lauren's wardrobe this morning. Her stuff is in my bag. There are a couple of skirts and a jumper."

"I can't wear your sister's stuff," I said.

"Lauren's not going to know," said Jody. "She's got more clothes than Barbie."

She tested the wax. "Okay, it's ready. Now lie down and be still because this is going to hurt—a lot."

The rest of the afternoon was spent in a festival of picking, primping, plucking and prodding. By seven, I was ready and my nose had returned to its natural color and my legs no longer felt numb.

I stood in front of my bedroom mirror and did a slow twirl. Lauren's stretchy purple skirt made me appear taller and skinnier. It helped that I'd borrowed Debbie's black stilettos. I still wasn't sure about Lauren's pink top with the sweetheart neckline or her black jacket with the fake fur trim. When I walked up and down the room, I felt like a young kid wearing her mother's hand-me-downs, everything looser than it should be, my little feet flopping in her big shoes.

"I hope I don't break a leg."

"You'll be fine," said Jody.

"I don't know about the hair."

Jody had curled it, so it cascaded in ringlets and then she had pulled some back on top with a diamanté clip. "Do you think the ringlets look like Medusa's snakes?"

"Don't be stupid," said Jody.

"I don't want to seem like I'm trying too hard."

"You don't want to seem like you're not trying at all." Jody dabbed away a splotch of mascara under my eye. "You're sophisticated," she said. "And slightly mysterious. Now go and floss."

"I've already flossed twice," I said.

"Sometimes meat can hide in those back cavities," said

Jody. "If you're going to kiss, you don't want your breath to smell like a carcass."

I went back into the bathroom and flossed and brushed my teeth one more time.

I felt nervous. I don't know how people can describe nerves in the stomach as butterflies. My diaphragm felt like an elastic band constantly twanging.

Jody passed me a small pot of passionfruit lip gloss.

"Make sure you're not lying down for your first kiss. It's harder to keep the saliva inside your mouth in that position. And only use your tongue if he uses his."

I sank onto my bed.

"Try not to clash teeth," said Jody. "That's fingernails down a blackboard."

"Would you stop it," I said. "We're only having dinner."

"Be careful what you eat," said Jody. "Only eat garlic bread if he does." She opened her makeup case and packed away her eyeliners and her pots of lip gloss. "It's probably best if you avoid all cabbage-related vegetables too."

"Oh my goodness." I took a deep breath.

"Laugh at his jokes, but not too hard," said Jody. "Take your floss and your gloss. Be attentive, but not overeager. And have a good time."

Mum popped her head into my bedroom. "Oh," she said. "Aren't you glamorous? Are you ready to go?"

"Yes," I said, exhaling slowly, my diaphragm twanging so hard it felt like it was bouncing up into my throat.

Jody squeezed me hard. "I am so proud of you," she said. "Have fun."

twenty

Mum drove me across town to Buranderry Heights.

All the houses were double story with trimmed hedges and lawns like green silk. Even the letterboxes were grand with wrought-iron curlicues. In fact, in most cases the letterboxes were flashier than the houses, gigantic exclamation marks proclaiming wealth and prosperity.

"Is this the one?" asked Mum. "Is this the boy? The one you like?"

"Oh," I said. "Yes. This is the one."

"What's he like?" asked Mum.

"He's caring," I said. "You know . . . committed to making a difference to the world. And his hair is curly at the back."

"He sounds very worthy," said Mum.

"This is his house," I said.

Mum pulled into the driveway, scraping the front guard on the gutter. She turned off the engine and stared at the house. It was huge and brick with large wraparound balconies and two white columns either side of the porch.

"It's very *Gone with the Wind*," said Mum.

In the middle of the front lawn was a statue of a naked lady holding a water jar on her shoulder. It was lit up, with water splashing out of the jar, over the lady's breasts into the lily pond.

"Goodness," said Mum. "That's almost indecent. Maybe we should have a little chat."

"Not the talk again." I cringed. "I'll be late."

"What type of family has a naked lady in their front yard?" asked Mum.

"What type of family has a cannon?" I asked.

I got out of the car and picked up my bag. I felt like my breath had been sucked out of my body.

"Okay," I said. "You can go now."

I watched Mum pull out of the drive before I walked up the sandstone path to the front door. I debated a few moments between using the big brass doorknocker or the doorbell. Sweat pooled in my waistband.

I rang the doorbell.

I stood close and peered through the stained glass window.

Nick opened the door. "Hiya," he said.

"Hi." It was like I had never spoken before, as if I had

had my vocal cords replaced and was trying out my new voice for the first time.

He took my hand. "I'm glad you came," he said. "Come in."

The hall was huge. There was another naked lady statue in an alcove with a ferny plant drooping discreetly in the right places. A chandelier tinkled in the breeze, like a million splintered diamonds.

"Come upstairs," said Nick, squeezing my fingers.

The carpet was creamy and soft and my high heels left a little trail of indents. I followed him into the lounge room. "This is my mum," said Nick.

"Hello, Sharon," said Mrs. Lloyd. She put down her wine glass, closed a catalog and stood up to shake my hand.

"This is *Gemma*, Mum," said Nick.

"Oh, Gemma! Good to meet you," said Mrs. Lloyd.

"You, too," I croaked.

The room was all dim lamps, leopard-skin throw rugs, soft cream leather sofas and fringed velvet cushions. A real fire crackled in the fireplace. Classical music burbled out of the surround-sound speakers.

Everything was pristine, elegant and artful. I was never going to let Nick see my house. Even thinking about Mum's cross-stitches made me shudder.

Mrs. Lloyd smiled at me, her lips perfectly outlined and glossed. Her cheekbones were round and smooth and her short hair was streaked with gold highlights.

"Dad's downstairs by the pool getting dinner ready," said Nick. "Come and I'll show you the library." He led me down a long corridor, past a gallery of photos of him as a child, most of them professionally taken.

"You have your own library?" I whispered.

"Yeah, but we don't read the books," said Nick. "The designer chose them because they make the right sort of statement."

I winced when I thought of Mum's library—the one whole shelf in the back sunroom dedicated to well-thumbed paperback romance novels with covers boasting windswept women, all with moist lips and heaving breasts.

Nick opened a huge, wooden door. "Here we are," he said.

At the end of the room was a long mahogany table. Sitting around it were Tea, Leonie, Eloise, Fatima, Serena, Dodi—and Jody's sister Lauren.

Lauren! What was she doing here? What were any of them doing here? They were dressed up too. Tight skirts. Tight shirts. Makeup. They dropped their pens and stared at me as if I had stepped off planet Mars.

"Now we're all here," said Nick.

Lauren glared at me. Her eyes said "kill." Suddenly, the fake fur trim on her jacket made my neck itch, as if I had brushed past a poisonous plant.

"Have a seat," said Nick.

The only place left was next to Lauren. As I sat down, she pinched me hard on the leg.

The room stunk of perfume. Musk, vanilla, rose, honeysuckle; a whole jangle of smells.

"Thank you for coming," said Nick, resting his hands on

the table. "Now that we're being denied the right of free speech at school, we have to be more active in our efforts to protect our town from the Rosefields conglomerate, which is why I've invited you guys along to 'P.R.O.T.E.S.T.—a new political lobby group for young people.' "

There were no guys here. Just seven girls—seven girls who each thought they were having a cozy dinner for two with Nick.

The world reeled as I mourned the loss of pumpkin soup, angel hair pasta, hazelnut gelato, crisp white napkins, my first kiss . . .

Nick slid a dossier across the table. "Here's a history of the whole sordid tale. Just read the summary for now. It'll give you a better understanding of the main players and the most important issues. Then we'll get going on phase one." His eyes shone with urgent zeal.

After we read the summary pages in the Rosefields dossier, Nick explained his plan, then we wrote letters. Handwritten letters. Nick said they made a bigger impact. Nobody spoke, unless it was to ask for help with spelling.

Lauren wrote to Mayor Glassoni, with her tongue poking out.

I wrote a letter to the Rosefields CEO, explaining why a large-scale shopping center would be totally inappropriate for our community. I wrote about Brian's proposal to my sister in O'Riley's supermarket, near the spice rack and how Stan announced it over the PA and gave them a gift voucher. I wrote about Ted's beautiful ballroom music and about how, every now and again, people danced down the aisles, waltzing their shopping trolleys around, and how Ted didn't care when Mum sent a pyramid of tomato soup cans flying. How tinny shopping center Muzak could never make us feel human or connected to one another. About how more important this was than the fact the food at O'Riley's was always out-of-date, the lights were dim, Stan's service was crappy and the aisles were often obstacle courses of mysterious boxes that were never unpacked.

Even though I believed everything I wrote, I felt a vague emptiness inside, a "feeling-sorry-for-myself" chasm.

At eight-thirty, Mrs. Lloyd popped her head into the room. "How's your political meeting going, Nick?" she asked. "Have you saved the world yet?"

Nick placed his pen on the table with a snap. "What do you want?"

Mrs. Lloyd was like a Labrador who had taken a kick in the guts. "Well . . . what I meant was . . . I . . . was . . . just . . . ," she stammered. "Dinner . . . your dad said to tell you it was ready."

• • •

We ate downstairs, by the pool under a galaxy of fairy lights.

I sat next to Mrs. Lloyd and watched her watch Nick constantly. She looked both hopeful and mournful.

"Your lawn is perfect," I said.

"Yes," said Mrs. Lloyd. "We're very proud of it."

"Does it take much work?" I asked.

"I don't know," said Mrs. Lloyd. "We have a gardener."

We sat in silence. I nibbled on a sausage.

Nick sat with Tea and Eloise, and their laughter burst out like trumpets.

Lauren glared at me, chewing on her turkey and pesto sausage, the way she'd like to chew on my head if she were given the chance.

"Do you know what type of grass it is?" I asked.

"No," said Mrs. Lloyd.

"We have 'Sir Walter' Soft Leaf Buffalo," I said. "It's a hard-wearing grass."

"I see," said Mrs. Lloyd.

"We had softer grass before," I said. "Santa Ana Couch. But army worm made quick work of that."

"You seem to know a lot about grass," said Mrs. Lloyd.

"The grass family contains 635 genera and 9000 species. It's the fourth largest family after the legume, orchid and daisy families. Economically and ecologically, the grass family is the most important family of flowering plants in the world."

"How fascinating," said Mrs. Lloyd. She sipped her wine and stared at Nick.

"Perennial grasses are good for lawns because they don't lose their basal meristems—you know, their growing points—when they're mown."

"Aha."

"My dad works in a nursery," I said.

"Oh," said Mrs. Lloyd. "How lovely. He must adore children."

"It's nearly time for dessert," said Nick.

Mrs. Lloyd leapt up like she'd been given a zap from a cattle prod. She snatched up our plates and darted upstairs.

"Why are you wearing my clothes?" hissed Lauren. "I'm going to kill Jody when I get home!"

"She thought you wouldn't notice if I borrowed them."

"You're wearing my best skirt and my favorite jacket!"

"They look a lot better on you than they do on me," I said. "If that's any consolation."

"I am not an op-shop!" spat Lauren.

Eloise, Serena and Tea wandered over and sat down at our end of the table. Their chunky silver and turquoise jewelry glinted in the fairy lights. Their lips were dark, as if they had been gorging on blackberries.

"I wouldn't have thought this was your usual scene, Lauren!" said Tea.

"What do you mean?" asked Lauren.

"Wasn't your last political activity lobbying the school council to allow body piercing on school premises?" asked Tea.

"What if it was?" said Lauren. "I also successfully lobbied for both girls and boys to wear nail polish to school. A lot of people were grateful for that."

"Spare me!" said Leonie.

"Let me give you a word of advice," said Tea. "Nick doesn't go for bimbos."

Lauren gazed at her hands. She was the most beautiful girl in our school, but her fingernails were bitten to the quick.

"And as for you, Gemma!" said Tea. "Where did you get that hideous outfit?"

Lauren glanced at me. A ripple of panic blew across her face. She clenched and unclenched her fingers.

"The op-shop," I said.

"Cool," said Serena.

After dessert, everyone rushed back to the library, leaving their dishes scattered around the backyard. I helped Mrs. Lloyd clean up and carry everything upstairs.

"Would you like me to stack the dishwasher?" I asked.

Mr. Lloyd was sitting on the sofa, watching football, a glass of wine twirling in his hand, the newspaper draped over his legs.

"No. It's okay," said Mrs. Lloyd.

"I don't mind," I said. "It'll only take a sec."

Mrs. Lloyd hesitated. "There *is* a program I'd like to catch on TV in a few minutes."

"Sure," I said.

I scraped the plates and bowls and opened the dishwasher and packed them in. I rinsed the knives, forks and spoons under the hot water and dropped them into the cutlery rack. I slid the glasses in on top.

Mrs. Lloyd washed up the wooden salad bowl and large diamond-cut trifle bowl, the hot steam billowing around her head. "What are you writing about tonight," she asked. "Freeing political prisoners? Saving whales?"

"The shopping center," I said. "We're writing letters to get the new development stopped."

"Oh," she said. "Are you? I think a proper shopping center would be so lovely. There's something beautiful about the cosmetics counters in huge department stores. All those shop assistants with their large, white teeth and smooth hair. And those cards with splashes of perfume. Every sense is stirred, don't you think?"

"I don't know. I haven't been to a big one," I said. "I did go to a bridal fair and I didn't like it."

"Is someone you know getting married?" asked Mrs. Lloyd.

"My sister."

"How lovely. Where are you having the reception?"

I closed the dishwasher with a snap. The cutlery jingled. "The Buranderry RSL."

Mrs. Lloyd squeezed out the wettex. "No! Not really?"

"Yes. Really."

"Opposite the tip? In the Flats?"

"That's where Brian took Debbie for their first date."

"What an interesting man!" she cried. She reached for her wine glass, her fingernails bright, polished jewels. "Would you like to see Nick's trophy room?"

"He's got a whole room for his trophies?"

"Oh yes," said Mrs. Lloyd. She dabbed her mouth with a tissue. "He's won so many awards. Freedom International has given him a special certificate of commendation every year since primary school for being the most prolific writer of letters."

"Wow! You must be proud."

"I am," said Mrs. Lloyd.

"I'd like to see it," I hesitated. "But maybe I should get back."

"Yes," said Mrs. Lloyd. "You're right. I'm sure that Nick's got a hundred different activities for you to do. Maybe another time then. It really is special." And the way she spoke made it sound as if it were a church. "Tonight went well. Didn't it?" she asked, touching my arm.

"Yes . . . it's been . . . great," I said.

"Are you sure?" She smiled, her teeth perfect, smooth, white gravestones all in a row.

"Yes. Thanks for having me."

The eyeliner underneath her left eye had smudged into a blue-gray bruise. "Good," she sighed, her breath tart and sour. "It's been a pleasure, Sharon."

• • •

Back in the library, everyone was busy writing. It was like an exam room. Heads down. Hands scrawling across the paper like racing cars on a track, competitive glances left and right.

"How many helpings of dessert did you have?" asked Tea, adding another letter to her pile.

I stopped still.

Dodi and Eloise smirked and wrote faster. Lauren nodded her head at me, encouraging me to sit down.

"I was helping Nick's mum."

"Like Nero fiddling on the roof while Rome burns!" said Tea.

The girls tittered. I didn't know what to do.

"Everyone else has written at least six letters and you haven't even finished one," said Tea. "Maybe you're not committed to the cause. After all, aren't you good friends with Raven De Head? And we know how he feels about the shopping center."

"I wouldn't say a good friend." My mouth tasted greasy.

"As long as you know where your loyalties lie," said Tea.

Nick stopped writing. The pages were piling up to his left. "Come on," he said. "We're running out of time." He smiled and made room for me. "I know Gemma's committed."

It felt great to sit next to him, to feel his leg pressed up to mine.

twenty-one

Debbie chose an oriental theme for her engagement party because Brian had proposed to her by the Chinese five-spices. It was Debbie's way of celebrating Brian's most original thought and extending it for as long as possible, in case he didn't have another one.

"Why is she so into themes?" I asked.

"It's just Debbie," said Mum. "Who are we to get in the way of her happiness? You only get engaged once."

"You hope."

"Stop grumbling."

"Why can't she have a normal engagement party like an ordinary person?" I asked. "For her, every single event needs frills, or icing, or add-ons or upsizing."

"She wants to be an individual," said Mum.

"It's wallpaper, Mum," I said. "It's just to cover the fact that she's exactly like everyone else."

"Why is everything so difficult for you today?" asked Mum. "Why can't you let things be?"

"Debbie doesn't even like Chinese food!" I said. "She thinks sweet and sour pork is too spicy."

"Gemma! Get changed into your costume!"

"But Mum, they're pajamas," I said. "What have they got to do with China? They probably don't even wear them over there."

"They're the only things we could find that were even vaguely oriental," said Mum. "At least we're not wearing the same color."

The doorbell chimed.

"Who can that be?" Mum shrieked. "It's far too early! I haven't even got my stays on!"

Stays are these weird corset pants that Mum wears over her undies, on special occasions. Watching her get into them is like witnessing a snake squeeze back into its old skin.

I poked my head around the bedroom door. "It's the Websters!" I said, as the Lieutenant Colonel moved into the light.

"Oh!" said Mum. "But I'm not ready!"

I closed the door. I pulled on my bright yellow Chinese pajamas.

"What is she wearing?" Mum demanded.

I peeked around the door again. I could make out Mrs. Webster's face but I couldn't see exactly what she had on. "I'm not sure."

"I bet something glamorous," muttered Mum, jigging around the bedroom.

"It can't be good for you, wearing those things," I said, glancing over my shoulder. "You'll have a cardiac arrest in a minute!"

"They keep my tummy in," heaved Mum.

"Imagine what they're doing to your internal organs!" I said.

Mrs. Webster's laughter trilled up the hallway. Dad laughed too.

"Move aside, Barry, and we'll show you!" cried the Lieutenant Colonel.

Brian stepped forward and fixed a large dragon's head on his father's head. Mrs. Webster threw an embroidered red cloth over Jackie and herself. Then Brian slid underneath to make up a tail. A long plume of smoke puffed out of the dragon's nostrils.

"Ready!" commanded the Lieutenant Colonel. "One, two, three!"

They danced up the hallway, as best they could with the Lieutenant Colonel leading the way. His crutches tapped and bells jingled and clouds of smoke filled the hallway.

"Watch the smoke detector!" Dad yelled.

Mrs. Webster was throwing everything into it in the middle. The dragon snaked and bucked as if it had been stabbed. Its golden eyes flashed and smoke whirled. They jived and writhed, aiming straight for the bedroom.

"I hope you've got your stays on!" I hissed to Mum.

"Go left!" Dad called suddenly from the back.

The dragon turned. It missed the dining room door entrance and knocked into the wall. A shower of golden sequins sprinkled the polished wooden floorboards.

"I think Jackie is better as the head!" the Lieutenant Colonel called.

"What's going on out there?" Mum hissed. "What is she wearing?" She stared at me in the bedroom mirror. Her curls were damp and beginning to loosen. She slid on her black pajamas.

"She's a dragon!" I whispered, closing the door.

"Don't start up again," Mum said, fumbling with her press studs. "I don't want another night of birketts."

"I don't mean *she's* a dragon," I said. "I mean she's dressed as a dragon! They all are."

"What?" said Mum. She plucked a tissue from the box and patted her face.

"The Websters are dressed in a full-sized dragon costume!" I said. "Like the dragons in the parades on Chinese New Year!"

Dad burst into the bedroom. "Will you two come and help me?"

Mum scooped up rollers and pins and plonked them in her cosmetics bag. "They're imaginative, aren't they?" she said. "I think they've embraced us, I mean to go to such an effort!"

"They might just want to have the biggest and best costume!" I said.

Mum scowled, the little lines around her mouth puckered. "Why are you so sour tonight?" she said. "Why are you so determined to think the worst of people?"

I ran my fingers through my hair. Why is it easier and more comfortable to see the truth about other people?

"I want you to be positive and uplifting," said Mum. "This is your sister's special night. Now, where are the Websters?"

"Out in the back garden!" said Dad. "Beryl thought she was seeing things when she saw a dragon prance through the dining room. She spilt her drink down her front."

"Goodness!" said Mum. "Things have got off to an exciting start."

"Let's get cracking!" Dad clapped his hands. "Before they destroy the entire lawn!"

Mum hurled the cosmetics bag into the bottom drawer of her dresser. She slipped on her embroidered slippers and put her arms around Dad. "Now, love," she murmured. "There's no need for you to chuck a birkett. I want you to take a deep, deep breath!"

Dad pulled his red silk pajama pants out of his bum. He took several deep breaths, huffing and wheezing as if he was suffering from an asthma attack.

• • •

People began arriving in a steady stream after that. Relatives and friends from both sides of the family flocked through the door. I kissed cousins I didn't know I had.

Every time a new guest arrived, the Websters stood up, pulled on their costume and danced around the garden. The dragon jerked and shimmied, prancing after the latest guest. Smoke rings coiled up in the night air and bells jingled and jangled.

Dad was right behind them, fluffing up the blades of grass.

After a while, the guests were coming so regularly even the Websters couldn't keep up.

Even though the night was chilly, the Chinese lanterns made the garden warm and romantic. Debbie loaded me up with plates of spring rolls and dim sums. Everyone was laughing and dipping and drinking. The scent of beer breath and onions floated like a haze above my head.

"I like your costume," I said to Jackie, as we sorted spring rolls onto trays.

"We're forging an alliance tonight—that's why we went with the dragon," said Jackie. "This engagement is the beginning of the joining of our two families, the uniting of our two forces, the contract, the seal of our pact, the treaty between the Websters and the Stones."

"Great!" I said.

"Once Brian and Debbie are married, your battles will become our battles, your victories will be our victories, your defeats will be our defeats, your joys will be our joys, and your sorrows will be our sorrows."

I spilt plum sauce onto the kitchen bench, filled with dread at the idea they might expect the reverse. There was no way I wanted to fight their battles and join in their victories and share in their defeats. Their enemies would be a lot more life-threatening than the local dogs crapping on Dad's lawn.

"Debbie's got potential," said Jackie. "She did the training course the other day. Dad was impressed with her time."

"She didn't mention it," I said.

The melding of Debbie and Brian had begun. Debbie

was becoming interested in war and military matters in the same way Brian was now becoming an expert on turf.

"And Dad's excited about the actual wedding," said Jackie. "He says it's like preparing for war. It's about strategy. He's getting dossiers made up on each guest. Their politics, their religion, their criminal records, the skeletons in their closets, their civic contribution to society, longstanding feuds."

"Why do we need a dossier on each guest?" I plucked a tray of dim sums from the oven.

"For the reception, of course," said Jackie. "Matching people up on the right table takes delicacy and tactical excellence. We want the night to run with military precision. In a war, failing to take care of the small details can lead to massacre and defeat."

"Right!"

"We pride ourselves on our tactical stealth and smooth reconnaissance," said Jackie, lifting her chin proudly. "Did you know your Uncle Bert and Aunty Beryl are card carrying communists?"

"Aunty Beryl and Uncle Bert!" I said. "They're ordinary old people who like sherry and Madeira cake."

"That's the idea," said Jackie. "Communists want you to think they're ordinary old people who like sherry and Madeira cake, meanwhile they're plotting the overthrow of democracy."

"All Uncle Bert is plotting is the punch line for his jokes," I said.

Jackie scrutinized me knowingly. She patted my arm. "You've been brainwashed," she said.

I was peeling extra lychees for the fruit platter when I heard the doorbell.

I skidded down the hall, half expecting the police. When I opened the door, Raven stood there, flapping moths out of his face.

"Hi," he said.

"Hi."

"I'm sorry to just rock up on your doorstep . . ."

I was too shocked to speak.

"I was in the area."

I cleared my throat. "Right."

"Actually, I had something to tell you."

"Oh." I felt a sharp pain grip my stomach.

"But now I've forgotten."

My stomach cramped again as if I'd eaten an off prawn.

"So," Raven said, laughing. "Now I feel like I'm standing onstage in the wrong play without a clue as to who I am and what I should be saying, wearing a pair of pink boxers—which I don't even own—with knee-length Ugg boots on."

I didn't say anything.

"Did I wake you up?" he asked.

"No," I said.

"You seem dozy. And you're in your pajamas."

I could feel the wet and smooth baldness of a lychee in my hand.

He grinned. "Can I come in for a sec?"

"We're having a party," I whispered.

I stared at him and swallowed again. He stared back, his grin fading slowly.

"I thought the party was last night."

I rolled the lychee around my palm and hesitated. "No."

I could hear the Three Rs swooping into the kitchen, squawking and honking. "It's cake time, Gemma!"

Rachael poked her head into the hall. "Gemma! Are you ready?"

"I'll be there in a minute."

Raven slipped his left hand into his pocket. He tapped a sneaker against the front step. "Did you get the dates mixed up?"

"No."

"Where'd you go last night?"

I rubbed my eyes. "To Nick Lloyd's."

A dozen different expressions flitted across his face. He smiled, sniffed, shook his head and leant against the wall. "I don't believe it."

"I'm allowed to have dinner with whoever I like."

"Are you going out with him?"

"No."

Raven raked his hand across the bricks left and right, as he tried to get his face straight. "I guess you had good food?"

"What's that got to do with it?"

"What did you have?" he asked.

"For your information," I said, "we had turkey and pesto sausages and salad."

"Gourmet!" he nodded.

I felt annoyed. "If you really want to know," I said, "the *gourmet* sausages lacked substance."

Raven pushed himself off the wall. "Well, they're probably gluten-free," he said. He wiped his hand across his face. More moths fluttered around the porch light. A car screeched around a corner. The babble of voices from the backyard rose and fell. "I'd better go," he said. "Mum's at work and Dad's out. I left the boys with Crow."

"With Crow?"

"He's out on parole."

We watched the moths banging into the porch light. "I'll be seeing you," he said. He lifted his hand in a half wave.

Even though I felt irritated, I didn't want him to go. "Do you want to come in?" I asked, my throat burning.

He stopped and turned back. He lingered, his face half in shadow, as though he was waiting for me to say something important.

"We could run through the scene," I said.

He shook his head. "I think we should leave it."

Raven traipsed down the middle of the drive, his feet crunching on white pebbles.

As I watched him go, my stomach hurt even more, as if I'd eaten a hundred off prawns.

twenty-two

On Sunday morning, Mum sent me to O'Riley's for milk and biscuits because people were coming over to watch Debbie and Brian open their engagement presents.

I thought it was bizarre that people wanted to watch Debbie sigh and clap every time a heavy-based aluminum saucepan appeared and hear her hiss with disappointment each time another set of salt and pepper shakers was revealed.

I didn't want to go home. I could imagine the Three Rs sitting in a circle in the lounge room, writing down each present on the list, cataloging and drooling over Debbie's gifts as though it was booty they had dragged back for her from some foreign invasion.

My trolley wheels jammed. I rested my head against

the handle and groaned. I must be turning into a Webster. The alliance was working. How else could war imagery slip so easily into my brain?

I nudged the trolley. It didn't move. "Bloody hell!" I grunted.

It would serve Stan and Ted O'Riley right if a proper shopping center was built on the tip, especially if it had a brand new supermarket, full of clean, fat aisles, bright, snappy lights and shopping trolleys with wheels that rolled where you wanted them to. It would be fair punishment for their stupid sloppiness.

I got down on my hands and knees and straightened the wheels. I pushed the trolley forward. It veered right and clipped the edge of the shelf. One after the other, like bricks in a crumbling castle, cereal boxes popped out and tumbled down.

"Help," I said, crouching and covering my head against a barrage of cereal.

"Bummer!" called a voice.

I swiveled around, my hands over my head. Sparrow and Robin were standing at the end of the aisle, grinning at me.

"Watch out!" said Sparrow.

Another box tipped and bounced off the trolley.

"Whoops," said Robin.

"That's a lot of fiber," said Sparrow.

"You should try psyllium husk," said Robin.

"If you've got problems *you-know-where*," added Sparrow.

"I don't have problems *you-know-where*," I said.

"It's nothing to be ashamed of," said Sparrow.

"I'm not ashamed," I said.

"Mum says psyllium husk fixed her right up," said Robin, peering into a box of unpacked marshmallows. "She's a three-times-a-day woman now."

"That's more than I need to know," I said. I tried to straighten up.

"Are you sure you don't have irritable bowel syndrome?" asked Sparrow, as if he were my family doctor.

I scooped up some of the cereal boxes. "What are you two doing here?"

"Shopping," said Robin.

"It's tacos tonight," said Sparrow. "Maggie's favorite." He walked down the aisle, kicking more stray cereal boxes towards me. "You're such a lady driver."

"All you need is a hat," said Robin.

"Yeah," said Sparrow. "A little white bowling hat with a gold-plated badge."

"For your information, I have a trolley with a disability," I said.

"Yes, I see," said Sparrow. He crouched and examined my trolley. "You got the one with ADD."

"Oh Lord, what have you boys done?"

Mrs. De Head arrived, clutching a rusted trolley. She wore nylon navy slacks riddled with static, and they clung to her legs like a second skin. She held a cracked leather purse tightly, bulging with receipts.

"Aw, Mum," said Sparrow. "Spare me! It wasn't us. It was her."

"Oh, for goodness sake, I turn my back for one minute to find a toilet duck and the next thing I know you've caused an earthquake." She pushed her trolley closer. "I'm really sorry. If anything's broken, I'm happy to fix it up."

Her cheap perfume hung in the air like a one-note song.

"Mum, I'm telling ya, we didn't do it," said Sparrow, standing up and shrugging.

"Raven's girlie knocked them over all on her own," said Robin.

"Raven's girlie?" She stared at me uncertainly.

"Hi," I said. "I'm Gemma. Raven's friend." I glared at Robin pointedly.

"Oh yes!" said Mrs. De Head. "Raven's spoken very highly of you."

"Very highly," said Sparrow.

"Cut that out, you," said Mrs. De Head, tapping him gently on the head.

"Yeow, Mum," yelped Sparrow. "Ya gonna give me brain damage."

"You're June Stone's daughter, aren't you?" asked Mrs. De Head.

"That's right."

"I used to play tennis in a day camp with your mother, years ago now," she said, smiling. "Back when Crow was small and I was a lot lighter on my feet."

Everything in her trolley was no-name brand. Biscuits. Fish fingers. Taco shells. Toilet duck. Tuna. All white packaging with black writing and a slash of red.

"Raven's a changed boy since he's been doing the play," said Mrs. De Head.

"Next thing you know, he'll want a karaoke machine," said Sparrow.

"So he can dance and sing as well as act," said Robin, swirling around the aisle, holding a pretend microphone. *"The Love Boat, soon will be making another run. The Love Boat, promises something for everyone. Set a course for adventure, your mind on a new romance. Love won't hurt anymore. It's an open smile on a friendly shore. It's Looooove! Welcome aboard— it's Looooove!"*

The more Sparrow laughed, the more Robin hammed it up.

"What's got into you two," said Mrs. De Head. "Stop it, and pick up those boxes."

"But we didn't knock them over," cried Sparrow.

"I didn't ask if you knocked them over," said Mrs. De Head. "I'm asking you to pick them up."

"Aw, ya killing us, Mum," said Sparrow. "Maggie's right. You'll get done for child slave labor."

"Not if I get done for insanity first," said Mrs. De Head, smiling, as she helped me slot boxes back onto the shelves.

• • •

When I finished shopping, I sat with Mrs. De Head and watched Sparrow and Robin play in the park. The sky was gray and our plastic bags rustled in the cool breeze.

"I'm glad Raven has you as a friend," said Mrs. De Head.

I thought about the night before and felt sick all over again.

"Not that you love one child more . . ." said Mrs. De Head. "But with Raven, I've always felt that if he had the right friends, he'd go a long way." She glanced at me quickly. Her face was thin and long like the hole in a darning needle. Her brown hair hung limply against her neck, as though she'd given up styling it a long time ago. Her cheeks had deep, graven lines etched vertically. She sighed. "It's hard to find people who are willing to look under the surface of things."

I felt uncomfortable knowing she was thinking I was that sort of person. My legs felt itchy, as though they wanted to leap up and run away on their own.

"It's funny," said Mrs. De Head. "When Raven was born I wanted to call him Paul. You know, after the famous actor."

I tried for a minute to imagine calling Raven such a plain, boring, non-descriptive name.

"I think Raven suits him better," I said.

Robin and Sparrow climbed over the orange barricades and onto the base of the new fountain.

"It's odd how things work out," said Mrs. De Head. "I didn't want to name the boys after birds. It was Mick's idea. But sometimes I think they couldn't have been named anything else."

Sparrow and Robin danced around lightly, laughing and shouting, taking turns, posing as statues.

"Wouldn't it be wonderful to be as carefree as a bird?" said Mrs. De Head, leaning back against the park bench.

twenty-three

We auditioned for the play on Monday afternoon. Even though we performed our prepared scenes, Mrs. Langton asked some of us to read different parts, opposite different people.

I read as Miranda to Jago, Nick and Juan, who each read as Ferdinand.

Raven read as Ferdinand, Stephano and Gonzalo.

Nick read for stacks of other parts: Alonso, Antonio, Caliban, Prospero and Sebastian.

Tea, Eloise, Serena and Dodi also read as Miranda.

Max and Juan read as Caliban.

Eloise, Tea and heaps of girls from Year Seven read for Iris and the other spirits.

When we finished, Mrs. Langton asked some people to improvise. Tea had a go in the hot seat as Miranda. Jago played Ferdinand and Serena soared as Ariel.

Then, when we thought it was over, Mrs. Langton asked Raven to improvise as Caliban.

Raven swallowed and tugged at his shoe. "I'd prefer not," he said.

"Do me this favor," said Mrs. Langton, in that gentle voice, which dignified you and made you want to do anything she asked.

Raven sighed, as if he had really bad indigestion. He dragged himself up onstage and sat on the hot seat, absolutely still, his hands on his legs, his head bowed. A shaft of spotlight lit him up like an insect caught in amber.

"Tell me about when Prospero first came to the island," said Mrs. Langton.

At first, Raven tried to shrug off the question.

"Were you happy?" she asked.

Raven lifted his head; his eyes were hot and bright. He spoke softly and deliberately, but resentment ran through his voice like a thick vein. "They stroked me. They made much of me. And I loved them. So I showed them . . . I showed them the secret places."

"The secret places?" said Mrs. Langton. "Where were they?"

Raven flinched. "Where the wild mint grows, where the mud crabs hide, where chestnuts hang in prickly husks, where the pink robin sings and seagulls perch, where stingrays glide, where the fresh springs flow, where the briny saltpits stew."

"Did they like the secret places?" Mrs. Langton asked.

"I kept them safe from the barren places, from fast sand, bogs and swamps. I laid the fertile plains in their laps like gifts."

"And then what happened?" asked Mrs. Langton.

"They took it," he spat. "Once they knew, they stole it."

"How did they do that?" she asked.

"They cheated me and made it theirs. No more making much. No more stroking. No more berries fizzing in water. No more learning. No more moon and stars and sun. Now I am their subject. Me who was King first! On this island which is mine. Subject to a tyrant, kept in a dank, dark cave."

"And what of Miranda?" asked Mrs. Langton.

"I am tormented! Prospero summons them. Goblins. Urchins. Apes. I am pinched, pricked and prodded. Beaten, bashed and bitten. Hissed into madness."

"You haven't answered my question," said Mrs. Langton.

He cowered, his arms across his face. "Don't hit, don't kick, don't bite! Don't pinch, don't poke, don't prod!" He cringed and trembled. "I'll carry the logs. I'll fetch the water . . ." His slid to the ground, on all fours, his eyes cunning. "But first let me lick your shoe! I'll not serve them anymore . . . let me serve you."

Everyone else had performed Caliban as if he were merely naughty. But Raven's Caliban was transparent with hunger. When he spoke, his skin was only a thin membrane around all the pulses drumming greedily in his body.

I could see how he could haunt Miranda. As I watched, I felt scared. Scared like a little child who was staring at the bathwater swirling down the plughole—that swirling, grasping dark hole that gobbled and sucked whatever it was given and was never full.

Raven's voice went hoarse and he finished. There was complete silence. A shiver prickled and arched its way across the room.

"Thank you, Raven," whispered Mrs. Langton. "Thank you."

Raven was dazed, as though he'd woken from a dream and didn't know where he was. He shuddered and climbed down from the stage and started stacking up the chairs with a forced cheerfulness. But I could tell he was embarrassed. It was like he had revealed something of himself he hadn't planned to, and now he wished he could snatch it back.

Mrs. Langton and Ms. Highgate conferred in the corner, their voices full of fierce murmurs. I had no idea who would get what part and I had no idea how Mrs. Langton and Ms. Highgate would come up with a decision by the end of the week.

But I knew one thing. Raven was good.

I had always thought Nick was the best actor. But now I realized that what I admired about Nick's performances was his voice—his vowels like songs and his crisp and tangy consonants. But when Raven was onstage I couldn't help watching him. He made me feel he was baring his soul, walking on a knife-edge, capable of something terrible and wonderful all at the same time.

Raven collapsed by my side, sheepish and exhausted. "If I get that role, I'm going to . . . I don't know."

"There are heaps of others who want it."

"I hate Caliban."

We were silent. Mrs. Langton and Ms. Highgate were still talking intensely in the corner.

I dug my nail into the gap of the floorboard. "I'm sorry about the other night."

"Nah, don't . . ."

"I should have told you . . ."

"I still would've been angry." He folded his script and put it in his bag.

"You could play any role," I said.

"You think so?"

"You're good."

"How good?" He was fishing for a compliment big time, I could tell by his dimples.

"I don't want to say in case it goes to your head," I said.

"Good enough to buy me a milk shake?" he asked.

"Maybe even good enough to buy you a potato scallop as well!"

Later, we got a lift with Serena's mum to Buranderry Village. I bought Raven a milk shake, four potato scallops and a serve of chips from Thea's. We took our food to a park bench in the Buranderry Memorial Park, and sat dissecting the afternoon, the mosquitoes circling.

When we were finished eating, we ran through the gardens, around the base of the new fountain, kicking piles of autumn leaves sky high like little kids. And even when Noddy, the Village gardener, darted out from Pete's pub and yelled at us, a schooner in his hand and a smoke hanging off his bottom lip like a water downpipe, we didn't care.

We were glad to be alive. Glad to have made it through auditions. Glad we hadn't dropped a single line or cue.

But we were mostly glad to be ourselves again.

twenty-four

When Ms. Highgate clopped down the stairs on Thursday afternoon and saw all of us standing at the hall door, she smiled knowingly. "What a crowd!" she said, fiddling slowly in her velvet bag.

"Tell us who's got the lead, Miss," begged Jago, as we parted like the Red Sea so she could get to the door.

"My lips are sealed," said Ms. Highgate, her mouth a tight crease.

She jiggled her key in the lock. The pink crystal on her key ring knocked against the handle. She tried again, turning the handle and pushing hard against the door until it scraped open. We surged in, pushing.

Mrs. Langton swept in behind us. Her hair was a silvery, twiggy mess. "Okay," she puffed. "Sorry I'm late."

We sat in a circle. Sitting in circles in drama is as automatic as the instinctive knowledge cows have that at four o'clock they should stop chewing and line up for milking. No one tells them to do it. They just know.

Raven sat nearby on my left, his legs scrunched up, his chin resting on his knees. Tea's face was flushed, as she sat clutching Eloise's hand. Nick reclined on the floor as if he were attending a Roman banquet.

"Right," said Mrs. Langton. "I'm going to read through the cast list."

And she began, reeling off the names, clattering through them, matching characters with real people. The spirits, the sailors, the boatswain, the ship's master, Trinculo, Stephano, Adrian, Francisco, Gonzalo, Antonio, Sebastian, Alonso, Ferdinand. The names flowed fast, almost too fast, like the bewildering blur of a foreign language. I held my breath and leant forward, watching Mrs. Langton's lips, a hot acid ache in my stomach.

There were gasps and sighs around me. Some kids punched the air with their fists and their eyes shone, while others stared stonily at the ground.

And then she was saying Miranda's name. And for a moment blood was roaring in my ears like a wild flood. But I could read her lips and they were saying my name. "Miranda . . . Gemma Stone."

Tea buried her head in Eloise's neck and her shoulders shook. Serena patted me on the back. Nick nodded approvingly. Jago stared at me from the other side of the circle, his mouth open.

And I felt this weird, fierce, wild sense of happiness burst up and out—a geyser of joy.

I turned to Raven. I reached across, to hug him or to dance with him, I don't know—but there were tears in his eyes. Not sad, feeling sorry tears, but hot, injustice tears. And he was shouting at Mrs. Langton, not caring how loud he was, his voice sharp rough angles.

"This is a joke," he cried, his face strained with fury.

Ms. Highgate stood behind Mrs. Langton, her small, teeth bared. "Stop it," she said. "You've got no right to speak like that."

Raven left the circle and snatched up his bag from the corner of the stage. "Shut up, you stupid cow!"

And the rage that always simmered under the surface of Ms. Highgate's cultivated niceness gushed out like blood from a wound. "You're behaving like a savage!"

"Don't you call me that!" said Raven. He kicked the stage so hard a panel cracked.

"See!" said Ms. Highgate.

"Julie," said Mrs. Langton. "Stop it."

Raven jerked his head at Ms. Highgate. "You cast me as Caliban!" He smashed a chair into the wall, his shoulders flung back, his whole body bristling with defiant bravado.

"I wouldn't have cast you at all," hissed Ms. Highgate.

"It was my decision," said Mrs. Langton.

Raven stood completely still, as if he'd been given bad news that he couldn't make sense of—a death in the family.

Then as Mrs. Langton's words sank in, his whole face punctured, the anger deflated by sharp grief. He took a step back, his shoulders hunched, the defiance in his eyes replaced with cornered despair.

"But now you've shown us exactly how well you were cast!" said Ms. Highgate.

"Julie," said Mrs. Langton, turning her head. "Please."

"I can't play Caliban," said Raven. "I didn't even want to audition for it."

Ms. Highgate snapped her mouth shut and turned away.

"I cast you, Raven," said Mrs. Langton quietly. "I cast you because you can give me a Caliban that isn't a stereotype and I truly believe the other roles won't stretch you in the same way."

Raven's mouth sagged. "Well, thanks," he said. "But no thanks." And he walked out without looking back.

And my geyser of joy fizzled out and dribbled away.

There was a strange, awkward silence. We listened to the clatter of Raven's footsteps as he ran down the stairs to the bottom gate.

"He is such a De Head!" said Tea, rolling her eyes.

"What an ungrateful git!" said Eloise.

Nick slid across the circle and patted me on the shoulder. "It's going to be good to be your dad!" he whispered. I stared at him. He tapped his chest. "You can call me Papa!"

Then it dawned on me. Nick had been cast as Prospero.

"Oh great!" I groaned.

So now not only was he Raven's master, but he was my father as well.

twenty-five

Raven didn't come to school the next day and on my way home, on the spur of the moment, I got off the bus at the Flats corner shop.

I walked past the little church with the slate triangle tile roof and the long narrow strip of bubbled windows tucked under the eaves. It was clearly built in a hurry: by people who didn't like looking out on the world or having the world look in on them. A lone, sickly cherry tree stood in the unfenced front yard. The lights were on and I could hear singing and the jingle of an out-of-time tambourine.

Kids roamed the streets, riding their bikes, their school shirts shiny, threadbare at the elbows, and half tucked into their jeans. Their faces were gleaming with wind and speed, as bright as headlights because school was finished for the week.

Dogs were running wild, sniffing at each other, chasing bikes, fighting on front lawns, barking and weeing, eating rubber hoses, rolling onto their backs for a scratch.

A little girl with a straggly plait sat in the gutter talking earnestly to a cat stuck down in the drain. When I walked by, she smiled, a trail of snot melting like wax over her top lip.

Cooking smells puffed out of each house like warm invitations. Fried chicken, onions wilting on the barbie, stinging garlic.

I turned into Raven's street. On the corner, a woman stood on her front porch smoking a cigarette. A red-faced toddler was tucked snugly at her waist, sucking on an empty Pepsi can. The woman waved as I went by.

At the end of the street, Raven's brothers were playing a game of tennis on the road.

"Hiya," said Robin when he saw me.

"Are ya staying for dinner tonight?" called Sparrow.

"Pies and peas with gravy," said Robin. "Yum!"

"Savory mince pies," called Maggie, from where he was sitting under a gum tree, smoking a cigarette.

"Not from the shops," said Sparrow.

"Nah," said Robin. "Mum makes her own."

"Mum's going to be home for dinner, too," said Sparrow.

"Gemma might have better things to do," said Maggie, ashing his cigarette into the tennis ball container.

"Pies and peas sounds yum." I picked up a tennis racquet with flayed strings. I thwacked a ball to Sparrow, but it spun into the gutter on the other side.

"Good shot!" Raven was sitting on a blue milk crate on the front porch, underneath the butterflies. He was rumpled, as though he had just woken up.

I stood on the gutter. "Why didn't you come to school today?"

"Why should I? I know what people think!" he said. "And now I know what Mrs. Langton thinks, too."

"Don't be stupid. She cast you in the role because you can do it best."

He shook his head, as though I had told him a lie. He leaned his arms against his legs. "The pies aren't gourmet," he said.

"So what!" I said.

"They're plain as."

"Plain as, is good."

I picked up another ball and served it hard. It bounced off a telephone pole and shot down the drain like a pinball.

"If you don't stop hitting our balls down the gutter, ya gonna send us broke," said Sparrow.

"Yeah," said Robin. "It'll be back to eating Spam for us."

I tried to hit a forehand, but it sliced into the front yard of the house across the road. "Hope she's a better actress than she is a tennis player," said Maggie.

"She got the lead role," said Raven.

"Good job," said Maggie.

"You've got a lead role, too," I said.

Mrs. De Head drove down the street in a battered green Torana. She waited as Robin and Sparrow moved out of the way, then eased into the driveway. Robin and Sparrow flocked around the car. They wrenched open the boot and lifted out the bags of shopping. Maggie opened the car door for his mum.

"Raven's girlie's here," he winked, leaning on the car door and nodding at me.

"She's not my girlie, you moron," said Raven. He chucked his milk crate at Maggie's head.

"You'd like her to be your girlie though," snorted Maggie, kicking the crate. It hit one of the sleeping giant cats, which hissed and bolted away.

"Hello, Gemma," said Mrs. De Head, climbing out of the car. "It's lovely to see you again."

"Hello, Mrs. De Head."

"Congratulations on the play," she said. "I heard you did very well."

"Thanks."

She picked up her purse and another plastic bag. "It must be hard for the teachers to have to decide."

"Not if they've already made their minds up," muttered Raven.

"I ran into your mum today at the butcher," interrupted Mrs. De Head. "She told me your sister is getting married in October." She glanced at Maggie. "I wish one of my boys would settle down with a nice girl."

"You just wish one of your boys would settle down," said Maggie with a wink.

"Raven's settled," said Robin. "He hasn't been suspended in months."

"He's letting the family down," said Maggie. "Next thing you know, he'll be elected Mayor."

"Cut it out," said Raven.

"If that's what love does for you," said Maggie, "you can keep it!"

"I said cut it out!" Raven glared at his older brother.

"Stop being a tease," said Mrs. De Head. "Come inside and help me get dinner."

"Aw, gees," said Maggie. "Can't one of the squirts help you, Mum?"

"I need you," said Mrs. De Head. "You're the best at making mash."

"Can Gemma stay for tea?" asked Robin.

"Of course, if she'd like to," said Mrs. De Head.

"Is that all right, Mrs. De Head?" I asked, glancing at Raven.

"That'd be lovely. It'll be good to have some female company," said Mrs. De Head.

After I had rung Mum, Sparrow and I played tennis against Raven and Robin.

Robin darted hyperactively around the road with a racquet the same size as his head. He was into the grunts and the groans and the whole show. Every time he hit a winner, he cranked his hand into a cobra snake and hissed. And every time we were about to hit a winner, he fluttered to the ground and pretended to be hurt.

Raven was a watchful player, lazy and languid. But his shots were sharp and low to the ground.

Sparrow was full of good advice, but had no practical skills to speak of, so by the time the streetlights came on, Raven was winning, and a lot happier.

"Do ya think she might be better playing left-handed?" asked Sparrow, as he crawled out of a blackberry bush at the end of the street with the lost ball. "I've got more scratches than the TAB!"

"Either that, or we could blindfold her," said Raven.

"Hey, leave her alone," said Robin. "I like playing against her. She makes me look *good*."

The moon had risen plump and blue-veined. The grass was wet with dew and our breath was coming out in swirls. We kept stopping the game as more people came home from work, their high beams flashing, sending us blind.

"It's too dark. I can't see the ball anymore," I said. "That's why I keep missing it."

"That and the fact your racquet has a bloody big hole in it," said Raven.

"Hey!" shouted Maggie, from the front door. "Grub's up."

We chucked the racquets on the front porch with the last ball and went inside.

twenty-six

I could tell there was something wrong straightaway.

Mrs. De Head was bustling around the kitchen with steaming pots. Mr. De Head was sitting at the table with his arms crossed tight against his chest. When he saw me, he barely nodded.

Mrs. De Head served up great clouds of mash. Maggie plopped the plates onto the table, not caring where they landed, his eyes bright with fuming.

"Your mum said there's some money missing from her purse," said Mr. De Head.

Raven glanced at me.

"I didn't say that," said Mrs. De Head. "I said I was short of money and I must have misplaced some."

"I didn't take it," said Robin, sitting down at the table. He poured a glass of Coke.

"Neither did I," said Sparrow quickly.

Mr. De Head sucked his tongue so hard it whistled. "If I find out any of you've been nicking money out of your mum's purse, I'll belt you black and blue."

Mrs. De Head poured gravy over Mr. De Head's three pies. A dollop fell onto the table. "Did I say I wanted gravy?"

"Oh," said Mrs. De Head.

"Where's the sauce?"

Mrs. De Head picked up Robin's pies and swapped them over.

"I hate gravy," said Robin.

"Shhh," said Mrs. De Head. She went to the fridge and got the tomato sauce. She slid it onto the table, next to Mr. De Head's plate. Mr. De Head said nothing. He picked up the bottle and squeezed it hard. The sauce spurted out in great, wheezy farts.

"I don't know what we did wrong to produce such a bloody pack of thieves."

"I wouldn't go blaming Mum," said Maggie, picking up the sauce bottle.

"Maggie," said Mrs. De Head.

"Shut ya gob, stupid," said Mr. De Head. "I never stole a thing in my life."

"What about the pension?" said Maggie, wiping the sauce crust off the bottle. "Some people reckon it's stealing if you get it when you can work."

"I'm getting what I'm owed," said Mr. De Head, before eating one whole pie in three big bites.

"Some people reckon you're getting more than you're owed."

"Shut up!" said Raven. "You can't talk."

"You need to watch yourself, Maggie," said Mr. De Head. "One day your mouth is going to get you into a whole lot of trouble."

"Please," said Mrs. De Head. She put down her knife and fork. "All of you. We have a guest."

We sat and chewed silently. Robin picked up the last pie. Sparrow yanked it out of his hand. It landed on the floor with a squidge. The cats were on it within seconds.

"You're a fat dork!" said Robin.

"You're a bloody dolt," said Sparrow, jabbing Robin in the ribs.

"Dill."

"Dropkick."

"Di—"

"Robin! Sparrow!" said Mrs. De Head, running her fingers through her hair. "That's enough."

The silent chewing again. The sound of swallows and slurps. I stared at Mr. De Head's freckled arms. He had an anchor tattooed on one arm and a rose on the other. The tattoos were both blue-green and blurred with age.

"The fountain's nearly finished," said Sparrow. "They're gonna put up the statue next week."

"Old Hairy dressed up in a soldier's uniform," said Robin. "They've got a picture at school."

Mr. De Head squashed his peas flat. "Old Hairy was never in the army."

"The RSL donated money to the project," said Raven.

"I did the town a favor thirty years ago and they still don't know it!" said Mr. De Head, scraping mince onto his knife and sliding it into his mouth.

"Who's up for a game tonight?" asked Robin.

"What . . . sort of game?" I asked.

"Any sort," said Robin, flicking a pea at Sparrow. "You can choose. Uno. Kerplunk. Mouse Trap. Yahtzee. Chess. Connect Four. Monopoly. Cluedo. Checkers. Snakes and Ladders. Twister."

"Not Twister," said Raven.

"Not for me," said Mr. De Head. "I'm going to watch the box. Get us a beer, Robin."

"Let's play Kerplunk," said Robin, going to the fridge. "I love Kerplunk."

"It's the only game you've ever won," said Sparrow.

"I am the Master," said Robin.

"Only because it's a game that doesn't require a brain," said Sparrow.

"How often do you play?" I asked.

"Whenever Mum's home and she's not too tired," said Sparrow.

"It's better than homework," said Robin.

"Well, this is cozy!"

Everyone stopped talking.

Crow was swaying at the backdoor. His skin was sallow, his flesh cutting over his cheekbones like sharp arrows. He was finely built; his faded jeans super tight. His eyes were like Raven's, but lighter; more the blue of the shallows around a tropical island; and bright like he had a fever.

"Hello there," he said. On his right arm, the curly tail of a sea horse tattoo poked out from underneath his sleeve.

"You're late, love," said Mrs. De Head.

"Any pies left?"

"Only one," said Sparrow.

"It's in the oven," said Robin.

"The cats ate the other one," said Sparrow.

"Bloody cats," said Crow.

Mr. De Head sat hunched and still, watching Crow. "Your mum's missing money from her purse," he said.

"Is she?"

"Do you know anything about it?"

Crow shrugged. "Might."

Sparrow peeled the lid off his last pie. Robin counted his peas.

"I needed a loan," said Crow.

"I'm not having drugs in this house."

"You're always thinking the worst, Dad," said Crow.

"You're in my house, so you'll live by my rules," said Mr. De Head.

"I'll pay it back." He opened the fridge and took out a beer.

"You shouldn't have taken the money without asking," said Mrs. De Head quietly.

"You were asleep," said Crow. "I didn't wanna wake you."

"Did you ask if you could have that?" said Mr. De Head, nodding at the beer.

"No," said Crow. "Is that the new rule? Do I have to ask

for everything? Is it okay if I take a breath? Is it okay if I smoke a fag?"

"Bloody oath, you do," said Mr. De Head. "I'm sick of you plundering your own family. You're just a filthy, dirty parasite sucking people dry."

"And you're not, you stupid friggin' old coot?" said Crow. "You've spent the last thirty years sponging off Mum and it's never kept you awake at night."

"Shut up," said Mr. De Head. The cats shot up and ran off, their tails flicking.

"She cans friggin' horse meat," sneered Crow. "And you spend the friggin' money she earns at the TAB."

"Crow," said Mrs. De Head.

"You're the friggin' dirty, filthy parasite!" said Crow. He popped open the can of beer, took a slug and wiped his lips with the back of his hand.

Maggie and Raven gazed at their empty plates. Robin edged closer to Mrs. De Head. Sparrow's plate was a pastry haystack.

Crow put his beer on the counter. He opened the oven and used a tea towel to pull out the tray. He picked up the pie and took a big bite. "Whooh!" he shouted. He dropped the pie with a plop back onto the tray. "Hot!"

Mr. De Head stood up. He grabbed the broom leaning against the wall. His stomach bulged and a spot of sauce soaked into his blue singlet, black as blood. He faced Crow, his left hand stretching and flexing around the broom handle.

"Are you going to whack me, Dad?" asked Crow.

"Bloody oath!" said Mr. De Head.

"Do you think anything you could do would be as bad as what I got in jail?" Crow sneered.

"We'll see," said Mr. De Head. He gripped the broom so hard his knuckles were white, and his eyes were fixed and mean.

Robin whimpered, his peas scattering everywhere. Sparrow slid off his chair and hid under the table.

Crow picked up his pie and took another big bite.

"Oh shit," whispered Maggie.

Raven sat in his seat, frozen.

"Show me what you've got, Dad!" said Crow.

"I'll show you," shouted Mr. De Head, lunging at Crow. He cracked Crow so hard on the forearm the pie flew out of his hand and smacked onto the floor.

"Do ya think that hurt?" laughed Crow, grabbing his arm.

"I'll make it hurt," said Mr. De Head.

And then Mr. De Head started whacking Crow like he wanted to kill him.

Crow lifted his arms up as the broom smashed against his body.

Mrs. De Head rushed out of her chair. "Stop it, Mick," she begged.

"Get out of my way," he yelled, hitting out, not caring where the blows landed. Pots fell off the kitchen bench. A glass vase toppled and shattered in the sink. Bills and advertising brochures sailed through the air. The dog barked madly and threw himself against the glass door.

Then one of the blows struck Mrs. De Head flat across the chest and she fell backwards and hit the kitchen bench. Her head grazed the corner of a cupboard and she collapsed heavily on the lino. She lay on the ground, her head resting on a calendar, stunned and winded, moaning softly.

"Mum!" shrieked Robin, scrabbling across the floor.

Maggie tore out of his chair and ripped into his dad. He grabbed him by the shirt and threw him against the fridge. Mr. De Head was so surprised the broom dropped out of his hand and clattered to the floor.

"That's enough, you shit!" Maggie shouted, pinning his dad down. "That's enough." And then he punched his dad in the face; and then again, over and over, his fists raining down like bombs. "Enough!" he shouted, each time his fist connected. "Enough! Enough! Enough!"

Blood was streaming everywhere. Mr. De Head crumpled like a spider, his legs and arms folding up. But Maggie wasn't going to stop, not until his dad was an ugly smear.

"For God's sake, Maggie," Raven cried. "Stop it! STOP IT!"

Raven wrestled Maggie and they banged hard against the oven, a pot of peas and a colander crashing to the floor. And then Maggie fell, weeping. And there was only sobbing and the soft sounds of wounded people.

Mrs. De Head lay staring up at the kitchen light, Robin almost on top of her, snot dripping out of his nose, his small hands pawing at her.

"You're crushing me," she murmured, blinking.

Mr. De Head staggered to his feet, his hands trying to

catch the blood shooting out of his nose like a tap. He grabbed a tea towel and jammed it against his face. He fumbled around for the keys, lurching against the fridge. He stumbled out. The front door slammed and a car engine started up.

Crow slid over to his mum. He lifted her up, his right arm quilted with welts. "Get some peas," he said.

Sparrow opened the freezer and pulled out a bag of peas. He crept over and gave them to Crow, who held them against the side of his mum's head. She flinched and Sparrow stroked her hair.

"Someone needs to clean the kitchen light," said Mrs. De Head. "I counted five dead cockroaches up there."

Robin slithered across the floor and picked up the calendar and the papers, sorting out the mess as he went.

And that's when I started to cry.

Big, scared sobs from the bottom of my stomach, they rolled out like sets of waves crashing hard on a beach.

"Oh, bloody hell!" said Maggie. "I forgot she was here."

Robin scuttled over and put his arms around me, but it only made it worse.

I couldn't get over what I had seen. I couldn't get over the suddenness of it.

Mrs. De Head dragged herself up and put her arms around me, too. She accidentally clutched the bag of peas against my back and I felt an icy trickle down my spine.

"We need to call the police," I sobbed. "Ring the police."

Raven and Maggie glanced at their mother then looked away.

"Shhh," hushed Mrs. De Head, stroking the back of my neck, her fingers callused and scratchy.

"If we call the police," whispered Raven, "who will they arrest?"

"The lot of us," said Crow. "Gladly."

"And then Crow will go back to jail, and Maggie too," said Sparrow.

"And maybe Dad," said Robin.

"It's better this way," said Mrs. De Head. "Let's pray. We'll pray to Jesus."

I couldn't help wondering where Jesus was when the punches were flying.

Sparrow and Robin patted my head. "Don't cry," said Robin.

"Everything's okay," said Sparrow.

"Jesus can use even the worst evil to bring some good," whispered Mrs. De Head.

But no matter how I tried, I couldn't stop the sobs.

"How about a cup of tea?" asked Mrs. De Head.

"Maybe we'd better call her mum," said Raven, his eyes avoiding mine.

"You can't send her home like this," said Mrs. De Head.

"Why won't she stop?" asked Robin.

"She's in shock," said Mrs. De Head.

"Her family doesn't carry on like we do," said Raven. "They talk properly to each other. As if they like each other."

"She sure cries a lot," said Sparrow.

"Sod off," said Raven.

Maggie crouched by my side. He put his hand on my knee. "How about a game of Monopoly?" he asked.

Robin stopped patting my head. "Are you gonna play?" he asked.

"Sure," said Maggie.

"I will," said Sparrow.

"I'll give you a run for your money," said Crow.

"In your dreams," said Maggie, with a flashy grin.

Mrs. De Head kissed me on the cheek. She smelt of oranges and too-strong musk. She tucked a strand of my hair behind my ear and brushed a pie crumb off my jumper. "See," she said. "Everything's all right."

Crow and Raven cleaned up the mess. Maggie boiled the kettle and set out some mugs and a plate of ginger nut biscuits. Sparrow and Robin rifled through the telephone table, searching for coins to use as replacement Monopoly pieces.

And before the tears had even dried on my cheeks, they were setting up the board, arguing over the pieces, then playing the game, screaming with laughter at each other's misfortune.

twenty-seven

Later that night, Maggie dropped me home. Debbie was still up practicing her capital letter calligraphy.

"You look like you've seen a ghost," she said. "How come your eyes are so red?"

I hesitated. I couldn't tell her. To even breathe a word would be a betrayal.

"You're not doing drugs, are you?" asked Debbie. "Because I'm not having some drug addict with rheumy red eyes wrecking my wedding photos."

"What makes you think I'm doing drugs?"

"You're hanging out with the De Head boys," said Debbie. "Everyone knows they do drugs for dinner."

"For your information," I said, "we had pies, mash and peas."

Debbie turned over a page in her art book. She used a ruler to draw straight, faint pencil lines. "You should be careful hanging around the De Heads'," she said. "They're a bad influence."

"What would you know?"

Debbie raised her eyebrows. A smudge of ink shadowed her cheekbone. "Everybody knows," she muttered.

I suddenly felt angry. "Everybody knows what?"

"Those boys could do with the army," said Debbie. "They need their craziness ironed out. That's all I'm saying."

"The army hasn't ironed out the Websters' craziness," I said.

"I beg your pardon!" said Debbie.

"Brian's family are nuts," I said. "Chock full of loonies."

"They are not," said Debbie. "Take that back!"

"I won't," I said. "What kind of people boast about having war in their blood?"

"They have served their country," said Debbie. "You're sitting in comfort here because for generations they have risked their lives for you."

"Yeah, right," I said. "We're sitting in safety because your in-laws like to kill people and get medals for their efficiency."

"Shut up!"

"You shut up!"

Mum came into the dining room, bleary-eyed. "What's all the shouting about?"

"Debbie is trashing Raven and his family."

"All I said was they needed the army," said Debbie. "They need discipline. Anyone can see that."

"I don't want to hear any more," said Mum. "Raven's lovely. I'm more than happy for Gemma to go out with him, if that makes her happy, as long as she gets her homework done. . . ."

"I'm not going out with Raven!" I cried.

"Oh," said Mum. "I thought . . ."

"He's a friend, that's all!" I yelled. "What makes you think *I'd* go out with *him*?"

"You . . . just . . . he . . ."

"You don't know what you're talking about!" I screamed. "Because you're a freak, too!"

"Gemma!" said Debbie.

"There's nothing to be—" started Mum.

"You don't know anything about me," I screamed. "Nothing."

"I think it's lovely—"

"Don't say another word!" I yelled. "I don't want to hear you!"

"Why is she chucking a birkett?" asked Debbie.

"We can talk this through, Gem," said Mum. "I'm sorry, I made a mistake."

"Instead of spending her time with that delinquent, she should take up calligraphy and help me with the name cards for the reception tables," said Debbie. "She'd be a whole lot better off."

"I . . . hate . . . youuu!" I screeched. "I hate you!"

It felt so good to scream out those words, to fling them into Debbie's shocked, comfortable face like hard, sharp slaps.

"She's lost it," said Debbie. "She's truly, completely lost it!"

I ran upstairs to my bedroom. I lay on my bed and stared at the wallpaper. I counted the petals on the same flower over and over again, holding everything back, holding everything in, because no place felt safe anymore.

twenty-eight

After that night, Raven avoided me. At first, I thought I was imagining it, that it was a coincidence that every time he caught sight of me, he'd shoot off in a different direction like a wild rabbit. Or he'd become engrossed in a conversation with someone else, his eyes fixed firmly on their face, as if the person he was speaking to was the most interesting person he'd ever met.

After a while, I began to feel invisible, as if I had become his blind spot. It was so weird. It was so weird not having Raven around. It was so weird not having him seek me out. I found myself looking for him all the time, and I was unable to concentrate on anything properly.

"Are you, like, listening to what I'm saying?" asked Jody, nudging my leg.

I stared at her. She stared back at me. Her face was devoid of makeup. Not a clump of mascara or a dash of eyeliner or a smear of lip gloss anywhere. I could barely see her strawberry blond eyelashes and, for the first time in two years, her freckles were visible, thousands of tiny golden clouds floating across her face.

"I'm sorry."

"Well, are you?" Jody asked.

"You haven't got any makeup on!" I whispered.

"Well, hello," said Jody, hugging her legs.

"Are you sick?" I asked.

"No!" She sniffed. "Haven't you heard anything I said? I got into the elite swim squad!"

"Because of Craigie?" I said.

Jody stopped peeling her orange. She stared at me, her eyes reproachful, juice running down her fingers.

"What?" I said.

"I just told you. Craig's going out with Lauren."

"Oh!" I said. "Blimey. I'm sorry."

"What's wrong with you, Gemma?"

For a second I felt tempted to tell her about everything that had happened at Raven's house. I knew she would be sympathetic. But I also knew there was something yucky about it. Something disloyal. Like the purpose of telling the whole story would be the side-effect of making us feel better about ourselves.

"Nothing's wrong."

"Well, I've discovered I *like* swimming," said Jody. "And Mrs. Porter told me that I have *talent*. She thinks I could go a *long way* if I'm willing to train."

"Great." I wrapped up my half-eaten ham sandwich.

"I'm giving it a go," said Jody. "I'm sick of thinking about guys, especially when they're not thinking about me."

"Long-term swimming is hard on the hair," I said.

"I don't care," said Jody. "Beauty is ephemeral. I don't want to enslave myself to it because one day I'll wake up and it'll be gone."

"I'm happy for you. Congratulations."

Jody broke her orange into segments. "You know, Lauren's been the most beautiful girl in her class since kindy and she's never been anything else and that's okay for a little while, but not for your whole life."

I gazed around the playground, my eyes flicking from group to group. "Have you seen Raven?"

"He was in English this morning," said Jody. "He read a sonnet. Drama must be doing him some good because his voice made a whole heap of girls swoon."

"Swoon?"

"Yeah. But I'm beginning to think you're right," said Jody, flicking back her fringe with her arm. "It's just a shame he's a De Head."

"I never said that!" I said. "Take that back!"

"Don't snap my head off," said Jody. "Gees, for a second you looked like a piranha!"

twenty-nine

Raven showed up for the first rehearsal of *The Tempest*. He snuck into the hall so quietly that at first no one noticed and when we finally did we were so shocked we stopped talking. His shirt pocket was hanging by a thread.

"Hi," he said.

"Hello, Raven," said Mrs. Langton, shooting a warning glance at Ms. Highgate. "I'm glad you came."

"I was . . ." Raven dug his hands deep into his pockets. "I was thinking . . ." His whole face was twisted with effort. "That I . . ."

Everyone sat waiting. He took a breath and stared up at the ceiling. He ran his hand through his hair. "I want to . . ."

"Why don't you sit down," said Mrs. Langton. "We're just about to start."

Raven wiped his hands on his shirt. "Good," he said, with relief. "Well, thanks." And he sat down on the other side of the circle without even glancing my way.

I felt a pain so sharp in my chest it winded me. I was proud of him for coming, but ashamed for him too. There was something humiliating about Mrs. Langton letting him get away without an apology. It was as though she knew how little he had to be proud of and this somehow excused his terrible behavior.

But if that pain felt bad, it was nothing compared to the pain I felt when Nick read through Prospero's speech to Caliban in Act One, Scene Two.

"Louder," said Ms. Highgate. "Voice up, please."

"Abhorred slave," cried Nick. *"Which any print of goodness*
    wilt not take,
Being capable of all ill! I pitied thee,
Took pains to make thee speak, taught thee each hour
One thing or other; when thou didst not, savage,
Know thine own meaning, but wouldst gabble like
A thing most brutish, I endowed they purposes
With words that made them known. But thy vile race,
Though thou didst learn, had that in't which good natures
Could not abide to be with; therefore wast thou
Deservedly confined into this rock,
Who hadst deserved more than a prison."

Raven's face was impassive, one hand following the text as Nick spoke, the other flicking at a rubber band wrapped around his finger.

I sat with my head bowed, wishing that Nick would swallow his words, wishing that he would gulp them back. They were poisonous words. What Caliban did was inexcusable. I couldn't deny it. He had broken trust with Prospero. He had tried to rape Miranda. He was full of plots and plans for murder. But was his nature worse than the others? Could some people be more naturally wicked?

I hated Nick's lines. He was so convincing as Prospero. I felt stupid ever thinking he could have played Ferdinand. He had the arm gestures right, even sitting down. The careless flick of his hand, his fingers full of dismissal and contempt. His big caramel voice booming through the hall, filling the corners, declaring Raven:

> *"A devil, a born devil, on whose nature*
> *Nurture can never stick; on whom my pains,*
> *Humanely taken—all, all lost, quite lost;*
> *And as with age his body uglier grows,*
> *So his mind cankers . . ."*

At the end of our rehearsal, Mrs. Langton asked Nick, Raven and me to stay back.

"Nick, I want you to go through your 'Abhorred slave' speech to Caliban again," she said. "At the moment, Prospero is coming across too much like the villain."

"Really," said Nick.

"It's a difficult speech," said Mrs. Langton. "Some versions of *The Tempest*—and some directors—assign it to Miranda. But to me, the sentiment and the rhythm of the language clearly makes it Prospero's speech. And how you deliver those lines is going to profoundly affect how we feel about your character."

"Right," said Nick.

"Caliban betrayed your trust. He tried to hurt your daughter. That's the wound you have to speak out of to make us truly believe you are speaking from his heart."

"Okay," said Nick, leaping up. "I'll give it a go."

Nick stalked around the stage, trying to feel his way into the emotion of the speech. I stood in the middle, facing Raven. Raven was silent, waiting, watching dust motes.

Nick stopped walking. He ran his fingers through his hair. He turned slowly and glared at Raven. When he spoke his voice struck fiercely, like a metal pick on ice, sharp, stinging, splintering.

"Savage"—"brutish"—"vile race"—"which any print of goodness will not take, being capable of all ill."

It wouldn't matter who said them. They were ugly and harsh. They were destroying words.

I hated them because even as they came out of Nick's mouth, I couldn't help wondering if they were true— the savagery, brutishness and vileness of that night at Raven's house; the tornado of violence, spinning in the air between us.

thirty

Debbie's female friends and family were sitting around the coffee table, which was heaped with "kitchen tea" presents. The Three Rs rushed about like traffic wardens, pouring cool drinks and reorganizing the seating arrangements just as everyone got comfy. Mrs. Webster and Jackie were huddled in the corner, looking on, as if they were visitors at a zoo, observing a cage of dangerous animals.

Renee clapped her hands together sharply and shushed us. When everyone was sufficiently silent, she ushered Rochelle forward.

"Okay," said Rochelle. A bracelet of perspiration had formed on her top lip. "The next game we're going to play is 'Name that Cake.' "

"Oh," said Aunty Beryl. "I really like this one."

"You were good at 'Pin the Tail on the Man,' " said Mum.

"It's the dart practice," said Aunty Beryl. "And he did have a gorgeous tail."

Mum was busy cross-stitching cluster after cluster of golden grapes, silver strawberries and bronze bananas.

"This is fun," she cried. "We never played games like this when I had my kitchen tea. Mine was a lot more serious. Everyone wanted to speak to me about my wifely duties."

"Now the person with the most correct answers to the questions wins this wooden-spoon bride with the chocolate heart earrings," interrupted Renee, waving the spoon around like a fairy wand, so that the earrings dangled frantically.

"Ooh," said Aunty Beryl. "Isn't it a darling? It would look lovely in my bridal doll cabinet."

"Here's another sherry for you, Beryl," said Dad, zigzagging his way over to her chair. He dashed out quickly, his hands over his bottom, as if he was scared of getting a pin in his tail.

"Okay," said Rachael, fanning herself with a piece of paper. "Ready. Set. Go!"

"What cake is an annual event?" asked Rochelle.

"Birthday," snapped Aunty Beryl.

"What cakes do monkeys like?" asked Renee.

"Banana," cried Aunty Beryl.

"What cake is the biggest flop?" asked Rochelle.

"Upside-down cake," screeched Aunty Beryl.

"What cake goes well in a saucer?" asked Rachael.

"Cupcake!" shrieked Aunty Beryl.

Renee glanced at Debbie and rolled her eyes.

"Aunty Beryl," whispered Debbie. "Let some other people have a chance."

Renee turned back to the group, took a deep breath and smiled sweetly. "What cake can be found on the ocean floor?"

Everyone stared blankly at her. Aunty Beryl jerked around on the couch as if she was undergoing a severe epileptic fit.

"Anyone?" asked Renee.

"Please!" begged Aunty Beryl. "Please!"

"Anyone else?" asked Renee, chewing on her glossy pink lip.

"Sponge!" burst Aunty Beryl. "Sponge cake."

"Aunty Beryl!" hissed Debbie.

"Good answer," said Mum.

"What cakes do mice like best?" Rachael asked.

"Cheese cake," squealed Aunty Beryl.

"I don't think that anyone will get this one," said Rochelle. "Which cake weights the most?"

"Pound cake!" bubbled Aunty Beryl. "Pound cake! Get it?" She gazed at us, her face gleaming. Her eyes had the hot, competitive glaze of an expert. "What cake feeds a rabbit?" she babbled. She jumped up and down on her seat. "Carrot!" She waved her hands around with sheer excitement. "What cake is a heavenly body?" She stood up. "Angel food cake," she gibbered. "Isn't that clever?" She stared at us, her eyes bulging. "What cake can be found at a seafood restaurant?" The bun on her head jiggled. "Crab cake! What—"

"Here," said Renee, handing over the doll. "You win."

"I won! I won!" Aunty Beryl rejoiced, tapping Mum on the head with the wooden-spoon doll.

"Again!" said Mum. "You're a true professional."

"Let's play another game," said Renee through clenched teeth.

"This one is just for the bride," said Rochelle, pointedly.

Renee whipped out a blindfold and placed it over Debbie's eyes. She led her to the leather pouf and sat her down. "Okay," she said. "We're ready."

Dad, the Lieutenant Colonel, Brian and Uncle Bert tiptoed into the room. Rochelle shepherded them over to the gas fireplace and made them stand in a line. The men pulled their trouser legs up over their right knees.

"Now," said Rachael. "We've provided a lovely selection of men here today. Your job is to feel their legs and guess which one is Brian's."

Debbie opened her mouth and screeched. She dragged her hands down her cheeks. "Oh my gosh!"

Renee helped her off the pouf and led her over to the first victim—Dad. Debbie felt his leg and knee for ages.

"I don't think this is him," she said, tugging at his skin. "This knee feels scabby and old, even withered."

"Uh-huh," said Rochelle. "Try the next one."

Rachael brought Uncle Bert forward. "I like this leg," said Debbie, rubbing her hands up and down Uncle Bert's calf muscle. Uncle Bert was staring up at the light, his arms crossed like he was undergoing cross-examination and wasn't going to crack. "The ankle feels right," she said. "But the knee is swollen and soft like an off honeydew melon. And the smell's not right either. No! This is not Brian."

Renee dragged Brian forward. She forced him to hoick his pants up higher. Debbie knelt down and touched his leg.

"This is not a leg," said Debbie, laughing. "It's a sapling. And far too prickly. It gives me the heebie-jeebies." She shuddered.

Brian stepped backwards and ran his hand up and down his leg surreptitiously.

"You're running out of people," said Aunty Beryl.

"I'm sure they're saving the best for last," said Debbie.

"Too true," said Rochelle, prodding the Lieutenant Colonel forward.

Debbie grabbed his leg. "Ooh yes," she said. "This is Brian. The leg is smooth and young. No yucky, prickly bits. No throbby, sticking out old veins. This is a strong, strong leg."

She ripped off her blindfold and stared up at the Lieutenant Colonel. She snatched her hand off his leg. "Oh," she said. "I'm sorry . . . I didn't realize . . . and it's your artificial leg too . . ."

"But it's a very good, young artificial leg!" said Mrs. Webster soothingly.

"But it was warm," said Debbie.

"I've been sitting out in the backyard with your Dad," said the Lieutenant Colonel.

"Giving it a tan," said Dad.

"This leg doesn't tan," said the Lieutenant Colonel, swiveling around to give Dad his most imperial stare. "Are you a bloody idiot?"

"It . . . it was a joke," stuttered Dad.

"Barry!" said Mum warningly.

"He's always been the type to make a joke about those less fortunate than himself," confided Aunty Beryl.

"Which leg was Brian's?" asked Debbie.

"The one that gave you the heebie-jeebies!" said Aunty Beryl.

"Let's have a break from the games," said Rochelle quickly. "Let's have lunch."

• • •

Throughout lunch, everyone talked about cutlery and glassware. Aunty Beryl spoke ad nauseam about the importance of getting a patterned forty-piece dinner set with a matching paper-towel holder.

Jackie and I ate our lunch in the sunroom, under the fruit cross-stitches.

"When I get married," said Jackie, "I'm going to have a weapons party."

"At least you're thinking about marriage," I said, taking a bite of my chicken drumstick. "That's a good sign."

"Getting married is one outrageous present-fest," said Jackie. "The engagement. The kitchen tea. The wedding. Then if you combine that with a number of marriages, you could be set for life." She sucked the gristle, her teeth chomping fiercely.

"How did your Dad lose his leg?" I asked. "Was it the war?"

"No," said Jackie. She wiped chicken grease off her chin. "He chopped it off himself. The electric chainsaw slipped when he was cutting down the trees in the front yard to make way for the flagpole."

"Oh, blimey! That's gross."

"It was pretty messy. Leg everywhere."

I dropped my drumstick onto my plate and held my stomach. "I assumed it was a war wound!"

"Most people do," said Jackie. "The worst part was he not only lost a leg, but he also copped a fine for cutting down native trees without permission."

"Jeez."

Jackie pointed at my chicken leg. "Are you going to finish that?"

"I don't think I can." I breathed out slowly.

"Can I have it?" asked Jackie. "My protein quota is low today."

"Help yourself," I said.

• • •

After lunch, everyone crammed back into the lounge room for more games. Aunty Beryl was unnaturally quiet because Debbie had told Mum to tell her to stop talking. She sat in Dad's recliner, a patient, martyred look on her face.

"Now," said Renee. "We're going to share the story of our first kiss."

"Debbie can go first," said Rochelle.

"I was in first class—"

"Not your first kiss ever," said Rachael. "You're first kiss with Brian."

"Oh yeah, of course," blushed Debbie. "It was at the

RSL on our first date. Brian was playing the five-cent pokies and he won ten dollars. He was so stoked, he turned to me and pashed me and my eyes whirred around like the lights in the poker machine."

"That's it?" I asked.

"What's wrong with that?" asked Debbie.

"That's beautiful," said Mum.

"Your turn, Mrs. Stone," said Renee, her hair fizzing about her head.

"Well," said Mum. "Barry was keen to inspect a turf farm, halfway across the countryside, but by the time we got there it was dark. So we climbed the fence and wandered about. After he had patted the lawns, we lay down on the Soft Leaf Buffalo grass and watched the stars shoot across the sky. And just when I thought I was going to go mad with itchiness, Barry leant over and gave me a kiss that was as light as the froth on a cappuccino."

"My first kiss was at a train station," interrupted Mrs. Webster. "When the Lieutenant Colonel was going into the army. He had two legs then, so he was fast. The train was about to leave, but he hopped off, ran over and gave me such a smacker. Then he had to bolt back along the platform because the train was leaving and his kit was on board."

"How romantic!" said Debbie, with a sigh.

"It wasn't a lingering kiss," said Mrs. Webster. "But then the Lieutenant Colonel has never been a man to linger."

"My first kiss was at my first Year Seven dance," said Rachael, her braces glinting brightly.

"So was mine," said Renee.

"Me too," said Rochelle.

"Eugene Walton," said Rachael. "Behind the hall."

"But that's who kissed me!" said Renee.

"You're kidding!" gasped Rachael.

"And me," said Rochelle.

"No way!" said Renee.

"His tongue made so much noise," said Rachael.

"He was like an octopus," said Rochelle. "I could hardly concentrate."

"And didn't he pong?" said Rachael. "Like he had taken a bath in Brut 33."

"I know!" said Renee. "But what a great kisser!"

"Mmmmm!" they all sighed.

"I've always found that postmen are good kissers," said Aunty Beryl confidently, her eyes swimming like two large blue tropical fish behind her glasses.

"How many have you kissed?" I asked, appalled.

"There was Ernie, he was my first. Then Stan. But he got the sack—too slow with his deliveries. Then there was Richie . . . well, I couldn't count them all. I've seen a lot of postmen come and go. But I'll say one thing for them, they always taste of sun and salt."

I couldn't believe it. Even Aunty Beryl had been kissed. Many times. And she was not the most attractive woman in the world. And yet, she had been kissed. And not just once.

Her story unleashed more kissing stories. Everyone talked at the same time. The stories went on and on. It was obvious that everyone in the universe had been kissed except for Jackie and me. I smiled at Jackie sympathetically.

"If you haven't been kissed before, you could always

tell a story of how you imagine your first kiss might be," I whispered.

"I've been kissed, you great goober!" said Jackie.

"You have?"

"Fred from the Barmy Army. We were having a skirmish day. I killed him fair and square and then somehow he entangled his lips with mine. He called it his Tour of Duty."

"You go, girl!" said Rachael.

I was the only one who had never been kissed. Me. The only one.

"What about Gemma?" said Renee with a smirk.

"Kissing pin-up posters and the mirror doesn't count," said Debbie.

I wanted to dig a hole and die.

Fortunately, Rochelle saved me. "Okay, everyone, let's move on to our last game," she said. "We've divided you into small groups and we're going to give you six rolls of toilet paper and you've got twenty minutes to make a wedding gown for the smallest person in your group."

"There will be a special gift for the most creative," said Rachael.

Rochelle ticked off our names and called out the groups. Mum, Jackie and I were together.

Mum picked up the rolls of toilet paper and we followed her into the dining room. "We don't have much time," she said.

"I'm not wearing a dress," said Jackie.

"It's a toilet-paper dress," I said. "For goodness sake."

"It's still a dress," grunted Jackie.

"You're the smallest person in our group," I said. "And Mum's the only one who can sew."

"I don't do dresses," said Jackie, stubbornly.

"Everybody knows a good soldier is flexible enough to go undercover," said Mum.

"That's true," I said.

"What would happen if your commanding officer wanted to send you into a country to do some covert work and she wanted you to wear a dress because it was the cultural expectation?" said Mum, looking over her glasses.

"A plum and exciting job would go to someone more willing to be flexible, but who might not have your skill or determination!" I added.

"What about my dad?" asked Jackie. "He'll think I've gone soft."

"He's gone," said Mum. "Barry's taken the blokes to the pub."

"Okay," said Jackie. "I'll give it a go. But only this once."

"Good! Let's get cracking," said Mum. "Gemma, you start on the rosettes."

Mum worked like a whirlwind, shouting out directions. She tacked together a skirt with a bustle and a perky, dainty bow, and a sweetheart bodice with rosettes along the neckline and a train. I made a tiara, a bouquet, a horseshoe and a pair of toilet-paper slippers.

When Mum had finished the dress, she undid Jackie's plaits and brushed out her hair. She raced outside and cut three of Dad's iceberg roses and pinned them to the top of the short veil, in front of the tiara. She ruffled in Debbie's makeup bag and pulled out a blush compact and brushed

Jackie's cheeks with pearl pink. She dabbed Jackie's lips with Debbie's favorite geranium-red lipstick.

"Oh, you look beautiful," said Mum. "But you need one more thing."

She pulled out a sturdy piece of thread from her sewing basket, scrunched up the last remaining scraps of toilet paper and made Jackie a pearl necklace.

"What a shame I don't have any more toilet paper," said Mum. "Gloves would have been the finishing touch."

Jackie was completely different. I'd never seen her, aside from her school uniform, in any color other than khaki. White suited her. Her skin had lost its yellow, pinched look and her hair rippled down her shoulders like Dad's port wine.

"Come and have a look at yourself," said Mum.

Jackie shuffled behind her and I held up her train.

Mum took Jackie by the hand and led her into her bedroom, over to the full-length mirror. "Voila!" she said, moving out of the way.

Jackie stared silently, turning left and right. She touched the rosettes and the toilet-paper pearl necklace. She turned side-on and stretched her neck, so she was queenly and dignified. She curtsied and then giggled. It was a lovely sound, like hearing a baby laugh.

"This is so weird," she said.

"You're gorgeous," said Mum. "And you've got a slender neck like Audrey Hepburn."

"Time's up!" shouted Renee.

When we walked into the lounge room, everyone stopped talking and stared at Jackie. All of the other brides in their toilet-paper gowns resembled embalmed mummies. Jackie, in comparison, was ready to model for *Mode Brides*. Her dress was a quirky work of art.

"Wow," said Renee. "You look beautiful."

"My baby," said Mrs. Webster, tears rushing into her eyes. She tore a piece of toilet paper from Debbie's dress and wiped her nose.

"You are our winners, hands down," said Rochelle, handing us each a ten-dollar gift voucher for Tupperware.

The girls buzzed around Jackie, touching the dress and admiring Mum's handiwork. And although Jackie couldn't get the dress off quickly enough, she let her hair stay loose for the rest of the day.

thirty-one

In my family, if you're upset with someone, you blurt it out, usually at an inopportune moment, such as when they're on the toilet. But with Raven, it was as if there were no moments. It was as though if I spoke to him, everything would fall apart.

One evening, after rehearsal, I trapped him at the school gate, as he waited for his brother.

The air was cold, the trees stripped and the sky a long way away. The stars were tiny and icy and there wasn't a moon, not even a crescent.

Raven stood pretending to read his script under the streetlight.

"Hey," I said.

He glanced up, then back down. "Hey," he grunted.

"How are you?"

"Fine."

"How's your mum?"

"She's fine."

"And the boys?"

"They're fine, too."

"So everything's fine?"

He flicked a page. "I guess so."

I gazed at the tree roots snaking up through the cement. I kicked a ribbon of silver foil glinting in a crack at my feet.

"Why aren't you talking to me?"

Raven lifted his shoulders. "Who said I wasn't?"

"Well, you're not."

"We both got into the play." Raven shrugged. "That's what our talking was always about."

My school bag slid down my arm. "It's because of that night," I said. "At your house. Isn't it?"

"I don't know what you're talking about." A hunted expression flashed across his face and he clutched his script and stared at me, daring me to say something more.

"You haven't talked to me since then."

"Don't be stupid," he said.

As I stared back, I realized that sometimes people who have the least to be proud about are the proudest people of all.

"I'm into method-acting." He turned over a page.

"You know, I've got to be Caliban, even when I'm not onstage. . . ."

I bit my fingernail.

He turned another page. "Given that our characters hate each other, I don't think we should hang out."

"You're a liar."

"I'm not." Raven closed his script and kicked an old cigarette packet into the gutter. "That's how I want to do the part."

At that moment, his mum's car screamed down the street and did a one-eighty, the tires screeching, before skidding to a stop.

"Hiya, Gem!" called Maggie, peering out through the open window.

Raven opened the car door and climbed in. He reached for his seatbelt and spent a long time clicking it in. Maggie shoved Raven's head. Even though it was freezing cold, Maggie only had a singlet on. He grinned. "How's it going? Haven't seen you for a while? Have you two had a lover's tiff?"

"Can we go?" said Raven.

"Everything cool?" Maggie asked, winking.

I sighed. "Yeah. I guess so."

My dad was driving slowly down the street as though he'd just finished playing Sunday bowls.

"How's the acting going? Raven says you're good."

"Okay, I guess."

"Do you need a lift?"

"No," interrupted Raven. "Here comes her dad now."

"Righteo then," said Maggie. "See ya round like a rissole."

"See you," said Raven.

Maggie revved the car and tore up the street, the tires smoking. He swerved out in a great arc, forcing Dad to veer left suddenly and run up the gutter, just missing a rubbish bin.

When I opened the car door, Dad was shaking. "Who was that dingbat? I've got a bloody mind to report him to the police? Did you catch his number plate?"

I hopped in the car and placed my hands over the heater. Dad kept raving.

"Can we go home?" I said. "I'm cold."

thirty-two

On the day the new fountain was dedicated, the main street was closed and crammed with stalls. At the top of the street were trestle tables devoted to toilet roll holders and second-hand books. In the middle were the white elephant stalls full of chunky enameled gold earrings and green glass ashtrays. The side street across from the Buranderry Memorial Park was crammed with Mrs. Wilton's craft stall, a corn-on-the-cob caravan, an oyster stall, a Lions barbecue sponsored by Tuffy's meats, a chocolate wheel, a fire-engine and an old clown sitting on the gutter, his face paint peeling, prinking balloons into swords.

At the top of the park, across the road, on the other

side of the war memorial, kids were leaping on a gigantic jumping castle, eating toffees and fairy floss and patting baby animals.

People were gathering in the main park, sitting in white plastic chairs around the new fountain.

Nick was onstage with men in suits whose sense of importance was as strong as perfume. Against his olive skin, Nick's crisp white shirt made him appear suave and more alive than anyone else on the stage. Mayor Glassoni was whispering in his ear, not pausing to even take a breath. Nick nodded, laughing at what the Mayor was saying.

Mrs. Lloyd sat on one side of the stage in the front row, staring at Nick, her face rapt. Mr. Lloyd was winking at a woman behind him who had her blond hair stacked up like a sandcastle.

Sadly, the fountain was hideous. There was nothing cute or quaint about it.

For some reason, Old Hairy in his fake soldier's uniform was sitting astride a horse rising up from the middle of the fountain. He was holding a rifle and aiming it at goodness knows what. But the expression on Old Hairy's face was that of a person trying to take a potshot at a duck in a sideshow alley. Half-brave, but mostly disheartened because they know the game is rigged.

Mum, Dad and I stood at the back of the crowd, under the shade of a gum tree.

Mum was eating a waffle swamped with maple syrup. "I heard the water is going to gush out of his rifle," she said. "But I still don't understand why that is."

"Better than his penis," said Dad, looking up from his paper. "That's all I can say."

"Out of the horse would have been more dignified," said Mum, squinting.

"Out of the horse's penis?" asked Dad.

"Oh for goodness sake, Barry!" said Mum.

"It says in the paper Old Hairy's eyes will light up at night," chortled Dad. "And turn the water a luminous lime green."

"You're not serious?" said Mum.

"That's what it says in the paper," said Dad.

The President of the Buranderry Village Progress Association was beside the fountain, being interviewed by a journalist, his wrists flicking out commas and dashes.

"I guess it's not so bad Old Hairy's aiming his gun," said Dad. "Apparently he shot anything that moved. They think that's how his oldest son died. Old Hairy mistook him for a roo."

After the mikes had been tested six times each, the proceedings got under way. Every significant figure in the local community was given a chance to speak: Mayor Glassoni, the deputy Mayor, the state member, the state opposition member, the federal member, the federal opposition member, the president of the Buranderry Progress Association, the librarian, the local priest, the sculptor and, finally, Nick.

"On behalf of the young people of Buranderry High who helped raise a significant sum of money for this project, thank you for coming today," said Nick, glancing at a palm card. "It's a great privilege to be involved in the re-building of this fountain. Hairy Buranderry was an enter-prising, daring and courageous man. And it's those qualities we're seeking to honor today. So without further ado, I . . . declare . . . this fountain . . . open." And with a big pair of gold scissors flashing in his hands, he cut the red ribbon with a dramatic flourish.

Water burst out from the gun, splashing people in the first row. Old Hairy's eyes flashed on and off like a broken-down traffic light. People everywhere gasped and took photos. Kids rushed forward, sat on the edge and paddled their feet. Some older people tossed in coins and made a wish. Everywhere people were hugging and kissing, as if they had found the missing link to bring the whole town together.

"I might go and look at those toilet roll holders," said Mum. She scrunched up her waffle plate and brushed some bark off the back of her dress.

"I'm going to get a sausage sanger," said Dad. "Do you want one, Gemma?"

"No thanks," I said.

I leant against the tree, soaking up the winter sun and the sounds of magpies warbling, trying to build a levee against a trickle of quiet sadness—maybe there was always going to be a disappointing gap between what we hope for and what we achieve.

"Hey. I didn't expect to see you here." Nick poked his head around my tree.

"Oh. Really?"

A cute dab of toothpaste laced the corner of his mouth. "I thought you might boycott the opening," he said.

"Why?"

"You know, Old Hairy Buranderry not being your favorite person."

"Oh yeah. Well, I'm a sucker for farm animals."

He glanced at the crowd pressing around the fountain. "Where are they?"

"Just past the war memorial," I said.

He touched my arm. "Let's go see," he said.

We wove our way through the crowd, past soaking kids with their scolding parents, around the rose beds, across the road and past the war memorial, down to the temporary farm which had been set up near the play equipment.

We watched lambs and piglets scamper around the pen, away from the snatching fingers of toddlers.

"What do you think of the fountain?" he asked.

"Ugly! Dismal. Horrid," I said. "Sorry."

"Yeah, you're right," he said. "It's unfortunate, but it's because everybody had to put in their two cents. That's local politics for you."

I bent down and stuck my finger through the fence. A baby goat ambled over and licked my finger. Nick bent down next to me, so our legs touched.

"So, has it turned you off? Does it make you want to give up?" I asked.

"No. Local politics is good training," he said. "For bigger stuff."

A lamb trotted up to the fence and baaed in our faces.

A hen strutted across the grass, chaff flying out behind her. A little boy in red overalls raced over to pick her up. She turned and pecked him on the big toe. The little boy burst into tears and ran to his mum.

"She thought your toe was a worm," called the farmer cheerfully.

"Speaking of bigger things, the protest letter you wrote to the Rosefields CEO was great," said Nick.

I stared at him closely. I thought perhaps he was having me on. He plucked a blade of grass and poked it through the fence. His fingers were long and splayed. One of the piglets stopped circling and came over to sniff at the grass. It snorted and moved on.

"Especially the story about your sister and her fiancé's proposal at O'Riley's," he said. "That was an excellent personal touch." A baby goat stood up and tottered over on wobbly legs. It nibbled on the grass before sliding down. "Did it really happen?" he asked. "Did he really propose to your sister by the spice rack?"

I wriggled a finger through the fence and patted the kid. "Yeah."

Nick reached out and flicked some chaff off my nose. "That was perfect. I couldn't have made it up, even if I wanted to." He ran his hand along my cheek and down my neck.

I was so taken aback, I didn't know what to say or do.

"What I like about you, Gemma, is you're unpredictable." His hand was warm against my shoulder. "Just when I think I've got you pinned down, you do something kooky." He leant over, his face beautifully carved and sun-lit like a marble angel. I closed my eyes. My tongue dried up and I felt shaky. Every nerve was singing. And just as I felt his breath on my lips, I heard the sound of a waterfall.

"Get out of the way," shouted the farmer. "Quuu-uuuicck!"

I tumbled back and scrabbled like a crab.

A black and white calf had her bum aimed in our direction and was sending out a super jet over the fence.

It squirted all over Nick. He jumped up. Cow poo streamed down his hair and neck, over his suave white shirt and tan pants in slow, steady thin streams.

"Ah! I'm meant to be going to a civic luncheon," he gasped. He had the dazed look of someone who had been in a serious car accident. I burst out laughing. I couldn't help it.

"Shit, Gemma! This isn't funny!"

I bit the palm of my hand.

He walked gingerly. "It's soaking in." He was holding his pants out at the side like a little ballerina. "These pants are ruined!" He was gazing at me, as if he expected me to do something about it.

"Crap!" called the farmer, before collapsing on a hay bale, crippled with laughter.

"Just go home and get changed," I said.

Nick reached tentatively into his pocket with his finger and thumb and pulled out a tissue. The woman whose little boy had been pecked handed him some wipes before she burst out laughing, too.

"Sorry," she said, and laughed again.

Nick grunted and started wiping off the clumps from his head. "I don't have time to go home."

"Maybe you could wash in the fountain?" For a second, I imagined him splashing around nude. I giggled.

"What are you laughing at now?" Nick asked, his marble face screwing up. "I'm meant to be receiving a certificate of commendation in twenty minutes. And now I stink like a fat cow pat."

"You don't see anything funny about that?"

"No, I don't," said Nick. "And I don't see why you do."

He chucked the wipe on the ground and started again on the other side of his face. "This shirt cost a fortune and now it needs to be dry-cleaned. I don't see why I should have to pay because that dill can't control his cow's arse!" And he huffed over to the farmer and abused him loudly, before tiptoeing squeamishly through the park.

thirty-three

The deeper we got into rehearsals, the more exasperated Mrs. Langton became. She had this quiet way of sucking in her breath whenever I was onstage. I tried to do what she asked, but I couldn't perform the way she wanted me to and I didn't know how to make it better.

I wasn't the only one who exasperated her, though.

Mrs. Langton gave Jago a lot of direction too. Every time she stopped him, Jago nodded his head eagerly and said, "Oh right. Yeah. Good, Miss. Got it." And every time, he'd go and do Ferdinand's scene exactly the same way as he did before, only louder. I could predict the exact pattern of his lines, where his voice would rise and fall and which words he would emphasize because they were the same each week. Sometimes I found myself completely distracted by this, even when he was declaring his love for me. But when I didn't react properly, I was the one who got into trouble.

Nick was smooth and professional, but I got the feeling he exasperated Mrs. Langton too. Sometimes he didn't listen properly. He'd cut me off before I'd finished speaking. Other times, when I was saying my lines, he went blank, like a switched-off robot, and he didn't come alive again until he heard his cue.

One afternoon, when we had finished rehearsing, Mrs. Langton asked me to stay behind. The chairs were packed in small, brown columns and the hall was empty and cold.

"How are you going, Gemma?" she asked.

"Okay."

She patted the stage. "Are you enjoying the play?"

I sat down next to her and nodded.

"I only ask because there's a lightness missing from your performance."

I could feel a golf ball rise up in my throat.

"Is there anything you can think of that's affecting it? Are you under some stress? I want to help you give your best performance."

She was so kind, her voice so considerate that everything exploded out of me like a cork from a champagne bottle. How I despised Miranda and hated Prospero and how I pitied Caliban when I should have been full of scorn.

When I finished my rant, Mrs. Langton simply nodded. "That would make it difficult," she said softly. She folded her hands over her knees and stared into the distance, taking a minute to think. She tucked her skirt around her legs. "It's a struggle to create a convincing character when you're sitting in judgment of them," she said.

"But it's so hard not to judge her!" I said. "Miranda and Prospero are so confident of their own goodness. So convinced they're different from Caliban. So sure his evil is race-related. And yet there they are hungering for Caliban's punishment to be more terrible than prison."

"What makes you think forgiveness is easy?" said Mrs. Langton.

"How can I play her when I hate her?" I interrupted.

"Mmmm." She tucked some stray wisps of hair behind her ears. "I think you're seeing Miranda through the eyes of the characters around her, which is not the same as seeing Miranda through her own eyes."

"How can I fix that?"

"You could try writing a journal," Mrs. Langton said. "Write about Miranda's life from her perspective, in detail. Include scenes that don't take place in the play. They're the scenes that shape Miranda and make her who she is. What was it like for Miranda to grow up with Caliban? Explore her hope of finding in him a true friend? Write everything you can about her, her daily routines and her dreams for the future."

"Okay," I said. "And then what?"

She shrugged. "And then we'll see."

We stared at the clock ticking on the back wall. In the distance, I could hear the cleaner whistling as he swept the paths outside the hall.

"Is there anything else?" she asked.

And suddenly I found myself telling her the whole horrible story of the night I had dinner at Raven's place. And how I hated hearing Nick speak Prospero's lines to Raven, in case Raven believed they were true; how I hated hearing those lines in case I found myself believing them too.

It was like a fresh wound tearing open. Snot, tears, words and sobs gushed out. Mrs. Langton put her arms around me and held me tight as I wept again for all the things that were lost that night.

thirty-four

After my talk with Mrs. Langton, I went home and wrote. I crammed a whole notebook with Miranda's thoughts:

I sit beside my father. I listen to his stories, the murmur of his magic. An owl hoots. The wind is soft against my skin. The fire crackles. The moon is close to sinking. And yet . . . and yet . . . I am filled with longing. Waiting for something I do not know. It blurs the edges of all I do.

I want to skip and flit, and skim and soar. But each day curls and falls like the one before, like waves eating away the sand.

He is there, Caliban, watching from his lair. He, who slept by my side! He, who shared my plate! We, who dug for

worms together; we, who watched the opal flowers burst
when the tide was full. We, who danced in fir groves. We,
who numbered stars and watched the moon wax and wane,
and the sun set and rise. My playmate. My childhood friend.
He, who I taught to sing and count.
He watches from his lair, waiting too.
It is hot. I collect pipis. I take a bucket. I walk along
the lacy edges of the sand, my feet sinking. He is behind
me, his feet in my footsteps. I know what he intends. It is
written on his face. A seagull circles. "Go home," I shout.
But the wind whips away my voice. I walk faster and so
does he. My dress drags in the sand. And then he is there,
his greedy hands pressing me down so hard, tiny shells
splinter against my skin. And I know I am no playmate. I
know I am no childhood friend.

I wrote and wrote and wrote.

Night and day.

All the things that bothered me, pouring out. Miranda's world filling my world so much, I was a citizen of two worlds.

And maybe it helped that winter was ending, the bite gone, the cherry blossom trees beginning to make their grand stand against the frost, the scent of spring as strong as a promise, but, amazingly, the writing began to thaw my hardness. I began to understand how Miranda felt about Caliban; how his betrayal had curdled her compassion.

I found things about Miranda to admire.

For years I have been filled with a longing I cannot
name. This longing so deep, that by dusk it pains me badly

and I close my eyes and turn my face from the blaze of the sky, my back against the dying sun. Because I have seen many noble wonders. Coral reefs in full bloom. Forests laden with dew. Rainbow-plumed parrots in foliage. Wild unicorns in full flight. Ripe peaches and purple sunsets. But none have checked this longing. Their beauty lasts for a moment, but rips open a chasm of aching.

And yet today, after the tempest, a man came to our shore, a man and not a spirit. He drifted into my path like flotsam from the sea, like the jetsam of a dream. And though his face was marred with grief, I saw that he was real, that he was solid, that he was good and flesh of my flesh. And for the first time this longing that no natural wonder could ever still was quiet. And I wanted to skip and flit and skim and soar like a child who has found a lost treasure.

But this man, this Ferdinand, my beloved, is not the only one on the island. He is one among many—some of whom my father has named as his enemies. My father's enemies. My enemies.

And yet . . . and yet when I see them, when I see so many of them, so much mankind, I can not help but be filled with amazement, with hope and terror, that such people, such glorious beings, can be contained by my same fragile skin and bone.

"O, wonder!
How many goodly creatures are there here!
How beauteous mankind is! O brave new world,
That has such people in it."

The best part was Mrs. Langton was no longer exasperated with what I was doing onstage. She didn't say anything, but I could read it in her eyes and in the half-smile of her lips whenever I performed.

Raven was still distant with me, yet sometimes I'd catch a friendly glimmer, especially on Saturday when we all came to school to build and paint the set. On those afternoons, when Raven and I stood side by side, painting the stage into a paradise, it was almost like the old days.

"You know," he said. "You've improved. Maybe the most of anyone."

"Really?" I was happy to hear him talk.

"I didn't believe you before," he said. "But now, when I'm onstage, I think of you as Miranda."

"Thanks."

"It's my pleasure. You're good."

I listened to the regular and comforting sound of the paint swishing onto the backdrop.

"How good?" I asked.

He stopped painting. He had a stripe of blue on his nose. "I don't want to say in case it goes to your head," he said.

"Good enough to buy me a milk shake?" I asked.

"You're far too good for that."

"How about four potato scallops and a serve of hot chips!"

"Maybe." He paused. He dipped his brush in the paint. "You're so good you should be made Dame Commander in the Most Excellent Order of the British Empire," he said. Then he splodged his brush on my shoulders and my head. "Arise Dame Gemma Stone."

thirty-five

And then it was opening night.

The audience was buzzing with laughter and conversation and the flapping of theater programs.

I stood in the wings, behind the red velvet curtain, waiting for my cue, soaking up the atmosphere, wondering if this is what it would be like to be a baby in a womb: to hear the world outside and to even feel it, but not be able to see it. I certainly felt like a baby jammed up and ready to go—but scared too—terrified to leave my warm, safe dark place, to go out into that harsh world of light and be exposed and maybe rejected.

Nerves spingle-spangled up from my stomach into my

throat. I felt sure I was going to vomit. The set sparkled, even under the dim lighting. I closed my eyes and breathed deeply, trying to ground myself as Miranda on the island. I tried to see wild unicorns rounding a rocky outcrop, their large hooves spraying out sea foam, their horns blinding silver points. I tried to taste the oysters shucked from the rocks and eaten fresh. I inhaled the scent of my bed of pine needles in our den, I heard the wind whistling through the caves, I traced my fingertips along the spines of my father's books on the natural rock shelves, kept safe from water.

My stomach had just settled down, when someone touched me on the elbow. I jumped and whirled around. "You scared the crap out of me!"

"Sorry."

Raven skulked forward and clutched my arm. His costume split his body in two. One half was scaled blue like a fish, his right arm deformed into a fin. The other half was cratered and bleached bony white, skeletal and ghoulish. He was a monster conceived by the moon and a stormy sea.

"I just wanted to say good—"

"Don't say it! It's bad luck."

"Chookers then." His lips were painted black and his teeth were bright yellow.

"Chookers."

His scales glinted in the light. He touched the frayed edge of the curtain. "I want to say sorry, too," he whispered. "For everything."

I didn't know which part of his face to focus on.

"I've been a dickhead," he said.

I felt relieved and proud that he'd been so brave, and so happy that we could be proper friends again, with nothing between us. I reached out and hugged him. He kissed me on top of my head, his fin around my shoulder like a wing.

Then the wind chimes pealed and I hurried to take my place onstage.

And the tempest began. The wind and thunder raging.

At first it was hard not to peek. Out of the corner of my eye, I could see Debbie sulking in her seat and Brian twiddling his thumbs. The Lieutenant Colonel was poring over the program and Mrs. Webster kept popping up and down, ostensibly to get comfortable, but probably so she could check out the people she knew. Mum couldn't take her eyes off me and Dad had the expression on his face he gets whenever Mum switches over to SBS.

Raven's family was flat bang in the middle. Mr. De Head was even wearing a tie. Mrs. De Head kept slapping Sparrow and Robin's feet off the seats in front but whenever Raven appeared onstage, they all sat up like an electric current had run through them.

After a while I got used to the audience and was able to forget them, except when they laughed in the places I thought they would be quiet, and were quiet in the places where I thought they'd roar with laughter.

Amazingly, everyone remembered their cues, their entrances and their lines. There were no moments where I wished a quicksand pit would open up and swallow either me or someone else.

And I learnt something new, which is good according to Mrs. Langton. She says every performance should throw up some new, strange or wonderful insight.

That night as I was listening, I was astonished at how desperately so many of the characters were jockeying for the position of king. Trinculo, Stephano and Caliban. Antonio and Sebastian. All of them plotting bloodshed and mayhem. And I understood for the first time why Prospero tested Ferdinand's love for Miranda by making him lug logs to a woodpile. It suddenly made sense. Because if all you have in your heart is a desire to be king, then you don't have room for love.

Mum was right.

Love is more than a "sit down on your throne while the doves swoon round your head and someone hand-feeds you grapes and chocolates" affair. It's just as much a "get down on your knees and clean dog poo off a shoe" kind of thing.

Prospero had set the cleverest test. Because if Ferdinand had absolutely no interest in doing the menial, grubby work of a servant for Miranda, he certainly wouldn't be able to face up to the bigger, harder things such as patience and forgiveness.

Love is doves *and* dog poo!

As I stood onstage, I felt both frightened and thrilled. Even as Jago's speeches rang out like well-known tunes, I felt I was hovering on the edge of a high cliff above a wild, wild sea.

thirty-six

When we got back to the dressing room after our fourth bow, Ms. Highgate was there with bunches of red roses for all of us. Tears poured down her cheeks. She hugged us so hard her brooch bruised our clavicles.

When she handed Raven his flowers, she held him tight and said, "Oh Raven! You were wonderful. Even at Caliban's most vile moments, sometimes I found myself cheering for him!"

Raven blushed. He was tongue-tied, gazing at me as if he was hoping I could conjure up a hole for him to plunge into.

Mrs. Langton simply beamed at us, unable to say a word.

After we got changed and had removed as much of the makeup as we could, we went back out to the hall and upstairs to the vestibule area.

It was packed.

People were standing in small circles talking loudly. The school's best trio was playing jazz in one corner, on a little stage. A makeshift bar was open and parents and teachers were lined up to buy beer and wine in plastic cups. White plastic plates with water crackers topped with cheese, salami and little green gherkins were being carried around and offered to the opening night crowd by the Year Seven ushers.

Well-wishers flocked from all directions to congratulate us on our performances. But it was mainly Raven they directed their highest praise to.

I spotted his dad, a beer in his hand, talking to a group of admirers. Raven's mum was standing by his side, clutching her brown purse, her face brilliant and alive with pride. Everywhere I went, I heard people whisper, "There's that De Head boy. Wasn't he marvelous?"

I found Mum and Dad standing behind a pot plant.

"Oh, you were very good, love," said Mum. "Mrs. McMahon was here, your Year Seven Home Group Teacher. She couldn't get over you speaking so well onstage. She said she always knew you had dramatic talent."

"She's still talking about the time you vomited on Mr. Daihatsu," said Dad. "She reckons it's her best party story."

"And what about Raven!" said Mum. "Who would have thought he could be so good."

"It was a weird play," said Dad. "Some of that poetry

went straight over my head. But you and Raven, you saved the show."

Jody came rushing up, screeching her head off. She thrust a big bunch of pink carnations and baby's breath into my hands. Then she threw her arms around me and hugged me so hard I almost fell to the ground.

"You were fantastic," she said. "You didn't look nervous at all. You were so good. I was sitting next to Mrs. McMahon and she was crying when you were onstage. Crying! Can you believe that! And what about Raven? Is he hot! Stacks of girls around us were drooling whenever he came onstage. Even though he was damned ugly in that costume."

"What about Nick?" I asked. "Did you think he was good?"

"Which part was he again?" asked Jody.

"Prospero," I said. "You dill!"

"He was a bit bossy," said Jody. She unwrapped a piece of chewing gum and popped it in her mouth.

The Lieutenant Colonel tapped me on the shoulder with his program. "You were excellent, young lady," he said, nodding firmly. "I'm going to have to come to you for advice on my wedding speech."

"You were wonderful," clucked Mrs. Webster, kissing me on the cheek. "We were so proud. We're delighted that Brian is marrying into such a talented family." She squeezed my arm.

"Just hope it rubs off on him," said the Lieutenant Colonel.

Jackie was behind them, holding her backpack like a

baby. She was wearing a skirt! A skirt! It was a khaki skirt, admittedly, and she was wearing it with her army boots, but to see her in a skirt was a miracle.

"Congratulations," she said, leaning forward. "The play was . . . interesting. Better than a bridal fair any day."

"You're wearing a skirt," I gasped.

"It's not a dress!"

"It's halfway there," I said. "In front of your dad?"

"Mum says he has to learn to accept that I'm a girl."

"Maybe we could wear skirts to the wedding?"

"It's too late," said Jackie. "Brian picked up the swans this morning."

Nick swaggered over, munching on a water cracker. He smiled at Jody and Jackie and nodded at Mum and Dad.

"Mrs. Langton said to tell you she'll give us our notes before tomorrow's performance," he said.

"Son," said the Lieutenant Colonel, stabbing Nick in the stomach with his program. "You'd make a great commander. Have you had any experience with cadets?"

"No," said Nick, coughing and holding his stomach. "I haven't."

"Well," said the Lieutenant Colonel. "Tonight you acted like one. Superb piece of work."

"This is the Lieutenant Colonel," I said. "My sister's future father-in-law."

"Great to meet you," said Nick.

The Lieutenant Colonel placed his program on Nick's shoulders and stared at him solemnly. "Have you ever thought about the army, son," he said. "All this poofy acting is all right, but if you want to be a real man, you need to be experienced in the theater of war."

"Ah . . . No, sir, I . . . I haven't," said Nick.

"You should," said the Lieutenant Colonel, smacking him hard on the shoulder. "You have the makings of a good soldier."

"Thanks," said Nick. He tucked in his neck as if he was expecting to be bludgeoned to death. He backed away into the pot plant. Green fronds hung over his shoulders.

Dad bailed him up. "You're the boy with the naked statue on the front lawn."

"We didn't put it there," said Nick, blowing a frond out of his mouth. "The previous owner did. His wife posed for it."

"It's a scandal," said Dad. "Tell your father it spoils your lawn completely. A well-kept lawn should be uncorrupted. No garden gnomes, no birdbaths, no tricky rose features and certainly no naked ladies. Nothing should distract the eye from the splendor of those lush velvety blades of grass."

"Leave the poor boy alone," interrupted Mum. "You were lovely, Nick. Your Prospero reminded me of a politician!"

Nick spoke very slowly as if he thought my mum and dad might suffer from some mental deficiency.

"Th-a-nk you-oo," he said. "Th-a-t's ve-ry k-in-d!" His lips stretched far and wide and he had a flap of gherkin obscuring his front left tooth.

"Isn't he a darling!" said Mum, as he dashed away. "He'd make an excellent news reader."

thirty-seven

Our third and last performance was the best.

Most of our families had seen the play and we were now performing for the general public, and we knew this was the last time we'd ever get to do the play. Everything was more vivid, as if each moment we lived onstage was the last moment we had.

After the curtain fell on the final scene, I had that same feeling I get on Christmas night; fierce joy, stabbing regret and an intense longing to do it again, folded together like nuts, raisins and glacé cherries in a fruitcake.

At curtain call, we held hands and bowed so low our foreheads grazed our knees, and then we lifted up our arms above our heads like champion relay runners. The applause was deafening. The audience threw streamers. Some stamped their feet and wolf-whistled. I felt happier than I had ever been—in love with everyone onstage because we had worked together to conjure something out of nothing.

"This is so good," said Raven, squeezing my hand.

We gestured to the lighting technicians and the musicians. The clapping cracked out even louder. I was laughing and crying at the same time.

Our school principal and another teacher dragged Mrs. Langton and Ms. Highgate from backstage. Nick presented them each with a big bouquet of native flowers and we clapped so hard our hands stung. Mrs. Langton kissed Nick, smiled shyly at the audience and left the stage. Ms. Highgate took Raven's hand and lifted it up and we bowed again.

When we got back to the dressing room, everyone was babbling about their mistakes and near mistakes. Tea was in the corner sobbing her eyes out because it was over. Jago hovered by her shoulder, patting her awkwardly on the head.

I was at the mirror, lathering cold cream on my face when Raven dropped a small gold box in my lap.

"What's this?" I asked. I wiped my hands on a towel.

"Open it." He grinned.

I slid the lid off. Nestled on tissue paper was a small white shell attached to some black leather cord.

"It's a necklace," he said. "In case you were wondering."

"I can see that," I said.

We stared at each other in the mirror. His face was still split in two and mine was white with cream.

"It's perfect," I said, and I took it out and slipped it on.

• • •

The cast party was at Nick's house, and his parents had transformed the whole place into a *Tempest* wonderland. They'd gone for the lush, tropical island look. The lawn was full of tall potted palms and flaming torches. Fishing nets, strung with shells, starfish and fairy lights, draped the walls and fences. The cabana had been converted into a tent cave, with swathes of red silk. It was scattered with plump burgundy and gold brocade cushions. In the corner, jutting out over the pool, was a dilapidated rowboat, which held a treasure chest spilling gold coins. A fire-eater was perched on a dais to the side of the yard, gulping flames. And underneath the balcony, there were two bulky blokes dressed as slaves, turning a pig on a spit.

A glittering silver disco ball hung from the top balcony like a full moon.

It was so beautiful. Even more beautiful than our set for *The Tempest*.

"Wow," I said, as I walked in. "Wow!"

Nick took me by the elbow and led me to the banquet table.

"You're here at last," he said. "I've been waiting for you. I thought you weren't going to come."

"Raven's makeup was hard to get off," I said. "He's still blue around the edges."

"Right," said Nick, grabbing me a plate. "Here. Help yourself."

"Thanks," I said, piling my plate with roast pork, crackling and salad.

"That's the way," said Mr. Lloyd, smacking his stomach. "I love a girl who's not afraid to eat."

"I'll get you a drink," said Nick. "Homemade punch?"

"Thanks."

I carried my plate to the pool. The giant palms waved gently in the breeze, bowing up and down. Raven lolled on the pool edge, scales still glittering around his hairline.

"Why is he all over you like a rash?" he asked, nodding at Nick, who was crossing the yard.

"He's just getting me a drink," I said. "Are you going to eat?"

"I'm not hungry," said Raven.

"There's homemade punch."

"No thanks. I hate that stuff."

We sat around the pool, eating and laughing, talking about the play and what Mrs. Langton might choose next year. Nick was stretched out on one side and Raven on the other. They spent their time trying to crack the wittiest jokes, competing against each other to keep my glass full. Small spurts of triumph raced through my veins, sharp and sweet.

It wasn't until I had begun to feel invincible that Mrs. Lloyd came down the stairs and confessed to us she'd given us the wrong bowl of punch.

"I'm so sorry," she said. "I don't know how it could have happened."

Raven stopped shredding a palm leaf and stared at Nick sharply.

"What?" asked Nick, innocently.

"You're an arsehole," muttered Raven.

"Careful," said Nick. "There are *ladies* present."

"My guests upstairs have been drinking the punch meant for you young ones," continued Mrs. Lloyd. "The punch you've been drinking is laced with vodka. Not just laced. Drowning in it. God, what are your parents going to say? We'll be arrested!"

"Mum," said Nick, garrulously. "It's okay. Everything's fine. You can go now."

Because by then, for most of us, it was far too late.

I was dancing wild dervishes by myself, spinning so fast that if Raven hadn't caught me, I would have fallen into the pool.

"Careful," he said. "Or you're going to split your head open."

I took my shoes off and fell onto the lawn. It was soft and springy like a marshmallow. I rested my face against it. I rolled over onto my back and gazed up at the disco ball. It was spinning in slow motion.

"What are you doing?" asked Raven, crouching beside me.

"This is the best turf in the world," I sighed. "It's softer than a cushion."

"Get up," he grinned, holding my hand. "It's wet."

"My dad would kill for this." Little beads of dew flung up through my fingers. The disco ball was spinning one way and the world was spinning another.

"If I profane with my unworthiest hand," said Raven.
"This holy shrine, the gentle sin is this:

My lips, two blushing pilgrims, ready stand
To smooth that rough touch with a tender kiss."

"No way," I said, sitting up. "I'm not ready for that."

"Why not?" asked Raven.

I staggered to my feet. The world rocked up and down like a seesaw. The fairy lights above the pool blurred like thousands of shooting stars.

"Because you should only kiss people you love," I said, trying very hard to keep my "s" sounds from turning thick and slushy. "It's wrong to do it so easily."

"What makes you think it's not love?" said Raven.

I shrugged his hand off. I couldn't deal with all that. I wobbled back to the dance floor where Serena and I whirled round together, wind charms in a gale.

Raven sat hunched on the edge of the pool, his face a sickly shade of aqua in the flickering light. I couldn't help glancing at him every now and again, to see whether he was watching me.

Nick was on the dance floor too. He swayed towards me and linked his arms around my neck, his forehead close to mine, staring with big, solemn eyes. The minutes strung out. The noise of the music faded. I wanted to laugh. Then his arms pressed hard against my neck. And suddenly, he was lunging forward, sticking his tongue down my throat with the urgency of a search and rescue party. For a moment, I was so shocked I didn't know what to do. I stood there, tasting his great, big, cheddary tongue.

"Yuck!" I said, wrenching my head. "Yuck! Nick! Stop!"

Raven stood by the edge of the pool, stricken.

Nick's mouth lunged for mine again like an industrial vacuum.

"Come on, Gemma," he said. He smelt of onion and waxy, greasy sweat. I pulled away, but he held on tight. "There are no bloody cows around now," he said, sliding his arms around my waist.

I turned my head and tried to wriggle away.

Nick swung me to the music. "What's wrong?" he asked.

"I don't want to."

"Don't be silly," he said, pulling at my shirt.

I pushed him off and barged through the reeling, jack-hammering bodies.

I staggered to the laundry and was sick in a peg bucket. I stayed there for ages, too ashamed to come out.

Later, Serena burst in and scooped the last glass of punch into a cup. "What are you doing behind the door?" she said.

"Nothing." I shivered. "Do you know where Raven is?"

My head was a flaming throbbing mess and I felt so cold.

"In the cabana, I think," said Serena.

I stuck my head into the cabana. Tea and Jago were lying on the cushions, pashing as though they were on a sinking ship.

Eloise, Pete and Dodi were holding their mobile phones like small, jeweled scarab beetles. "Do you know where Raven is?" I asked.

Eloise glanced up. "Gone home."

"He used my phone," said Pete, his eyes glued.

"Brother picked him up," said Dodi. Her thumb darted over the keys, agile and quick.

I hurried down the side path, past the fountain and out onto the front lawn.

The street was empty.

Just neatly trimmed lawns and white, leafless gutters.

Back in the yard, plastic plates floated in the pool, swirling white discs. The pork hung slumped and half-eaten. Nick was dancing with Serena, his mouth slightly open.

I wanted to go home. The magic of the play, the feeling of being linked and in love with everyone, was gone.

thirty-eight

One of the things that scares me most is the feeling I'm going to drown in the flow of other lives. You can be celebrating because your sister's given birth to a healthy baby or you've won lotto or the lump in your knee isn't cancer after all, and yet, across town, someone is devastated because their grandma died, or they failed an important test or they have no food. Sometimes when I think about these competing lives, even in my own town, let alone the whole world, I feel too tired to move.

When the explosion boomed in the Buranderry Memorial Park, I didn't hear it. I was busy toying with my cheesecake and raspberry coulis, wondering why my dad hadn't come to pick me up.

It wasn't until Serena's parents arrived that we learnt the town fountain had been blown up.

We milled on the front lawn. Mr. Lloyd had his mobile on one ear and the portable house phone on the other.

"Oh Nick, no," said Mrs. Lloyd. She rushed to him, shoeless, her feet thin and bare like slivered almonds. "Oh sweetie," she said. "After all your hard work."

Nick shrugged off her hand. Mrs. Lloyd's immaculate face, those eyebrows pruned into perfect arches, those lips so carefully bordered and contained, went slippery with grief.

"Several shops are damaged," called Mr. Lloyd. "I'm going down there." He stalked self-importantly up the drive. The garage door opened and he reversed the silver Mercedes out, the breeze lifting his fringe. Nick opened the passenger door.

"Well, I'll stay here and wait for the other parents, shall I?" said Mrs. Lloyd.

She stood on the lawn, waiting for them to answer, the naked lady hovering over her shoulder like a guardian angel. Mr. Lloyd zoomed off, the car a silver streak.

When Dad arrived, he was apologetic and agitated, late because there was chaos on the roads.

"Come on, Gem," he said. "Before it gets worse."

But the traffic was bumper to bumper all the way down the long, sweeping curves of Buranderry Heights. "You'd think it was Christmas," said Dad, "and people were going to look at the lights."

As we came to the first roundabout into the main part of

town, we gave way to two ambulances, their lights flashing and sirens wailing. "Oh, gosh," said Dad. "That's not good."

There were emergency service vehicles everywhere. Two fire-engines were parked askew and a policeman stood in the middle of the street, directing traffic.

"Move on," he said, waving. "Don't stop. This is no time for sightseeing."

The fountain was a smoldering hole and the windows of all the shops behind were completely shattered.

"Good heavens," said Dad.

Police and SES volunteers swarmed everywhere, murmuring into their walkie-talkies, looping orange and white barrier tape around the park.

"What sort of person would do that?" asked Dad.

A long line of cars had come to a complete standstill. The car in front of us had three heads jammed out of a rear passenger window.

And then I saw it.

Mrs. De Head's green Torana. With its windows blown to smithereens. Parked out the front of Thea's Milk Bar.

And I began to feel hot. Everything pressed in on me. Dad's breathing. The roof and the dashboard with those clever flashing lights. I rested my head against the window.

"I have to get out."

"Nearly there," said Dad. "Hold on. It's okay. Looks like the police have everything under control." The line of cars moved forward. Dad touched the accelerator.

"Stop!" I said. "Stop the car!"

"Not here," said Dad. "I can't stop here."

I unclicked my seatbelt and opened the door.

Dad jammed his foot on the brake and I jumped out. I ran towards the fountain, my feet crunching over rubble. An SES volunteer grabbed me by the arm.

"No one's allowed in here, love," he said, leading me back to the road.

"But that's my friend's car!" I said, pointing at the Torana.

"That's no good, love," said the volunteer. "But no one's allowed past this point."

A large crowd had gathered at the war memorial. I crossed the road, past the town clock with its unlit glass face sparkling like a sequin. My lungs burned.

People were huddled in small groups, talking, talking, their voices blending like swarms of bees.

"What's wrong?" asked Dad, panting.

I pushed forward into the crowd and found Mr. Lloyd and Nick.

Thea was sitting on the edge of the war memorial sobbing openly. Her husband knelt at her feet, his arms around her, while their son looked on helplessly.

Egg Tuffy, the butcher, was near the cannon, his elbow crooked around it, regaling the crowd. "I was in a deep sleep, mate," he cried. "And then I heard an explosion, this almighty, bed-shaking boom. Next thing I know me window's blown in and there's friggin' glass over my bed. Jules, me girlfriend, she's going hysterical. She thinks it's her ex-boyfriend tracked her down. I've got glass cuts to me chin and blood's pouring out over the bed. So I grabs me shorts and thongs and chuck 'em on and I goes over to the window and glass is crunching under me feet and I peek out and there's no friggin' fountain, just three guys lying in the park. One of them is moaning and the other two are in a heap. The one on the bottom is screaming like a stuck pig but the one on top is quiet and I know he's a goner. So I calls the police and I don't go down till they get here."

He paused to take a breath, delighted to have such a large crowd hanging on his every word. "And me shop's stuffed. Windows shot to buggery. And then I'm starting to worry about looting. I've got me some top quality meat in those freezers. Some of it delivered fresh yestieday and me shop's friggin' hanging open for the world."

"Who did it, Egg?" called Mr. Lloyd authoritatively, his hand on Nick's shoulder.

Egg's face flopped like a windless sail. His story had only just begun and now someone wanted the ending before he'd even got to the middle.

"It was the De Head boys," he said. "Those friggin', good-for-nothing shits. I'm telling you one of them's dead for sure."

My legs felt like unset jelly. My heart skipped a beat, the whole world stopped still and my ears rang with the rush of my own blood.

"Which one?" I called. "Which one was killed?"

"Couldn't tell," said Egg. "It doesn't matter, does it?"

The brick memorial rose above us like a chimney. The gray slab of marble fixed to the bricks glimmered in the light, the names indecipherable dints.

"They're friggin' losers," said Egg. "The only thing they ever bought from me was mince. Cheap mince that I wouldn't even feed to me friggin' dog if I had one." He gazed around at the crowd in mock horror, checking to make sure he still had them on his side. "They wouldn't know a friggin' piece of rump steak if it upped and bit them."

There was a smattering of laughter. And then everyone began to speak at once.

"Crow, the older one," said a woman, with curlers wound tight like cocoons. "He stole my sister's Subaru."

"I hate the tall, skinny one," said a girl with sleek, dark hair, puffing on a cigarette. "The one with the dragon tattoo."

"Magpie," said an older man, tying the shoelaces of his runners.

"Yeah. He's creepy," said the girl with sleek hair.

The older man gazed mournfully at the stars. "Once a De Head, always a De Head," he said.

I couldn't stand to hear any more. I felt as though I was lost on the shore in a fog and a huge tide was flooding in.

"Can you give me a lift to the hospital?" I whispered.

"Okay," said Dad, squeezing my arm.

Nick turned a clod of grass over with his foot. "They're sick," he said. "It's genetic."

And as he stood there staring at me under the war memorial light, I saw he was perfectly proportioned and beautiful like a trophy but all gold-plated and empty on the inside.

"You're a dickhead!" I said.

And I ran, ran on my jelly legs—running, running, running.

And I could hear Dad running behind me, his breath like ragged sobs.

And words were spilling out of my mouth; frantic, frenzied words.

And I realized I was praying, praying to that God of thieves and dumbheads.

Praying, praying, praying that Raven and his family would be safe.

And praying, praying, praying for myself. Tears streaming down my face. Praying for the hate banking up in my own heart towards Egg Tuffy and Nick and all those people in the park.

Praying, praying, praying because I knew I was always going to be shipwrecked by the requirements of love.

thirty-nine

It took ages to get to Buranderry hospital, and when we did we found Sparrow and Robin alone in the waiting room.

Robin was sitting on a chair, swinging his legs, his hair mussed and his racing car pajama-top buttoned up funny. When he saw us, he slid off his seat, ran over and put his arms around me.

Sparrow was standing at the snack machine pressing the buttons hopefully. "Do ya have any money?" he asked, and banged his hand hard against the glass. The chip packets quivered. Taped to the machine was a sign that said no change was available at the front desk. The sticky tape was curly and stained.

"No," I said.

"Bum!"

Two styrofoam cups with teeth marks rolled from the magazine table as though an invisible wind had puffed them off.

"I have some," said Dad. He handed Sparrow three dollars.

"Where's your mum?" I asked.

Sparrow shoved the money down the coin slot and pressed the buttons. A packet of Cheezels slid out and fell to the bottom.

Robin pointed up the brightly lit corridor. "Mum's with the doctors."

Sparrow flicked open the slot and dragged out his Cheezels. He opened them up and sat down, munching loudly. "Dad's been out all day," he grunted. "We don't know where he is."

"Maggie's dead," whispered Robin.

"Dead on arrival," said Sparrow, his fingers furry yellow.

I could feel my heart seize up. Dad put his arm around me.

Maggie.

Maggie dead.

Maggie.

"And Crow's lost an eye," said Robin, squinting. "Like a pirate." He pressed his hand over his left eye like a patch and looked up at us, his right eye filled with fear.

My heart slashed in my chest. "What about Raven?" I swallowed. "What about him?"

"We don't know," said Robin. "He's cut up bad, though."

"Do you reckon Maggie's in heaven?" asked Sparrow, rolling a Cheezel between his fingers.

"Do you reckon there's a skate ramp there?" asked Robin.

"I don't know," I said, reeling.

"Mum said that's where he is," said Robin. "That's what she said."

"I'm really sorry," whispered Dad.

Sparrow stared into his Cheezels, a big tear dropping off the end of his nose. He wiped it away with the back of his hand. "They did it for a joke," he said.

"And now Maggie's dead," said Robin.

"This time he's not coming back," said Sparrow. "Not like jail or detention center." And he dropped his packet of Cheezels and put his head down on his knees and sobbed.

Robin edged away from me. "But we'll see him again," he said. "When we get to heaven."

"Who cares about heaven?" said Sparrow.

I sat next to Sparrow. He turned and buried his hot, runny-nosed face against my knee and his tears soaked through my jeans.

We sat there for ages, the three of us, holding hands, waiting for news. I stared at the black smudges on the floor, curled like commas. After a while the boys fell asleep, their heads lolling and jolting.

Dad rang Mum and told her what had happened. Then he bought me a cup of hot chocolate and we sat opposite each other in that white, glaring light that made the pouches underneath his eyes look like two puffy beanbags.

I told Dad what had happened at the party. About getting drunk and not caring. About the feeling of power that had run through my body like a fire. And about the way I had shrugged and walked away from Raven when he had all but said he loved me. About the kiss Nick had stolen.

And about how maybe I was to blame for everything that had happened.

Dad nodded and let me talk. Then he walked over to the window.

"Oh Gem. I don't know what to say. Nothing's going to make it easier," he said. "But we've got to be answerable for our actions and that's true for Raven, too."

We listened to the rattle of the Coke machine and the tick of the clock and stared at the flicker in the exit sign for hours, mesmerized.

Eventually, Mrs. De Head shuffled down the corridor like a sleepwalker. Her hair was greasy and limp and her thin face shimmered like the spidery, punched-in windscreen of a car after a head-on collision.

"He's going to live," she said, hugging Sparrow and Robin tight, whispering baby words into their hair, her bloodshot eyes swimming with tears. "Raven's going to live." Every line on her face splintered into a million fragments of rejoicing and mourning.

And I couldn't help feeling it would be easier to love like Nick, dumping all your affection into a charity bin, than to face the large, sprawling, aching, messy catastrophe of loving people up close.

On the way home in the car, when I saw the sun rise up

in the same old way, I thought I would break into a million pieces. It seemed like a rotten trick that the grass could still be silver-white with dew. That a crescent moon could still hang in the sky like a crooked smile. That early-risers could still be traipsing down garden paths to pick up their plastic-wrapped newspapers.

That life could still go on without skinny, belligerent Maggie.

forty

The town was full of talk. Everyone had a theory on how Crow, Maggie and Raven had gotten hold of the gelignite they used to explode the fountain.

Everyone had a theory on why Maggie died.

Everyone wanted to expound his or her theory and it didn't matter where. On the street, in the bus, outside the newsagent, inside church, under a hairdryer and over a beer.

People yacked on about where they were on the night and what they were doing, even what part of their dreams were disturbed.

Nothing could divert them. Not even the news that the tip was going to be made into a park with cycle ways, duck ponds and play equipment.

Because in the end, bad news is so much more compelling than good news.

The *Buranderry Voice* seized on the story. It compared the two explosions in great detail. Showing before and after explosions of the first fountain, destroyed by Mr. De Head, and before and after explosions of the second, destroyed by his sons.

They ran photos of Crow, Maggie and Raven. Photos that made them look like surly criminals. No nudie-rudie photos of little boys running through a sprinkler; no bashful photos of two little brothers sucking on lollipops. No photos of them when they were at school with floppy collars, their grins happy and gappy. No cheesy, hopeful photos of them at their first school dance. Just photos with harsh light, so they looked like people nobody would want to know or love.

The newspaper editorials ranted against the dangers of working mothers, alcohol abuse, welfare dependency, the high incidence of ADD in boys and the benefits of medication. The letters pages spewed out hate. How the De Head boys had it coming and deserved everything they got. How this would learn them.

They didn't report the fact that Maggie had saved Raven's life. How he had leapt into the path of those flying fragments.

They didn't report that every single window in the De Head house had been smashed by vandals or how Robin and Sparrow had been bashed at school.

They didn't report that when Mr. De Head found out

about Maggie, it was like he had been struck a blow to the head that made him as simple as a child. Or that he sat by Maggie night and day in the morgue and eventually had to be torn away.

They didn't report the way Mrs. De Head walked to and from the hospital every day.

They didn't report the fact that Raven was so sick with grief he wanted to die and wouldn't see anyone but his mum.

None of these things made it into the paper.

In the end, even Maggie's funeral notice was typed so small, slotted in between the "Lost & Found" columns, it could hardly be seen.

forty-one

Maggie's funeral was the saddest thing.

There was hardly anyone there. Mrs. Langton came from school and there were some people from Mrs. De Head's church, mainly elderly women wearing small fussy hats, but that was all. It was like a funeral for an old person whose close friends had already all passed away.

Jody arrived late. I was glad to see her, and surprised too. She was dressed in black; her eyelids red and bloated and she carried handfuls of tissues. She sobbed by my side from the moment she sat down. I know she was crying for Maggie, but I think she was crying for herself too, maybe because she'd realized for the first time she wasn't safe from death just because she was young.

Throughout the service, Mr. De Head was like a jack-in-the box. Every few minutes, he'd stand up and gaze at the door, as if he was at the movies minding a seat for a friend who had gone to the bathroom or to get some popcorn. He didn't pay attention to what was being said and he didn't seem to notice the coffin at his side. Every few minutes, Robin tapped him on the arm and helped him sit back down. And for a while, Mr. De Head nodded his head along to the prayers or the poem that Sparrow read or the eulogy that the pastor faltered over. But then he would be up again, looking at the door, his fists poking out of his too-short suit sleeves like turtle heads. When he cried out loudly— "Maggie?"—the elderly women rustled in their seats. Mrs. De Head started weeping and Raven tugged him down.

I don't know why people sing at funerals. Usually we only sing when we're happy and never in groups unless it's the national anthem and then it's more often than not out of time and out of tune. But it was actually a release to sing at Maggie's funeral. Even though the songs were in the wrong key and too high. As soon as the first note of the organ was played, everyone leapt to their feet because then Mr. De Head was no longer a lonely sentinel.

After the service we waited to speak with Mrs. De Head, outside the church. Sparrow and Robin hovered by her side, their eyes downcast, their hair so slick with gel they looked like they had just hopped out of the bath. Crow puffed on a cigarette by himself, his missing left eye bandaged and hidden by reflective, dark glasses, his right arm in a sling.

Mr. De Head was sitting in the gutter, next to the

hearse. When Mrs. Langton came over to him, he was delighted, completely taken by surprise. He let go of Raven's arm, stood up and shook her hand and patted her back. Then while Mrs. Langton was speaking, Mr. De Head leant slightly forward and peered around her, his eyes searching further down the road.

When Mum, Dad and I finally made it to Mrs. De Head we were struck dumb; we had no words worth saying. We sort of fell into her arms and it was as though she was comforting us. The shoulders of her powder blue silk dress, which smelt of mothballs, were splotched with our tears like little dark lakes.

The air was as soft as feathers. Somewhere in the streets behind us, a bird droned for a mate. The cherry tree out the front was cobwebbed with pale pink blossoms. Across the road, a cloud of jasmine draped over a broken paling fence like a white fur coat.

Everything was new again. A whole season of newness.

Except for Maggie in his tidy honey box, awash in a sea of blue irises, their yellow tongues like flames.

I wanted to speak to Raven. I wanted to go to him. I wanted to touch his shoulder or put my arms around him. But when I turned to him, I saw his face. He was like one of those trees, one of those ghost gums, stained with grief, his anguish frozen and congealed.

And I was frightened. I was too frightened to step forward.

forty-two

Then suddenly, Debbie's wedding roared towards us like a freight train.

Last-minute fittings and alterations, last-minute meetings to argue about the reception seating, honeymoon destination dramas because the airline Brian had chosen had plunged into receivership, and then the hen's big night out singing bad karaoke at a Thai restaurant in Jindleburra.

And life had to go on—even though most of the time it felt as though tinny Muzak was blaring in my ears making a mockery of everything ordinary.

On the morning of the wedding, Mum dashed around the house trying to mend the icing on the wedding cake while sewing the last stitch onto Debbie's veil.

Debbie was upstairs screaming like a banshee because Dad had left the chocolate bonbons in the boot of the car and they had melted into blobs.

"There's so much to do!" she cried. "And no one capable to do it. Who's going to the reception center to be there when the ice sculptures are delivered? I can't go now. I'm about to have my makeup done."

"I'll go!" said Dad.

"You!" Debbie snorted. "You've already destroyed the chocolates."

"It's not the look, Deb," said Dad. "It's the taste."

"And now it's raining . . ." said Debbie. "And we haven't had a rehearsal. I told you we should, but you wouldn't listen to me. And it looks like it will rain all day. My hair will go limp. My dress will be muddy. And I'll start my married life with a bad omen."

"Debbie?" I said then, hesitating, as I peeped into her room. "Do I really have to wear these feet?"

Debbie ran at me, her arms flapping and her eyes wide like an attack dog. "Yes! Yes! Yes! Yes! This is my wedding day. And you'll wear webbed feet if I say so!"

"Debbie!" cried Rochelle. "Come back! Your dress!"

"Watch your train," cried Renee. "It's caught under the bed!"

Debbie's head snapped. "Yee-oow!" she screeched, whacking into the wall.

"I'll get her an ice pack," said Mum. "Before the muscles stiffen."

"Calm down, Deb!" called Dad, sidling down the stairs.

"Who put that dirty great footprint on my train!" she screeched.

"She's chucking the biggest birkett I've ever seen," said Aunty Beryl, passing Dad the packet of frozen peas.

"You think that's bad," said Dad. "Earlier this morning she wanted to immerse me in a vat of boiling oil."

"What's wrong with her?" asked Aunty Beryl.

"It's prewedding syndrome," said Mum. "It's similar to premenstrual syndrome, only worse!"

"I'm so glad I've never been a bride," said Aunty Beryl.

"I'll be glad when this is over. It's worse than getting married myself," said Dad.

• • •

Later that afternoon, when Con the wedding photographer saw Jackie and me coming down the stairs in our swan costumes, his wad of chewing gum dropped out of his mouth and got stuck in his red carnation.

He aimed his camera at us. "Turn your beaks to the left," he urged. "Now give me the look of two big lovebirds on the run!"

"Are they white flamingos?" asked Aunty Beryl.

"No, Bell," said Dad, patting his bow tie smugly. "Anybody with any sense can see they're swans!"

"Oooh," said Aunty Beryl. "They don't look like swans to me. Their necks are extra long. Are you sure they're not flamingos?"

"That's great," said Con, smirking. He flicked his hand at me. "But maybe not so aggressive. Give me something a little more demure."

"They look like football mascots," said Uncle Bert.

"Can you dip your beaks?" called Con. "It'll bring out the sequins."

"They're symbols of love," said Mum.

"Stretch out your wings," suggested Con. "As if you were about to take flight."

"Careful of the lights," said Mum.

"Get in the car!" screamed Debbie, a soggy bag of peas clutched to her neck. "The chauffeur is waiting. If we delay any longer, we'll have to pay him overtime."

Con kept shooting, making sure he got every angle of our costumes. Debbie tapped him on the shoulder.

"*I am the bride*," she seethed. She grabbed me by the wing and tugged me down the hall.

As soon as we walked outside, the neighbors whistled.

"You've got great legs for a stork," said one.

"Hello, birdie!" said another.

"I told you this was a mistake," I whispered to Debbie as Jackie hopped into the second Rolls Royce.

"Just shut up and get in the car," she muttered.

I spent ten minutes trying to maneuver myself next to Jackie. I tried climbing in head first, but my neck was too long and my beak kept jabbing the Three Rs.

"You smeared my mascara," yelled Rochelle.

"Watch out," snapped Rachael. "You just pecked my boob."

"There's not enough room," cried Renee. "Try hopping in bum first."

I reversed back out. "They want me to hop in bum first," I said to Debbie.

"Just get in," she cried.

"She could hang her head out the window," suggested Mum.

"We can't drive to the church with a swan head hanging out the window," said Rachael. "We don't want our hair to get messed up by the wind."

"Would you stop taking photos!" cried Debbie. She whirled around on Con, who was snapping photo after photo and reel after reel on both his cameras. She stalked towards him.

"You told me to take action shots," he said. Debbie flung the bag of peas at his head.

"There's not enough room in this car for two swans," said Rochelle.

"She can ride with me on the bike," said Uncle Bert.

"No, Mum," I begged. "Please."

"It looks the best solution," said Mum.

Dad glanced uneasily at his watch. "We don't have time to argue."

"Get on the bike," said Debbie menacingly.

Uncle Bert hopped on and revved his engine. I climbed on behind him. My tail feathers hung over the back. Debbie's driver bipped his horn and Uncle Bert sped off so fast I nearly lost my beak.

As we roared around the corner I looked back and saw that all our neighbors were buckled over on their front lawns.

I knew it wasn't from food poisoning.

• • •

Although we didn't go to church much, Debbie wanted to get married in the Catholic church that Mum and Dad were married in, so she had held out against the Lieutenant Colonel and the Church of England. He finally gave in when Debbie promised that any male grandchildren she produced would be brought up experiencing, from infancy, the Buranderry Army League Hornets.

Uncle Bert and I arrived at St. Monica's Catholic Church at least ten minutes ahead of the rest of the bridal party. The wind had ripped off quite a lot of my feathers so I resembled the type of bird other birds picked on.

Mrs. Webster and an altar boy with a face full of freckles were looking anxiously up the street.

"Where's the bride?" asked the altar boy.

"They're on their way," I said. "They couldn't keep up with Uncle Bert."

"Are you a cockatoo?" asked the boy.

"No," I said. "A swan."

"Why would you wear that?" he asked, his eyebrows raised.

"For the same reason you're wearing a dress," I said. "Because somebody made me."

Father Nolan dashed out with a big warm, welcoming smile on his face.

"How are we doing, Paddy?" he said to the altar boy. "Has the bride arrived? The groom is getting a little—" He glanced at me and his smile faltered. "Oh . . . goodness. Are you an ostrich? Are you looking for the preschool party?"

"No," I groaned. "I'm Debbie and Brian's flower girl."

"Oh. I'm terribly sorry," he said. "I'm not up with the fashions these days." He rubbed his hands. "The bride is coming, isn't she? She's more than fashionably late. Ah, here she is now. Excellent."

The Rolls Royces slid into the curb. The chauffeur unrolled the red carpet as Debbie and Dad lurched out.

"Well, let's get this show on the road, shall we?" called Father Nolan.

"I can't!" said Debbie, her eyes brimming. "Mum, my buttons have popped."

"Don't worry," said Mum. "I've got the needle and thread here. Barry, thread it, will you, I can barely see in this light."

"Come on, Dad!" called Debbie.

"You're making me nervous," said Dad. "Stop breathing on me."

"Good heavens," cried Father Nolan. "How long does it take to thread a blooming needle? Here, give it to me!" He snatched the needle and thread out of Dad's hands. "I'll thread it in a second." He adjusted his bifocals, stared at the needle and mumbled under his breath.

"Come on!" screeched the Three Rs. "We're freezing out here!"

Aunty Beryl poked Father Nolan in the stomach. "Here, give it to me," she said. "Oh, God, I've dropped it."

"I only brought one!" cried Mum.

Father Nolan stared at a large silver watch. He pasted down the long, greasy strands of his hair. "We have to hurry this up," he said. "I have another wedding in forty-five minutes. With a nuptial mass."

Everyone was poring over the grass, searching for the missing needle. Father Nolan's vestments were flapping in the wind and as he bent over and flicked his fingers through the grass, I glimpsed his bright, striped clown-socks.

"Here it is!" screamed Aunty Beryl. "Oh, no. Sorry. False alarm."

"Here it is!" cried Mrs. Webster. She held the needle up triumphantly.

Uncle Bert swiped it out of her hands. He licked the thread, held the needle up into the light and pushed it through.

Mum started sewing away. Debbie stood under a huge white umbrella as soft rain fell, beading everything with fine, silver glitter.

Jackie and I huddled together. Latecomers dashed past us, panting, their heads bowed.

"How old was your friend who died?" asked Jackie.

"Maggie," I said. My throat felt tight and dry. "He was twenty-two."

"I've never known anyone who's died that young."

The street was lined with bottlebrush trees. The blooms danced in the wind like red lanterns. A car zoomed up the street, the speakers booming.

"It's really young," I said.

A flicker of panic whipped across Jackie's face. "I'll be trained to kill people that age."

"I guess so," I said.

"It seems a waste," she whispered. "A whole lot of possibility gone."

"You don't have to do it," I said.

"But what would Dad say," said Jackie, splashing her giant, webbed orange foot into a puddle. "He'd kill me."

"As if he would," I said. "Would he?"

Jackie shivered as a gust of wind sent leaves flying.

"Maybe I'll wait and tell him after Debbie's had a baby boy," she said.

"Good idea."

"Okay!" called Mum. "We're ready to go!"

The Three Rs' dresses were speckled with rain. Jackie and I shook the water off our feathers and took up our positions at the head of the bridal party, completely dry.

"Good luck, Debbie," said Mum. She prinked the train before she dashed into the church. "You look beautiful."

forty-three

And then the bridal march swelled up and Debbie grabbed Dad's arm and the Three Rs nudged us through the door.

And I learnt the first rule of being a member of the official bridal party, which is: It doesn't matter how shocking you look as a bridesmaid or a flower girl because the moment you enter the church, no one has eyes for you anyway. They're standing on their tiptoes, desperate to catch the first glimpse of the bride.

By the time we had waddled our way to the front of the church, Debbie was leaning on Dad as if she was about to fall over, and he was leaning just as badly on her. In the oblong entrance, they cut a perfect triangle. When Debbie started to walk down the aisle, little gasps rolled down the length of the church like a minor avalanche.

Every head was turned towards her. Except for one. One shining face in the back row, staring at Brian up the front, watching him greedily, as if her life depended on it. Mrs. De Head. Sitting alone. In the last pew. I didn't know where to look. The organ buzzed and people whispered as Debbie ducked her head and smiled. I closed my eyes, dizzy with sadness.

As Debbie drew near, Brian stepped forward in his purple velvet suit. His hair was cut so short there was a white outline around the edges. His Adam's apple was huge and every time he swallowed his bow tie waggled. But his eyes were blazing at Debbie. He was jubilant. He was elated. He didn't look afraid of what was around the corner: he was ready and willing to drink up joy and sorrow, right to the last drop.

I glanced back at Mrs. De Head and I wondered if there was envy in her eyes. Envy because she'd be watching for Maggie in the milestones of other people for the rest of her life.

At the front of the church, in an alcove, was a statue of Mary. She was gazing serenely at row after row of candles lit in prayer. I found myself wanting to turn and run. To bolt at top speed. To get out of the church. To find a cool, safe place, a cupboard, somewhere I could lock myself into and swallow the key. To seal myself up.

To seal my heart away from love.

Because no one who loves is immune from its fire.

No one.

All those burning, waxy candles silent witnesses to that truth.

And when Father Nolan asked if there was any reason why Debbie and Brian should not be joined in marriage, it took all my strength not to holler out a warning.

Then after the songs, readings and prayers, Father Nolan asked the big questions, his voice velvet wingback chairs and glass balloons of golden cognac.

"Brian and Debbie, have you come freely and without reservation to give yourselves to each other in marriage?"

"I have," said Debbie.

And I was so proud of her.

"I have," said Brian.

And I was so proud of him, too.

"Will you love and honor each other as husband and wife for the rest of your lives?"

"I will," said Brian.

"I will," said Debbie.

"Will you accept children lovingly from God, and bring them up according to the law of Christ and his Church?"

"We will," they said.

Father Nolan held out his hands, his voice booming in such a way that it was obvious he had come to the part he really liked. "Since it is your intention to enter into marriage, join your right hands and declare your consent before God and his Church."

Brian took Debbie's right hand. His left leg quivered.

Father Nolan stared at Brian over his bifocals, his sea-green eyes smiling. "Brian, do you take Deborah Lea Stone for your lawful wife, to have and to hold, from this day forward, for better, for worse, for richer, for poorer, in sickness and in health, until death do you part?"

"I do," said Brian, his leg shaking even more.

Father Nolan turned to Debbie. "Debbie," he said. "Do you take Brian Winston Webster for your lawful husband, to have and to hold, from this day forward, for better, for worse, for richer, for poorer, in sickness and in health, until death do you part?"

And there was a beat of silence.

Debbie was so tiny under the tulle—as though she had been swallowed by a gigantic, frothing wave and was drowning in sea foam.

You could see it dawning on her that Brian was not some doll she could eventually put out on the front lawn for council pick-up the moment his right eye went gummy and his head popped off.

She stood there trembling and indecisive, not sure she had it in her to sign up for a little war with a front line moving against her own selfishness. You could see she wanted to raise her hand, so a big, bronzed lifesaver could come save her.

The silence was agonizing. Not even a nose whistle.

"Debbie!" hissed Mum.

Father Nolan wiped the sweat from his brow. "Debbie, do you take Brian Winston Webster for your lawful husband, to have and to hold, from this day forward, for better, for worse, for richer, for poorer, in sickness and in health, until death do you part?"

Everything swirled in my head.

Brian.

Nick.

Raven.

And skinny, laughing, Monopoly-mad Maggie.

This whole sick, crazy, glorious world.

"I do," I said.

"I beg your pardon," said Father Nolan.

"I do," I said. "I take Brian to be my lawful brother-in-law, to have and to hold, from this day forward, for better, for worse, for richer, for poorer, in sickness and in health, until death do us part!"

Everyone stared at me.

"I do," I said. "I take Debbie to be my lawful sister, to have and to hold, from this day forward, for better, for worse, for richer, for poorer, in sickness and in health, until death do us part!"

I swiveled and faced Mum and Dad who were sitting in the front pew, their mouths open like the clowns at the Royal Buranderry Show.

"Mum and Dad," I said. "I take you to be my lawful parents, to have and to hold, from this day forward, for better, for worse, for richer, for poorer, in sickness and in health, until death do us part."

"What's wrong with her?" cried the Lieutenant Colonel, rapping the floor with his sword.

"I do to you, too," I said. My beak jutted over my eyes. "I take you to be my lawful in-laws, to have and to hold, from this day forward, for better, for worse, for richer, for poorer, in sickness and in health, until death do us part."

"Any one else?" asked Father Nolan.

I glanced at Mrs. De Head with her crooked blue cocktail hat perched like a landslide above her eyes and at the Three Rs who were staring at me, their mouths thin pleats.

"Yes," I said. "To every person I've ever loved or hated and to those people I'll want to love or hate: I do. I'll love you, as best as I can, from this day forward."

"She's chucking the biggest birkett I have ever seen," whined Renee, hoicking up her rain-streaked, pink bubble-gum strapless dress. "And nobody's doing a thing."

Father Nolan flapped his vestments. "This is very un-usual," he said.

"Once they start chucking a big birkett in this family, it's hard to stop them," said Rochelle.

"It's the acting she's done," said Rachael. "It's sent her crackers."

"I guess that about sums it up then," said Father Nolan, wiping his forehead with his stole.

"No," I said. "It doesn't."

"It doesn't?" said Father Nolan.

"I'll take him, too," I said, bobbing my head.

"Who?" asked Father Nolan. He glanced over his left shoulder at the altar boy. "Paddy?"

"Not him!" I said. I jerked my head. "Him!"

"Who?" he asked, glancing over his other shoulder.

I pointed at Jesus, hanging above his head like a pale white arrow. "HIM!" I cried. "I'll take him."

"What in Heaven's name do you mean?" asked Father Nolan.

"I'm not sure," I said. "But I guess I'm not so certain I won't need his help."

"Is she a nun now?" asked Uncle Bert, his hands outstretched.

"Who knows?" cried Aunty Beryl, screeching as though I had just confessed to murder.

Finally, Debbie took Brian in her arms and kissed him full on the mouth. "I, Deborah Lea Stone, take you Brian Winston Webster, whatever way you come, until death do us part."

And some sad sack in the middle of the church got so excited, they let loose with the confetti and rice. Father Nolan didn't seem to mind; he was grinning with relief, confetti stuck in his hair like a bad case of cradle cap.

Everyone was kissing and hugging and laughing, the whole place ringing with life.

forty-four

By the time we got to the Buranderry RSL, all the ice sculptures had melted into frosty poles. But nothing could dent Brian and Debbie's happiness, not even the fact that the origami serviettes were floppy mush.

Every thirty seconds, someone "ting tinged" a knife against a champagne glass, until Brian dipped Debbie backwards and pashed her head off.

Uncle Bert was the official MC. For the first time in years, he was able to take his time with his punchlines without fear that people were going to run off in the middle of the joke. His jokes were still as corny as ever, but everyone was in such a good mood they killed themselves laughing all through dinner.

Jody had told me that wedding speeches were the worst

part of a wedding, but that night I wanted the speeches to go on forever.

Dad was beery and teary and he forgot to speak into the microphone most of the time. He held the mike out from his body as if he were a sound recordist specializing in insect noises. But his wobbly bottom lip spoke more powerfully than words.

The Lieutenant Colonel was also overcome, but it wasn't as easy for him as it was for my dad. So he kept sitting down to ride the emotion out. On the fourth attempt, he broke down and hugged Debbie and Brian so fiercely, Debbie's train split at the seam and Mum had to do another emergency repair.

Brian was shaking when he stood up to speak. "This is from the 'Song of Songs,' " he said. His face was as white as the piece of paper fluttering in his hands. He gazed at Debbie.

"Place me like a seal over your heart, like a seal on your arm; for love is as strong as death, its jealousy unyielding as the grave. It burns like a blazing fire, like a mighty flame. Many waters cannot quench love; rivers cannot wash it away. If one were to give all the wealth of his house for love, it would be utterly scorned."

Debbie hugged Brian and burst into tears so that globs of her mascara tracked down his white shirt.

Dad was so amazed at how many words Brian had strung together in a row, he gave Brian a standing ovation, until Mum dragged him back down.

• • •

After Debbie and Brian had cut the cake and danced the bridal waltz, Uncle Bert called for everyone to join them.

"And here is a special song for our two flower girls!" he said, beaming.

The chicken dance came on.

People rushed to the dance floor, pumping their arms, cackling away. Jackie and I danced on the edge because our sharp beaks were like deadly weapons.

"I told Dad about me not going into the army," said Jackie, as she snapped her beak up and down in time to the music.

"When?" I asked, flapping my wings.

She wiggled her tail feathers. "Just before he got up to give his speech."

"Blimey," I said.

"I think he's okay," shouted Jackie, as we dunked beaks. "He didn't want Brian to marry Debbie at first and look how good that's turned out." She clapped her wings and darted away to dance with Brian.

A warm breeze blew through the doors and I could smell the rich stench of the tip across the road.

Dad, who was pretending to be groovy by shuffling aimlessly in the one spot, gave me a big hug. "Hello my swan," he yelled. "It's been a huge day for you."

"Are you happy?" I shouted.

"Ah yes," cried Dad. "Even if Brian doesn't know a screw-driver from a wand or a Commodore from a Camry, at least he's not Birkett." And we looked at each other and laughed.

Mum bustled over. "Come on you!" she said to Dad. "Show me how it's done!"

As I watched them bumble around on the dance floor, something inside me hurt. Some sadness at knowing that time can't be stopped and that these perfect moments can't be preserved like fruit.

It hurt so much, I went out on the balcony and into the pong.

It was empty except for the overflowing ashtrays and the glasses half-full of flat beer, and the sticky plastic chairs arranged in circles.

I tried to imagine what the tip would be like once it had been transformed into a park with lush grass, ponds full of lily pads and ducks, bursting with the noise of bike bells and dogs barking.

I leant against the railing. In the distance, I could hear the squawking of seagulls, a cough and the eerie shimmer of a train braking on the rails.

And then a voice.

"But, soft! what light through yonder window breaks?
It is the east, and Juliet is the swan!
Arise, fair swan, and kill the envious moon,
Who is already sick and pale with grief,
That thou her maid art more fair than she."

I leant over the balcony railing.

"See how she leans her beak upon her wing.
O that I were a feather upon that wing,
That I might touch that beak."

"Raven?" I said.

His face was pale in the starlight, shattered with scars.

"Mum said I missed the best wedding she's ever been to."

We stood staring at each other. All the words we should have said and didn't and all the words we wanted to say and couldn't, swooping in the air around us.

I took a deep breath.

"I do," I said.

His face crumpled as easily as eggshell. "No," he said. "I don't want you to say that to me."

"Why not?" I asked.

He stood there, frail, like every certainty had been beaten out of him. "Because I'm a turkey, a goose, you name it."

I lifted my wings. "Look," I said. "We're birds of a feather."

And I walked across the balcony, past the ashtrays, plastic chairs and beer glasses and down the stairs, my webbed feet slapping against the tiles.

Because it's not for me—that cool, safe place, that little cupboard with a swallowed key.

Because even though this life scares me, I still want to fly.

acknowledgments

i would like to express my deep thanks to the members of my writing group, Monica, Lynne and Kate. This book has taken a long journey and without your timely words of encouragement and your sometimes fierce, well-aimed kicks—it might never have been finished!

To Mum, who is constantly anxious that she is going to make an appearance in one of my books, and to all my family—thanks for every sweet, terrible, glorious moment.

Big thanks to my friends for the countless occasions you have helped me have space to write. It was very comforting to know my two darling boys were in your care. A special thank you to Gaz, for his sound technical advice and for always being kind and gracious even when I'm chucking a big birkett.

To Barbara, thanks for believing I could do it and for reassuring me that it was a good thing to take my time. Thanks also for the huge, earthy belly laughs along the way.

Thanks so much to Erica for seeing the glimmer of something worthwhile in those early drafts and for encouraging me to press on. I really appreciate your warmth, your consistent generosity and great skill.

A thousand thanks to Jodie, for being so full of tact, grace and editorial wisdom. Thanks for the long conversations, the delicate attention to detail, and those completely necessary moments where you mercilessly laughed at my rueful insecurities. And finally thanks for always pushing me to make it better.

Lastly, big, big buckets of thanks to Keiran and to Bryn and Riley—for all your pats, hugs, kisses, laughs, cups of tea and unbelievable patience, for all the ways you make this life so wondrously good.

The author and publisher would like to thank the Hal Leonard Corporation for permission to quote the:

Love Boat Theme

from the Television Series

Words and Music by Charles Fox and Paul Williams

Copyright © 1977 (Renewed 2005) by Love Boat Music and LBC Music, Inc.

All Rights for Love Boat Music Administered by Ensign Music LLC

All Rights for LBC Music, Inc. Administered by Famous Music LLC

International Copyright Secured   All Rights Reserved

lisa shanahan trained as an actor at Theatre Nepean, University of Western Sydney. While completing her studies, she taught drama and wrote her first play for children. Thereafter, she enrolled in a children's writing class, where she discovered a great passion for creating stories for young people. Already a prolific author of books for children in her native Australia, Lisa Shanahan has now written her first novel for young adults. She lives in Sydney.